THE RIDDLE OF SPHINX ISLAND

THE RIDDLE OF SPHINX ISLAND

R.T. RAICHEV

This is a work of fiction.

All the characters are imaginary and bear no relation to any

living person. Gutenberg *Lite* is an invention.

R. T. Raichev

Original cover photograph courtesy of Graham Richardson.

First published 2013

The Mystery Press is an imprint of The History Press
The Mill, Brimscombe Port
Stroud, Gloucestershire, GL5 2QG
www.thehistorypress.co.uk

British Library Cataloguing in Publication Data.
A catalogue record for this book is available from the British Library.

ISBN 978 0 7254 9244 5

Typesetting and origination by The History Press
Printed in Great Britain

To E.G., who is 'Ella Gates',
and to Jane, in tribute to new beginnings.

'I have devised for my own private amusement
the most ingenious ways of carrying out a murder.'

Agatha Christie, *And Then There Were None*

CONTENTS

1

A MATTER OF
LIFE AND DEATH

'I have reason to believe that at some point in the course of the weekend party, a murder will take place. I am perfectly serious. It's not the sort of thing I'd joke about.' Sybil de Coverley's expression didn't change. She had one of those long oval faces one saw in Gainsborough's paintings. 'Your aunt said you'd find the prospect tantalising if not irresistible. Your aunt has little doubt that you'll come to the island the moment you hear about the murder.'

Major Payne cocked an eyebrow. 'My aunt has little doubt, eh?'

'Those were her exact words. She said you were interested in the more refined expressions of violence and lawlessness and particularly in murder as a fine art. Dear Nellie. She believes the whole situation is exactly up your street.'

'My aunt thinks she knows us so well …'

'She says she has had the chance to observe you "in action".'

'A murder,' said Antonia. 'A real murder?'

'Well, yes. A murder that hasn't taken place yet but which is real enough. Would I have come all this way about an imaginary murder?' An impatient note crept into Sybil de Coverley's voice.

'You might have done,' Payne said. 'It could all be a game. Something concocted at my aunt's instigation. One of those Murder Weekends, perhaps?'

'It isn't a game. It's a matter of life and death. The most awful part of it is that I am the only one who *knows*. I really am at my wits' end. I am desperately anxious about the whole thing. I may not look it but I am. A Murder Weekend, did you say? I wouldn't dream of staging a Murder Weekend on Sphinx Island. That's the very last thing I'd ever do. It would be so much trouble, besides, I wouldn't have the foggiest how to set about it. Goodness, the idea!'

The faded gentlewoman with the vague, pale blue eyes, neat snuff-coloured hair and two-piece in fine heather-coloured wool gave a little laugh. No, it wasn't a game, Antonia decided. Only a moment earlier she had observed Sybil de Coverley dig the fingers of her right hand into the palm of her left hand. She *was* worried. Unless she was acting. Could she be acting?

Here we go again, Antonia thought wearily. It is our tenth wedding anniversary on Saturday and we have been asked to spend it on a privately owned island off the Devon coast, trying to catch a would-be murderer ...

No, they were not going. Of course they were not going. Out of the question.

She said, 'You have reason to believe that a murder will take place. What reason precisely?'

'Precision has never been my strongest suit – as we used to say at the bridge club. It's so terribly difficult to explain. Something happened. Several things, in fact. Seemingly unrelated incidents, some of them puzzling, some, well, very silly. At first I thought it was all nonsense but I found myself wondering – then I made a discovery, which left me speechless. You see, I realised that I'd been looking at the thing *the wrong way up*.'

They expected her to continue, but she didn't. She went on sitting quietly, a little frown on her face.

Payne leant back in his chair and reached out for his pipe. 'I wonder if you'd care to give us some more details?' Of all the idiotic rigmaroles, he thought. The *vagueness* of it. He resented being edged into a mood of suspense and irritated curiosity. Pure fiction, he thought. It was fascinating but it didn't touch the ground. Nobody could be so vague. The bloody woman was putting it on, he was sure she was putting it on, must be.

'I'd rather *not* be too specific,' Sybil said. 'I haven't completely discounted the possibility that I may be making a fool of myself. John – my brother – says I don't need to make a fool of myself since I am already one. I believe you have met John?'

'I don't think we've had the pleasure,' said Payne. Something stirred at the back of his mind. Hadn't there been something in the papers concerning a John de Coverley and Sphinx Island – some years ago – what was it? – some freak accident?

Sybil said that most people thought of her as the most rational person on earth, but sometimes she had to admit she had fancies about things. 'I blame the island. If one lives on an island as small as mine – one can walk across it in twenty-five minutes – one tends to lose one's sense of perspective *completely*. But this is different. I am sure it is different. That's why I am here. I need your help. On the other hand,' she reasoned, 'it would be awful if I opened my mouth and besmirched the reputation of someone who was perfectly innocent. I can't simply say I am awfully sorry but I have reason to believe that A is planning to kill B, can I? Not the done thing. That's why I would very much like a second opinion. A second opinion is always helpful – wouldn't you say?'

'It can be helpful, yes, though not invariably so.' We mustn't encourage her, Antonia thought. We are *not* spending our wedding anniversary on her island.

Payne asked if their visitor had considered talking to the police.

'The police? Oh but I couldn't possibly. Not to the *police*,' Sybil drew back a bit. 'You see, I am not in possession of anything approximating "tangible evidence". I don't believe the police would take my story *au grand serieux*. They would laugh at me. I am sure I'd be dismissed as yet another neurotic rich woman who's got nothing better to do than suspect her guests of wanting to murder each other.'

'More tea?' Antonia picked up the teapot.

'Yes, thank you ... This room is not in the least oppressive or demanding or colour-coordinated ... What magnificent embroidery.' Sybil patted one of the sofa cushions. 'I don't suppose you do it yourself, Antonia? You do? How perfectly splendid. I thought you'd be too frightfully busy with your writing. I must say I *am* impressed. So wonderfully soothing, embroidering. Not my sort of thing at all, but I do admire people whose sort of thing it is. You are clearly a woman of many talents, Antonia.'

'No, not at all.'

Payne started filling his pipe with tobacco. He'd changed his mind. He didn't think Sybil de Coverley had come to deceive them. He had to admit his natural inquisitiveness was piqued. Only the day before he and Antonia had decided that they were a little bored. Antonia had written the last sentence of her new novel and, having submitted it to her editor, was feeling at something of a loose end. He had been asked to conduct a private inquiry into the affair of that terribly peculiar friend of the disgraced defence secretary, but that had also been brought to a successful conclusion. He and Antonia had lamented the fact that nothing much seemed to be happening, that their minds were like racing engines, tearing themselves to pieces because they were not connected up with the work for which they had been built.

Payne had quoted Sherlock Holmes. *Life is commonplace, the papers are sterile; audacity and romance seem to have passed for ever from the criminal world.*

Sybil de Coverley raised the teacup to her lips. 'It's Thursday today, isn't it?'

'No, it's Wednesday.'

She sighed. 'If you live on an island, you tend to lose track of time. Everything seems to happen in limbo. Well, I have reason to believe it will happen on *Saturday evening*. This gives us three whole days, doesn't it? Saturday evening has been – how shall I put it? – *indicated*. Sorry, I've got a bit of a headache. Nothing like the kind of headaches my brother gets but bad enough. The truth is my nerves are in a terrible state.' She opened her bag and produced a bejewelled pill box. 'Neurophen Plus. Have you ever tried it? It's heaven.'

'You believe that on Saturday evening an attempt will be made on someone's life? At your house on Sphinx Island?' said Antonia.

'It does sound absurd, put like that. Or maybe it was the way you said it? No, I don't blame you, Antonia. I don't mind one little bit, I really don't. My reaction would have been very much the same. If I were to meet someone who said the kind of things I'd been saying in my kind of voice – well, I'd take against them right away! A friend of mine once described my voice as "clipped and staccato – simply made for instruction, chastisement or summing up." That is not exactly a compliment, is it? I said a "friend", but she is nothing of the sort, really. Little more than a fifth columnist, as we used to say at school.'

'Let me get this thing clear. You know who the would-be killer is,' Payne said slowly, 'and you also know the identity of his intended victim?'

'I do know, yes. Actually, I never said it was a man. I never said "he" or "his". You are trying to catch me out, aren't you?'

'I can't help wondering *how* you know. Perhaps the would-be killer talked to his accomplice about the murder and you overheard the conversation? Or else he wrote something which you happened to read? The only other possibility I can think of is that you saw him – or her – look at the victim in a certain way?'

Sybil shook her head resolutely. 'No, no, I couldn't possibly tell you what it is, Major Payne. It wouldn't be right. I am sorry. I have no doubt you think me frightfully irresponsible, playing games with human lives. I must say I did deliberate whether or not to warn the victim – I mean the person who is going to be the victim. I suffered *agonies* of uncertainty! I had the idea of writing an anonymous note and leaving it in their room!'

'*Beware of X. Don't let X get anywhere near you,*' Payne murmured.

'Something on those lines, yes.'

'But you didn't write the note?'

'I didn't. In the end I decided that that was one road down which I most definitely must *not* go. I was suddenly riddled with doubt. What if I'd made a mistake? What if I'd got the wrong end of the stick after all? It would be so terribly awkward, wouldn't it?'

'I suppose it would be.'

'More than awkward! It would spell the ruin of somebody's good name! These things do matter, even in this irresponsible day and age. I'd never forgive myself if that did happen – never. You know how accusations tend to stick? No matter how wild? Pitch, as they say, soils.' Sybil de Coverley smoothed out her gloves on her knee. 'Well, when you come to the island on Friday afternoon, you'll be able to meet everybody and of course I'll show you the – the thing.'

2

TEN LITTLE
SAILOR BOYS

'What thing?' This time Antonia didn't try to keep the exasperation out of her voice.

'It's an object. I found an object,' Sybil said evasively. 'What I believe to be proof of someone's guilt. Your aunt says both of you are astutely analytical, which means you will have no problem seeing the object's significance at once. I am sure it will come to you in a flash.'

'How much does my aunt know about your suspicions?' Payne asked.

'No more than you do, I assure you. Dear Nellie. She was one of mama's greatest chums, you know. She's been on the island since Monday. I think she's enjoying herself. I have told her exactly what I have told you. Not a word more not a word less.'

'I don't suppose you have told your brother about your suspicions, have you?'

'No, of course not. My brother is the very last person I would ever tell. John would say I was bonkers. He often says that. He once compared me to the woman in the Chekhov play who lived in a cupboard because she believed herself to be a seagull! John has a thing about seagulls.'

'I think he got Chekhov mixed up with Strindberg,' said Payne. 'The woman who lived in a cupboard believed she was a parrot.'

'My brother has a thing about seagulls,' Sybil repeated. 'I am afraid relations between me and my brother have been strained for some time. I think he suspects I intend to sell the island, you see.'

'The island belongs to you?'

'Indeed it does.' Her father had left Sphinx Island to her. Sphinx had been her albatross. She got a sense of floating melancholy each time she thought about it. 'Well, it took me quite a while to make up my mind, but then I decided that enough was enough. It's *my* island, so I can do with the damned thing as I jolly well please. John can't really prevent me from selling it. He's got no legal right. I'll sell it and then I'll buy myself a nice little flat in South Kensington, so there.'

'Would your brother be very upset?' Antonia asked.

'He wouldn't be "very upset". He would be terribly upset. He'd kick up a hideous rumpus. There would be ugly scenes. He would try to stop me in some way. John said once he would rather cut his throat than live in South Kensington.' Sybil heaved an exasperated sigh. 'Would *you* live on a small island, Major Payne? If given the choice?'

'I am not sure. I don't think I would.'

'Antonia?'

'No. Not on a small island.'

'What if someone left you an island in their will?'

Payne said he would sell it. He put a match to his pipe.

'That's *exactly* what I intend to do. I am so glad we are singing from the same hymn book. If my lease of life were suddenly to run out, the island would go to John. I have made a will to that effect, though of course I have no intention of kicking the bucket. Not in the foreseeable future at any rate,' Sybil said brightly.

Payne looked at her. 'Does your brother know that you've left him the island in your will?'

'I have an idea I told him. I believe I said, "If I were to snuff it before you, dear boy, Sphinx is yours for life," or words to that effect. I do try to be fair.'

Sybil went on to say that she hated the sea as much as she hated the island and of course you couldn't have one without the other. *The cruel alien sea.* Either layered in purple and blue or muddy green or gun-metal grey. She'd got to know the sea so well, she could write a paper on its changing colour. The island used to bear their name – De Coverley Island – but it was popularly known as Sphinx Island. Crackpots seemed to be drawn to it as bees are to honey. There were pictures of the island on the internet, if they wanted to look at them before they came. Aerial photos and so on.

'You can read about the island's history, it's on Wikipedia, all about the secret military experiments during the Second World War, the UFO landing in the fifties and so on and so forth.'

'Where is Sphinx Island exactly?' Antonia asked.

'It is situated three miles off the Devon coast. From some angles, it does bring to mind a crouching, smiling kind of Sphinx. It looks absolutely hideous. We've got our very own launch, *Cutwater,* so you won't have to hire a boat or anything like that. Oswald said he would collect you himself. Oswald is terribly keen on sailing. Mad about it. He said he would be at Wanmouth to meet the 4.50 from Paddington. I'm talking about Friday afternoon … Unless you decided to drive?'

Payne smiled pleasantly. 'We haven't yet said that we are coming.'

'You'd recognise Oswald right away by his rather superior-looking yachting cap. Thank God for Oswald Ramskritt! He is an American. He is the man who's going to take the island off my hands. He is awfully zealous and territorial. The frontier spirit, wouldn't you say? Apparently, at one time, *before* the Crunch, he was so frightfully rich; he seriously considered the idea of buying Venice and turning the Grand Canal into a six-lane expressway.'

'Can one buy Venice?'

'Perhaps not in the normal course of things, but he said there was a way round it. Oswald has the smiling self-assurance of a man who has achieved success early and easily. I believe he is a self-made man, but then aren't all Americans? He and his entourage are already on Sphinx. He's got a yacht. Not a particularly vast one, but it's terribly smart. Are you a sailing man, Major Payne?'

'I'm afraid I am not.'

'Poor John used to do a lot of sailing himself, when he was younger, before the attack, but he is a virtual recluse these days. He never goes anywhere and he tends to keep to his room when we have visitors. Expecting him to come down and say how-do-you-do would be futile, like waiting for a badger to start tap-dancing. Nobody seems to mind. Oswald says he loves English eccentricity in every shape or form. I am sure he means it. Mrs Garrison-Gore of course is too busy to notice anything. I must admit I find Mrs Garrison-Gore's kinetic intensity a little exhausting.' Sybil bit her lip. 'Oswald's secretary – *not* Ella, the new young one – seems to *like* John. Her name is Maisie, I think. The other day I saw her standing outside John's door, talking to him through the keyhole.'

Antonia had the impression Sybil regretted mentioning Mrs Garrison-Gore's name.

'I wonder if she's been attempting to nudge him into a more enlightened direction? That's the sort of thing an American girl *would* do. She is terribly well-meaning and of course she is pretty as a picture. So refreshingly innocent and unspoilt, a *tabula rasa*, as papa would have put it – unless she turns out to be an accomplished little actress who's after Oswald's millions. I find American girls incomprehensible, don't you? Apparently John told her that he liked fried chicken best, he whispered it through the keyhole, which suggests some kind of a bond might have been forged between them. He also told her she mustn't think he *enjoyed* chewing blotting paper.'

'Does your brother chew blotting paper?' Antonia asked. I want to see these people, she thought.

'He does. As it happens, there's a perfectly rational explanation for it. I bet you'll never guess what it is.'

Payne cleared his throat. 'Old-fashioned remedy for headaches that develop as a result of shooting?'

'You *are* clever. I don't believe I've ever said that to a Major before. That's the reason he does it, yes. John is a shooting nut. He is the proud owner of several guns. He shoots at seagulls, mainly. He is tormented by blinding headaches, which he insists on explaining with the fact that he is left-handed. He is, to use an awful phrase – please, you must forgive me – *in denial.*'

'Who else is on the island?' Payne asked.

'Well, there is Ella. Ella Gales. She works for Oswald. General dogsbody and so on. Ella's got the patience of a saint, though she is too clever for straightforward virtue. I believe she was born a Swede. "Stoic and isolate". Quite distinguished-looking, a former beauty queen, apparently. The epitome of style and sheer *chic*. Ella and Doctor Klein are thick as thieves, which I find intriguing. If you could imagine Beauty and the Beast … Shall I tell you who they remind me of? Those two hunted outcasts, Hagar and Ishmael, abandoned and wandering in a psychic wilderness of their own creation. Whenever I happen to walk in on them I get a palpable sense of having interrupted some cabal in its scheming.'

'Who is Doctor Klein?'

'He is Oswald's doctor. Doctor Klein is what papa would have called an "Americanised Kraut". Papa used to refer to America as a "land of sanctimony and barbarism". Papa would have detested that awful senator with the vests, what was his name? Why would anyone in their right mind want to be the President of America, I simply can't imagine. Papa was one of the most zealously xenophobic people you are ever likely to meet, yet when he was confronted with *real* aliens, he didn't turn a hair.'

'What real aliens?'

'There was an incident in the early 1950s. A landing of sorts. All part of the Sphinx Island mythology. I keep getting letters from madmen asking questions about it. They call themselves "ufologists", or something like that.' Sybil waved a dismissive hand. 'Doctor Klein is enormous – and I mean enormous. It's odd since he eats next to nothing and invariably declines pudding.'

'Why does Oswald Ramskritt need a doctor?' Antonia asked. It occurred to her that she had heard Mrs Garrison-Gore's name before, only where?

'I am not sure. All I know is that Doctor Klein holds reflexology sessions with him, if that's what they are called. Rich Americans appear to suffer from all kinds of peculiar conditions, have you noticed, or perhaps they only imagine they do? Oswald is surrounded by nice and helpful people. It makes me green with envy. You wouldn't believe this, but the moment they realised there were no servants on the island, Ella and Maisie offered their services!'

'No servants?' Payne's left eyebrow went up.

'Not a single one. Mod cons are in somewhat short supply on Sphinx. Remember the old Punch cartoon? Oh dear that was so *funny*. "Good night, Mrs Jones, you must forgive our primitive ways." Well, Ella alone is worth ten servants. Ella makes sure the flowers are right, she organises the menu and she actually cooks for us. She is efficiency personified. I have an idea she was once involved with Oswald. I don't think she

THE RIDDLE OF SPHINX ISLAND

is awfully happy, but then who is? Maisie, as I said, is Oswald's brand-new amanuensis, if that indeed is the word I want, though what exactly she *does* is anybody's guess.'

'There is no Mrs Ramskritt?'

'No. Dead, I think. Strictly *entre nous*, Oswald's completely smitten with Maisie, poor man, as only a middle-aged man can be, though I somehow doubt he's declared undying love for her yet. The girl, on the other hand, is in awe of him.'

'They seem to be a fascinating bunch of characters.' Payne shot a glance at Antonia.

No servants, Antonia was thinking. That was a bit unusual. A house party on a minuscule island and no servants …

'Who is Mrs Garrison-Gore?' Antonia asked.

'Oh, just a friend of a friend … I am afraid John has been making things a little awkward for everybody. What started as a mild neurosis has developed into what some may call a morbid obsession. He leaves his room *only* in the dead of night. He likes to walk about the island, even when there is a storm. He wears an oilskin and a slouch hat and carries a lantern and a gun. I'd better explain. A couple of years ago John was attacked by two seagulls and he's been quite different since. Sometimes, in the morning, we find the little beach below the rocks littered with the bodies of the seagulls he has shot during the night.'

'I assume he has a licence for his guns?'

'He has, though in my opinion it should be taken away. He is *not* a responsible person and accidents do happen, don't they? I loathe the idea of reporting him as that would make me a snitch, but the truth is that John and I can't agree about a single thing. Strangers to matters of any importance, as they say.'

Payne looked at her. 'This murder mystery of yours – is it perhaps something to do with your brother?'

21

She gave a sad smile. 'You ask the kind of question I can't possibly answer. Incidentally, no one must *ever* know that you are on any sort of urgent mission. When you arrive on Friday, you will be introduced as Lady Grylls' nephew and niece-by-marriage, which of course is who you are.' She lowered her voice. 'I am sure you wouldn't dream of giving the game away. Your aunt said you make a religion of being discreet in every case you undertake.'

'I don't think we are up to undertaking anything. I am not sure we'll be able to come, really.' Antonia spoke in sudden panic. 'As it happens, we are extremely busy this weekend, aren't we, Hugh? It's rather a special kind of weekend for us, you see. An exclusive kind of celebration, you may say –'

'How many people are there on the island altogether?' Payne asked.

'Let me see. Oh dear, I am so terribly bad at arithmetics! Seven – no, eight – that includes your aunt and Doctor Klein.' Sybil de Coverley counted on her fingers. 'When you join us, there will be ten of us … Ten, yes – that's right, isn't it?'

3

BETRAYAL

Doctor Klein's hand went up to a point above his right eyebrow where it hovered for a second or two. It was a curious gesture. She had observed him do it before. He asked if she really wanted to hear the results of his assessment.

'I do. I want to see whether you will tell me anything about Oswald which I don't know already,' Ella said. She was tall and attenuated and very fair. Her ash-blond hair was bobbed and she wore pearl earrings. She looked extremely elegant in a silk trouser suit with narrow trousers and tunic top in a subtle shade of a very pale greenish-gold. From a distance she looked no more than thirty. In fact she was fifty-nine.

'You think you know him well?'

'I believe I do, yes. Oswald enjoys talking about himself, doesn't he?'

'Yes. He is quite uninhibited. He believes I am one of the few people who understand him. He says he can trust me. I don't know why he should think that. He is so pleased with my services, he promises to double my fees.'

'Oswald is certainly generous to people he wants to impress.'

'You realise, don't you, that you are asking me to betray my patient?' Doctor Klein's lips twitched into what might have been a smile. He was a large shapeless man with white marsupial cheeks and he spoke in soft and uninflected tones, without a trace of any accent. He reached out for his notebook.

'Is patient confidentiality part of the Hippocratic oath?'

'I never took the oath, actually … *I hereby swear by Apollo Physician and Asclepius and Hydieia and Panaceia and all the gods and goddesses* – I have no idea how it goes on.' He put on his rimless glasses, opened his notebook and started leafing though it.

They were in Ella's room, sitting beside one of the long curved windows. It was a pleasantly furnished room. Off-white rugs on the gleaming parquet floor – fawn-painted walls – an oval mirror surrounded by lights – a dressing table with intricately shaped scent bottles and two hairbrushes with ivory handles. The only splash of colour was provided by a bowl containing blood-red roses.

The window was open. The sea outside was liquid sapphires that sparkled in the sun. Ella watched the waves rise up and move apart – 'in planes of blatant impossibility'. She shaded her eyes. There was something magical about an island; the mere word suggested fantasy. But the sea would be truly terrifying if there ever was a storm. None of the mainland was visible. Ella had the strange feeling that all contact with the world had been lost. An island was a world of its own – a world, perhaps, from which you might never return?

Doctor Klein was speaking.

'Oswald has an overweening sense of his own infallibility and his confidence in his own talents and powers is quite alarmingly exalted. He has a grandiose self-image and is reluctant to concede the possibility that he might ever become the subject of valid criticism. He compares himself to Rommel and Napoleon. Even if infinitesimally challenged, he becomes offended. He has difficulty masking his indignation and when his voice rises, it is –'

'Staccato with outrage?'

'Yes.' Doctor Klein looked up from his notes. 'You certainly know him well. He sees no need to justify himself or his actions on any count, regarding it as self-evident that he is right, in spite of all the evidence to the contrary. His capacity for self-analysis is limited.'

'Non-existent, surely?'

'A typical response to a question he doesn't want to answer is to deflect it with a question of his own. He demonstrates a marked reluctance to examine his behaviour or the consequences of his actions. He lacks insight and the concept of a wider responsibility is completely alien to him –'

Ella had the peculiar feeling that she had known Doctor Klein a very long time, well before he had joined Oswald's entourage – that perhaps he and she had met in some other life, that they had some shared destiny. In his company she found peace. She had chosen to turn to him for solace the way some people turned to open spaces, to a forest in spring, or to the sea. There was something mythical about him … Something *mystical* … A figure out of some strange dream … The gentle ogre … The benevolent behemoth …

It occurred to her that Doctor Klein must hate Oswald as much as she did. He had never said so, but he wouldn't be sitting here with her, betraying his patient's confidences otherwise …

'You are lost in a brown study, Ella,' she heard Doctor Klein say, as though from far away. 'Are you all right?'

'Yes. Sorry. Please go on. I know it is terribly perverse of me, but I find it extremely comforting listening to you dissecting him so mercilessly.'

'Oswald has mastered the appearance of affect, but it is unlikely that this is more than a convenient mask. He is insensitive, overbearing and emotionally immature –'

'He is a tyrant and a bully,' she whispered. 'Does he say anything about me? Does he ever try to justify the way he treats me?'

'He mentions you from time to time, yes.'

'What does he say? Please, tell me. I want to know.' She prepared for the blow by clenching her hands into fists and half-closing her eyes.

'He says you "provoke" him, sometimes by design, sometimes unintentionally. He admits he was in love with you once, deeply and passionately, but that was "aeons ago". He still has an overriding need for physical love, though he is no longer attracted to you. In his opinion, you have never been able to understand the way he "operates". You have no idea what makes him "tick". He describes you as "clinging". He catches you looking at him "with distaste and scorn". Is that true?'

'I suppose it is true.'

'You are the "grudge-bearing type". You tend to "live in the past". You seem incapable of "cutting your losses". You don't smile enough. You don't know the meaning of "letting go". He refers to you alternately as "saintly Ella" and "that masochistic martyr". He is annoyed by what he perceives to be your self-righteousness.'

'Am I self-righteous?'

'Not in the least. Oswald hates your "passivity". He resents the way you refuse to get angry with him and have a "proper fight" … He admits you are extremely competent in most things you undertake. No, he doesn't seem to see anything wrong with the way he treats you. He regards himself as your benefactor. He believes you should be grateful to him –'

'He actually said that?' Ella was aware of her senses becoming preternaturally acute. Her ears throbbed with the crash of the sea and the wild shrieks of seagulls. Her nostrils twitched at the reek of something loathsome, some detestable putrescence that came from the direction of the little beach below the rocks.

'He said you were consumed by sexual jealousy because of his affectionate interest in Maisie. He suspects you of wanting to harm him – or her.'

Although the day was very warm, Doctor Klein wore a black suit and a black tie. He always wore a black suit and a black tie. It was impossible to imagine him dressed in any other way. Ella believed he had three or four identical-looking black suits hanging in his wardrobe.

As she watched him, he started melting –

She was crying. It happened often these days. Silent tears ran down her cheeks. She didn't make a sound.

'I am sorry,' she said, pressing her handkerchief against her lips. 'Please go on.'

'Are you sure you want me to?'

'Yes.'

'You are upset.'

'I am not. I am fine, really.' She dabbed at her eyes. 'Please go on.'

'Oswald sees himself as a Julius Caesar kind of figure. Unappreciated, tragically misunderstood, threatened, betrayed, doomed. He suspects that members of his staff in the city are in the pay of some of his big business rivals. He's got it into his head that they are plotting his assassination. He has a recurrent dream about it.' Doctor Klein paused. 'Oswald believes he will be safer living on an island, but is afraid that he is going to die a violent death.'

Ella said slowly, 'Sometimes when people believe strongly enough that they are going to die, they do die …'

4

SUNSHINE ON THE SPOTLESS MIND

Oswald was the nicest man she had ever met. Kind-hearted and natural and always cheerful. He was very informal and even called his mother by her Christian name. He was supremely intelligent. He was an extremely important man. He was the owner and manager of Spectron Futures, did Lady Grylls know that? He was considerate and thoughtful and very, *very* generous. He liked nothing better than giving presents –

A large amethyst-and-gold bracelet slid down her slender tanned arm.

Oswald said *such* clever things, Maisie Lettering went on; only the other day he told her he wasn't really vain, *simply conscious of his own genius*. He had also said he was not the kind of man who ever became oppressed by a sense of general unworthiness.

'I don't know many people who are conscious of their own genius. In fact, I know no one,' Lady Grylls said. 'But perhaps he was joking?'

'Maybe he was. I do think Oswald *is* a genius.' Maisie's eyes were very bright. She said she considered herself extremely fortunate. Working for Oswald had been an honour and a privilege.

'I understand he's interested in buying this house as well as the island on which it stands.'

'Yes! Oswald has a lot of ideas. It's like a – like a never-ending spring! Sometimes his ideas come to him in the middle of the night and he has to turn on the light and write them down for fear of forgetting them.'

'Is that so? How very interesting. In the middle of the night? Fancy!' Lady Grylls chided herself for assuming the girl had witnessed Oswald Ramskritt's nocturnal inspirations at first hand. He had probably *told* her about it.

She had first entered Mr Ramskritt's employment as a nurse for Martita, Mr Ramskritt's invalid wife, Maisie explained. Martita had been extremely difficult, she'd had terrible bouts of temper, but then she'd died, which everybody thought very sad but it was also a merciful release, really. Oswald had then asked her to stay on and be his secretary!

'At first I thought I'd misunderstood. I raised a number of objections, but Oswald insisted I was the right person for the job. He was adamant. He said no one else would do.'

'You are awfully pretty, my dear,' Lady Grylls said.

'I am certainly very healthy. I am never ill,' Maisie said thoughtfully. 'I can't remember the last time I had the flu. I haven't had a headache in my life and I don't know what a nosebleed is. Mr Ramskritt told me he had every confidence in me. He said the work wouldn't be difficult. Just obtaining certain data from the internet, listening to him whenever he needed to air his views on some subject as it brought clarity to his thoughts, making phone calls, sending emails, preparing his cocoa and – well that's it, really!'

'Cocoa? I thought he drank nothing but champers.'

'He has a cup of cocoa before turning in.'

'But how perfectly extraordinary!' Lady Grylls might have unearthed a wondrous fragment of Attic pottery. '*Tea, although an Oriental, is a gentleman at least* … Chesterton, I think … Must ask my nephew … Cocoa in the poem was a vulgarian. A cad or a bounder, which, my dear, I am sure, your employer is not.'

'Is that the nephew whose wedding anniversary it is on Saturday?'

'The very same, my dear. My nephew and my niece-by-marriage.'

'That surprise we've got for them –' Maisie broke off. 'Do you think they will like it?'

'I very much hope they will. In my opinion it's the kind of present that's so much more suitable than anything one could buy at Fortnum's or Selfridges ... I still have coffee at Fortnum's sometimes, though these days I find myself spending more time in Harley Street than in Piccadilly ... I don't suppose you like England much, do you, my dear?'

'Oh but I do! I love England!'

'You love England? Really? I am told that some people – foreigners, mainly – are fascinated by the *idea* of England but they get bitterly disappointed when they come face-to-face with the real thing ... A *soggy little island, huffing and puffing, trying to catch up with* – with something or other. One of your fellow Americans said that, I do believe, though don't ask me which one. It was some famous American writer.'

'I don't read as much as I should. I need to improve my mind,' Maisie said. 'Oswald keeps recommending books to me.'

'Keeping up with one's reading can be quite a task.' Lady Grylls pushed her glasses up her nose. 'I am now compelled to use a magnifying glass which is rather a bore.'

'Would you like me to read to you sometime?'

'Kind of you to offer, my dear. Yes, why not? Your voice is as clear as a bell. Perhaps you could try to get something racy? Or maybe a murder mystery, of the kind my niece-by-marriage writes?'

'I don't really like murder mysteries. They scare me.'

She seemed a genuinely nice gel, Lady Grylls decided. She couldn't have been anything but an American. There was the earnestness, the simplicity, the complete lack of self-consciousness, the kindness and friendliness, all of which one associated with Americans. Might have been deemed gushing, garrulous and gauche, but, oddly enough, Lady Grylls didn't for a moment think of her in those terms. And she was so awfully pretty. Didn't she really see how pretty she was? Hadn't it occurred to her that her quite exceptional looks might have had something to do with her rapid promotion from nurse to secretary and the great trust her employer had to chosen to put in her?

At some point Lady Grylls seemed to doze off and she woke up with a start.

'That's right, my dear, how perfectly extraordinary. What was it you said about the house?'

'It's very old, isn't it?'

'No, not all old. It was built in the early 1930s. There's nothing special about it, really, though it seems to have generated its own mythology. I believe it was used for something terribly hush-hush during the war, then there was the alien thing.'

The girl's eyes had opened wide. 'The 1930s is *very old*. Oswald said he is enthralled by the lullaby the sea waves sing to him at night. Oswald is very romantic, but I think he is worried about something. I am not sure Ella likes it much here. She hasn't complained or anything, mind. Ella never complains.'

'No, she is not the complaining type.'

Lady Grylls found herself contemplating the Ramskritt ménage – tragic queen Ella and ingénue Maisie – not a *ménage-à-trois*, surely? It was curious that Oswald should have brought his very own German medico along. A Doctor Klein. Though of course anyone less *kleine* one could hardly imagine. His name should have been Grosse, something like that. Each time their orbits intersected, she had the disconcerting feeling she was seeing *two* people. Doctor Klein's eyes didn't seem to belong to Doctor Klein's body. She didn't quite know what she meant by that ... Not a well man ... Metabolism as sluggish as a frozen Thames. Breathing like a suction pump ... One always expected doctors to enjoy perfect health but this one clearly didn't ...

The girl was telling her something about her parents, elder sister and younger brother who lived in a place called Vermont ...

The drawing room door opened.

'I'd like to see everybody in the library in a couple of jiffies, if poss,' a voice said. 'Oh sorry, Lady Grylls. Were you having a nap? I do apologise, but we've got *very little time* and I am not sure we've got everything right yet. So let's put our best foot forward, shall we?'

Lady Grylls blinked. It was the woman with the pudding-bowl hairdo of course, the dreadful draperies, the smudged make-up and the costume jewellery. A Mrs Garrison-Gore. At the moment she was wearing something else, not the draperies and the jewellery – something in *aubergine à la crème d'oursin* – Goodness! – clung to her like a uniform – were those epaulettes?

'The good news is that Feversham will be with us very soon. Oswald phoned to say he'd fetched Feversham and they were on their way. I pray to God that Feversham is the right person. We'd be lost if he turned out not to be, lost! I'll have to reshape the whole thing. Doesn't bear thinking about! Maisie, would you help Lady Grylls?'

'The right person for what?' Lady Grylls was now fully awake.

'The right person for the job.'

'What job? Hate it when people talk in riddles.'

'*The takeover.* That's how I think of it.' Mrs Garrison-Gore spoke with an air of aimless defiance. 'I keep my fingers crossed he is the right man. If he is not, it's back to the drawing board and square one!'

What a tedious woman. Mrs Garrulous-*Bore*. Brought to mind a scout mistress. Lady Grylls couldn't abide scouts mistresses. Self-preoccupied, interfering, bumptiously self-important and *such a loud voice*. Lady Grylls then remembered Mrs Garrison-Gore served a very definite purpose – but surely Sybil could have hired someone less annoying?

'Maisie, I really do think you should –'

'Leave the gel alone. I can manage. My good woman, you fuss too much. You make it sound as though my time to depart to the shades has come.'

'Not to the shades, Lady Grylls, only to the library,' Mrs Garrison-Gore said.

Lady Grylls suppressed a groan. Who was it who said that the meaning of our lives was the impact we have on other people, whether we make them feel good or not? If that were true, she reasoned, then Mrs Garrison-Gore led a singularly meaningless life.

'I have not yet reached the stage gerontologists call "twilight senility". Whenever I am asked what it feels like to be eighty-six I invariably say that it's *so* much better than the alternative. My doctor warned me I have the typical physical constitution of a likely centenarian. Apparently my mind is most likely to go some time before my body, but then one can't have everything, can one?'

Clasping her stick, Lady Grylls rose to her feet. She gave Maisie a little wink.

Mrs Garrison-Gore stood in the corridor outside the library, frowning down at the open folder in her hands. Although she had managed to work out all the details now, she was assailed by the ghastly feeling the whole thing was all going to be a complete fiasco … Chin up, she murmured as she pushed open the door.

5

THE WAR
IN THE AIR

The Game Book, bound in black morocco leather, lay on his desk and the sight of it cheered him up considerably. He knew of no other morale-booster that could ever rival the Game Book!

It had belonged to his great-grandfather; it had then passed to his grandfather, then to his father. His grandfather had shot with the Prince of Wales, later Edward VII. Screwing up his face, John de Coverley adjusted his silver-rimmed monocle in his left eye. *Pheasants 456, Hares 90, Rabbits 99, Woodstock 57, Boar 15, Grouse 47*. He turned a page, then another.

He picked up his pen and started writing. *Herring-gulls 18. Lesser black-backed gulls 4. Bonaparte gulls. 3 Black-legged Kittiwake 4. Sybil gulls 4 –*

No, not Sybil – *Sabine* – Sabine gulls! Funny mistake to make – a 'Freudian slip'. Well, sometimes he did see Sybil – his impossible older sister – as a seagull. It wasn't only his imagination. She *did* resemble a seagull. The way she walked, the way she put her head to one side, the quizzical look she gave him. Most irritating of all, there was her cawing laugh. He had nearly taken a pot-shot at her the other day. There were times when he felt like wringing Sybil's neck.

John knew the exact number of seagulls he had killed the night before. Also the precise *genus* they belonged to. He had examined each corpse carefully by the light of his lantern. Every time he shot a gull, he made an entry in his little note-book; he later transferred all the entries to the pages of the Game Book.

The gulls were familiar with him by now and they tried to fight back in various ways. Sometimes they were too lazy for a full-on attack, then they tried to scare him off with their ominous 'gagagaga' and when they failed, they subjected him to a low pass. One of their intimidation tactics was to drop oyster shells on his head, another to vomit on him, or worse, and, if he let them, they would certainly succeed in bespatter-ing him since they had the precision of stealth-bombers. Only he didn't let them. As soon as they started descending, he took aim and pulled the trigger – *boum-boum!*

He never missed. He was a crack shot.

Most of his male ancestors had been big game hunters. De Coverleys had travelled the world over, looking for beasts to kill, to places like India, the Amazon, the Zambezi, even the Siberian steppes. Papa's hunting lodge in the Upper Hebrides, he remembered, had been full of 'trophies of the chase'. Antlers and tusks gracing every wall, elephant's feet serving as umbrella stands, and, best of all, there had been the mounted maws of snarling *tigris* and *ursa*.

The difference between me and my ancestors, John thought, is that I don't shoot *pour le sport*. No – this was war! He regarded himself as a soldier. He had moved his bed to the middle of the room and it now occupied a diagonal position, like a battleship of the paper game Jutland, which, forty years ago, he had been extremely fond of playing.

There wasn't anything *wrong* with him, was there? He took off his monocle and held it up between his thumb and forefinger. He thought back to that fatal day in June when he had been nearly scalped by the two herring gulls, which had swooped down on him and attacked him simultaneously, in a synchronized manner …

Perhaps he had suffered some kind of brain damage after all. Or was there something in the de Coverley genes that caused male members of the family to cling tenaciously to some *idée fixe*? Or, for that matter, to remain partially stuck in their childhood? John smiled at the idea.

The doctor who examined him had described his wounds as 'superficial', but sometimes these chaps didn't know what they were talking about. The funny thing was that he had never so much as considered the possibility of subjecting himself to a proper, more comprehensive examination. Sybil had made the suggestion, several times in fact, but then he *knew* she was eager to have him despatched to a loony bin, blast her.

Had he been born with a rogue gene or was he catapulted into non-conformity by the seagulls' attack? He found the question endlessly fascinating. As a matter of fact it was his sister who was the bedlamite. Sybil frequently did things that defied logic, like filling the house with crowds of people and then going off to London.

Extreme gregariousness was a form of madness, of that he had no doubt. And she had dismissed the servants. She was up to something, he could tell. Not that he minded a servant-less state. The fewer people there were about the better. He needed neither a daily woman nor a night nurse.

He would have preferred the island 'not honour'd with a human shape'. He'd told Sybil time and again – *no more house-parties, please* – but he might have been speaking Eskimo. It stuck in his craw that his sister never seemed to understand what he told her. Or pretended not to.

If gulls pose a particular threat to health and safety, a cull should be conducted, either by shooting or poisoning. He had seen that written somewhere. He was doing society a favour, not that he expected society to show any appreciation, let alone return the favour.

Gulls could live up to forty years, which was an awfully long time. They bred excessively. Their wingspan was three to five feet and they had fearsome hooked beaks. They were evilly-inclined and full of malice. They knew he went to bed at about two every morning and they woke him up at five with their shrieks. They tried to punish him for the destruction of their brethren.

John glanced at his watch. Tea-time. Marching up to a side table, he turned on the electric kettle. There were the Spode teacup and pot with the hunting scenes which he rather liked. Sybil, he had to admit, was awfully adept at providing him with regular supplies of eatables. And if she wasn't around, it would be that obliging American girl who answered his call. The other day he had asked for a dish of *fritto misto* – and he'd got it – hey presto! – piping hot – done to perfection!

The American girl had also brought him a whole cherry Bakewell tart. He had tried to lure and entice the Enemy with pieces of cake, which he had left lying on his windowsill. His intention was to capture a seagull alive, put it in a cage and subject it to some refined nastiness worthy of Dante, but the blasted things were too clever to fall for such a ruse, it seemed.

There was still some cake left. Goody! He swung his monocle on its black silk ribbon.

The American girl was actually the kind of girl he'd enjoy making friends with. But she seemed to be at the beck and call of the chap in the yachting cap, another American, whom John suspected of coveting the island. It was the kind of aberration that urgently needed correcting.

As John poured boiling water over the Gunpowder tealeaves, he felt the beginnings of a headache. The fellow in the yachting cap looked ruddy and hearty and he had discussed the island with Sybil. They had been standing on the terrace below. The fellow said the island was *exactly* what he needed …

There should be an eleventh commandment. *Thou shall not covet thy host's island.*

He carried his cup to his desk and sat in the swivel chair. The window was open. Such a magnificent day – not a single cloud in the sky! He couldn't see any gulls either. He took a sip of tea.

No, he didn't care at all for the chap in the yachting cap. Not one little bit.

What was that – voices? There were people in the library – which was immediately below his room.

His headache was worse now, so he reached out for the rose-wood box that lay on the desk before him. Taking out a sheet of blotting paper, he tore out a large piece, crumpled it up between his fingers and popped it into his mouth. Then another.

The trick was to concentrate and chew *slowly*. Once the blotting paper was transformed into paste, he would insert it between his front teeth and the upper lip and thus prevent the vibrations of the skull which caused the shooting headaches.

The voices in the library were becoming louder. He was a perfectly reasonable man, but if they went on like that, he wouldn't be responsible for his actions. Should he get his gun and fire a warning shot in the air?

He could actually hear what was being *said*. Nellie Grylls asking when Sybil was coming back. He knew her voice well enough. Once, years ago, he and Nellie Grylls had sat next to each other at dinner. He then heard the chap with the hearty American accent – the chap who coveted his island – ask the girl called Maisie to sit beside him. Damned presumptuous of him.

John put down his cup. He heard a door open and then there was a sudden hush.

Be not afeard; the isle is full of noises. Sounds, and sweet airs, that give delight and hurt not.

He didn't see himself as Caliban, but the Bard might have had Sphinx Island in mind when he wrote *The Tempest*. I wouldn't mind a Miranda, John thought. Or for that matter, a Maisie. It was some time since he had enjoyed female company of the right sort. That American girl would be quite perfect.

He glanced out of the window. *L'isle, c'est moi*, he murmured. Sybil and her American could go to hell. He believed the skies would be clear tonight. There was going to be a moon – a full moon?

The next moment a voice started speaking. It was a school-marm-ish sort of voice. Some bossy middle-aged woman. Really, the people his sister mixed with!

What was it the woman just said? John sat up. No, ridiculous, he couldn't have heard properly. The teacup shook slightly in his hand and tea spilled in the saucer.

'Ladies and gentlemen, allow me to introduce you to John de Coverley!'

6

INVASION OF THE BODY SNATCHERS

Immediately he saw what was happening. Everything had fallen into place. This was a conspiracy. His sister intended to sell the island to the American fellow in the yachting cap. His sister hated the island. His sister had been receiving glossy brochures from various estate agents. He'd seen them when he came out of his room at night, neatly stacked on the coffee table in the drawing room. St John's Wood. Bayswater. *South Kensington*. Sybil was mad about South Kensington. He'd heard her on the blower the other day, talking to someone. *Really, darling, South Ken is heaven, my idea of heaven*. Well, he would rather live in South Korea than in South Ken. Wild horses wouldn't drag him to South Ken.

He tended to forget that the island belonged to Sybil. Papa had left it to her. Papa had never had a good opinion of John, for some reason. Papa had been a notoriously poor judge of character. Papa had been in the habit of wearing tartan gloves, John remembered. Green and yellow tartan. *These gloves impart special powers to whoever wears them*. That's what papa told him once, when John was a little boy. It was again to Sybil that papa had bequeathed the gloves.

There was a reason why his sister had filled the house with people. The guests were part of the *plan*. Sybil intended to make things difficult for him. It was always harder for someone to put up a fight if there were a lot of people around. All the guests had been carefully selected. *They were all on Sybil's side.* And was it a coincidence that one of the men, the fat Teuton, was a medico? The fat Teuton was a member of Oswald Ramskritt's entourage. Not an ordinary medico, oh no. The fat Teuton was a *loony doctor.* John had gathered as much from a conversation he'd overheard between him and the tall woman called Ella Gales –

John knew exactly what was happening. His sister intended to have him certified and put away somewhere – no, not certified – having him certified would be too much trouble – Sybil wouldn't want her smart friends to talk about it – *he was to be killed.*

John ran his hand over his face. Yes. Sybil intended to have him killed. Killed and disposed of. They would do it the civilised way of course – they wouldn't smash his skull with a croquet mallet nor would they strangle him with the cord of his monocle – oh no – a tiny prick on the side of the neck would be enough. That's where the medico came in.

They would drop his body in the sea. They would probably use the paperweights from the library, the large triangular ones with the Etruscan motif, to weigh him down. He would be gone in a jiffy. He would never be found. He might never have existed. The fish would have a feast. The seagulls would rejoice.

Ladies and gentlemen, allow me to introduce you to John de Coverley.

It all made perfect sense now. His sister intended to have him *replaced.* She had already found a replacement. His replacement was downstairs. It would have to be someone who looked like him, though the resemblance didn't have to be too great. Very few people knew the precise details of John de Coverley's physiognomy. He had been, as they say, out of circulation for, oh, for quite a bit. One tall, distinguished-looking middle-aged man with grey hair carefully brushed back, looked very much like another.

All the chap had to do was put on an old shooting jacket with leather patches, wind a Paisley scarf around his neck, stick an eyeglass in his eye and – *voila!*

He knew how his sister's mind worked. What Sybil wanted was a brother who didn't embarrass her, who refrained from sneaking out of his room at the dead of night on one-man battues. A brother who observed *les convenances*, who came down to tea, brimming over with vacuous bonhomie, who haw-hawed and how-do-you-do-ed and spouted well-bred banalities.

Aren't we having marvellous weather? Would you like me to show you round the garden? It's a bit soggy after last night's rain but we have galoshes galore. We get Admirals and Painted Ladies regularly vying for supremacy over the honeysuckle. The Painted Ladies invariably win.

Sybil liked Society too much. She enjoyed gallivant-ing. Calling on people. Staying with people. Dining out. Attending matinees. Eating violet creams. Having tea at Brown's. Going to the Chelsea Flower Show. Filling the house with crowds of people.

If Sybil had managed to bag a husband, it would have been the husband who made the expert small talk and poured the drinks – but that, alas, wasn't to be. Too late now – poor old Syb was the sexual equivalent of one of those 240-volt electric kettles plugged into a 110-volt socket – doomed never really to come to the boil.

The woman with the booming voice was probably a matron on loan from some psychiatric institution. She certainly sounded the kind that imagined they knew exactly what was to be done about the toff *fou*.

John pulled at his lip as he sat considering his next step.

He could always barricade himself in his room. He was, after all, a soldier; being under siege was something soldiers took in their stride. Or he could write an SOS note, shove it in a bottle and throw it into the sea. As soon as the police found his message, they would send a chopper and have him rescued. But that would mean leaving the island and once he left, it might be a little difficult to get back. By the time he did manage to get back, the man in the yachting cap might already be in residence. That was something he should never allow to happen …

'I don't want to leave the island,' John de Coverley said in a defiant voice. '*Ever.*'

For a moment or two he remained deep in thought. Then, putting up his monocle, he turned his head and gazed at his gun.

It was extremely important, Romany Garrison-Gore said, that everybody should act in a coordinated but natural enough manner, even when performing trivial and seemingly irrelevant acts, like opening a paper or asking the time, adding cream to a cup of coffee or complimenting someone on the freshness of their complexion.

She appeared to be in complete control of her audience, but she wasn't truly at ease. There was something in the air. She was aware of certain vibes. She couldn't quite put her finger on it, but she knew she wasn't imagining it. She had always been sensitive to atmosphere, ever since she was a girl. Where *were* vibes coming from?

Not from Oswald Ramskritt, she didn't think. She rather liked Oswald. Something engagingly *boyish* about him and he had a vast fortune, which was again something she admired … Ella Gales looked composed and dignified as she always did, and she was holding her head high – that's what Queen

Christina must have looked like – if the Greta Garbo film was anything to go by … Little Maisie Lettering was smiling her artless smile – butter wouldn't melt in her mouth – a Daisy Miller kind of figure – ten minutes in Maisie's company and Romany felt like being suffocated by candyfloss … Doctor Klein brought to mind a giant balloon that had been inflated to bursting point and was about to rise at any moment … Lady Grylls had fallen into a doze again. Really, the upper classes were so terribly rude … Feversham was the picture of gentlemanly nonchalance, very smart, yet very languid, which was so English, smiling in an amused fashion as though at a joke which only he had understood. His eyeglass wasn't exactly like John de Coverley's – it was tortoiseshell-rimmed, while John's was silver-rimmed, she couldn't help noticing. Not that it mattered.

They probably thought she was enjoying haranguing them, but that was far from being the case. Like the characters that populated her books, Romany Garrison-Gore was *not* what she seemed. What most people took for breathtaking conceit was actually a cover for a deeply seated sense of insecurity. She was frequently tormented by a dreadful sense of approaching danger, by a feeling of imminent disaster – even of encroaching death!

I mustn't become *too* anxious, she thought. When I become too anxious, I make snap decisions, which are not always the right decisions.

The next moment she gave a little gasp. It was Doctor Klein who was causing her unease. The vibes were coming from him. *Yes*. She didn't know exactly how she knew, but she did. It was her intuition. She was curious about Doctor Klein. She felt with absolute certainty that Doctor Klein had become Oswald Ramskritt's doctor for the wrong reasons. It was her gypsy blood. Sometimes it allowed her to see things.

She was curious about all of them, actually …

Was Maisie aware that she had started leaning against Oswald Ramskritt's arm? Was Ella really the epitome of decency? Was Feversham going to be any good? Why couldn't Lady Grylls make the effort to stay awake?

If she ever saw their thoughts written out, would she be able to match them to their faces?

The door suddenly opened and a voice spoke.

'What's this, a wake?'

It was John de Coverley. Startled, they stared back at him. His face was red. His monocle glistened.

In his hand John de Coverley was clutching a gun.

7

WARNING TO
THE CURIOUS

Sybil de Coverley had come to see them on Wednesday afternoon.

The letter arrived the following morning, Thursday, about half an hour before the Paynes sat down to breakfast.

'Well, that's that. The die is cast. I don't imagine they dress up for dinner, or perhaps they do. We could always phone and ask.' Major Payne poured himself some coffee.

'We made a terrible mistake,' Antonia said. 'We should have said no.'

'We did say no.'

'Yes, but then we changed our minds and said yes. It was the wrong decision. We allowed ourselves to be won over.'

'Unless the talk is about cancer tests, it's always better to be positive than negative. Let's think of it as an adventure, shall we?' Payne helped himself to some bacon and eggs. 'We've never been on an island before. Think of it that way.'

'Of course we have, Hugh. We *live* on an island. It's our wedding anniversary on Saturday. We could go to the Caprice and have fun or we could fly to Capri and have fun … Why oh why didn't we say no?'

'Toast, my love?'

'Yes, thank you … No, no marmalade … I suppose we could always ring her and say we have reconsidered the matter – or plead a prior engagement, which, I'll say, we'd completely for-gotten? I can lie really well if I put my mind to it. How about it?'

'We wouldn't have any peace if we didn't go to Sphinx Island. We'd be eaten away by curiosity.'

'Curiosity killed the cat,' said Antonia.

'I don't suppose you would go so far as to describe us as pathologically curious, would you?'

'I would,' she said firmly. 'We like nothing better than stick-ing our forks into other people's dinner.'

'You make us sound perfectly hideous.'

'We become restless and intense and we feel wretched and irritable if our curiosity is not gratified. We suffer withdrawal symptoms and when that happens we are hell to be with. That's why people hate us.'

'Nobody hates us. You are being neurotic.'

'Our friends are very careful when they talk to us. They think we suspect them of having things to hide.'

'How do you know what they think? Have they told you?'

'No, of course not. But it's written on their faces.'

'You are imagining things. Writers have a permanent need for fantasy.'

'Once we become curious, there's no stopping us. And we have started craving instant gratification, which I regard as a sinister development. At the moment we feel restless and out of sorts because we have allowed the riddle of Sphinx Island to take possession of our minds.'

'I don't think I am feeling particularly restless,' said Payne. 'And I am most certainly not irritable.'

'You raced through *The Times*. Earlier on you snapped at the milkman.' Antonia took a sip of coffee. 'You shooed Dupin off the sofa.'

'I always shoo Dupin off the sofa. The milkman is a fool. He doesn't seem to know the difference between half fat

THE RIDDLE OF SPHINX ISLAND

and full fat … There is nothing wrong with craving instant gratification, nothing at all. Children crave instant gratification. So did Ava Gardner and J.F. Kennedy. Joan Collins craves instant gratification, if an article in the *Enquirer* is to be believed. It's a common enough condition. I am surprised that you should be making such a song and dance about it.'

'I had no idea you read the *Enquirer*.'

Payne picked up the letter from the top of the pile that lay on the table between them. 'Look at this. *Major and Mrs Payne*. When was the last time we got a letter addressed to *both* of us? Written with a pronounced old-world formality with a stylo that looks as though it's been dipped in blood.'

'Let me see … This isn't blood. Can't be … It's some purplish ink, isn't it?'

'Looks like blood to me.' Payne held the letter close to his nose and sniffed at it.

'Who's it from?'

'No sender's address. Looks ominous. May be anonymous. I don't recognise the writing – do you?'

'No. Looks like someone who's been taking calligraphy lessons and is showing off.' Antonia put down her cup. 'Why don't you open it? Come on, open it.'

Payne cocked an eyebrow. 'Instant gratification, eh?'

'Very well, don't open it then.' Antonia started buttering a piece of toast.

There was a pause. Payne picked up *The Times*. 'I can't understand the way the crossword man's mind works. Yesterday one clue read, "This turn is rather offensive" – four letters – and the solution given today is "star"!' He looked up. 'How and in what way can a star turn be offensive?'

'A star turned becomes "rats" … We don't get many letters these days, have you noticed?'

'Would I be stating the obvious if I pointed out that's because we conduct all our personal correspondence via email?'

'We get bills of course. The Inland Revenue seem to be particularly interested in me. They seem to suspect I am earning millions from my books, which I am *not*.' Antonia's eyes kept going back to the letter, which Payne had propped up against the silver sugar bowl. 'I wish I were. I am not *popular* enough.'

'Popular taste is not to be encouraged. Down with Brown and Rowling, says I.'

'Do you think my books are an acquired taste?'

'Your books seem to divide public opinion if a website called brillread.com is anything to go by. Some of the so-called readers who leave postings on it give the impression of being markedly deficient in flair or literary taste altogether. You do have some discerning aficionados, though.'

'Not many. Not enough.'

Payne reached for the letter and held it up, squinting at the stamp. 'Posted in Torquay ... How very interesting ... That's not too far from Sphinx Island ... So the killer *is* on the island ... Wouldn't you say?'

'I wouldn't. I don't believe there is a killer. I think you should open the letter now. We might as well see what it's about. It may be a fan letter. Someone who is fascinated by our detective work, if one could call it that.'

Payne slit open the envelope and took out a single sheet.

He stroked his jaw with his forefinger as he read.

His expression changed. He lowered the sheet.

'What is it, Hugh?'

'I'd rather you saw for yourself. Otherwise you'll say I am making it up. I am sick and tired of being accused of making things up.' Payne tossed the letter across the table. He crossed his arms.

Antonia read aloud:

Dear Major and Mrs Payne,
I fancy you consider yourselves experts at solving murder mysteries
that are too subtle and intricate for our thick-headed police? Let us
see, clever Major and Mrs Payne, just how clever you can be. Perhaps
you will find this particular riddle not too hard to crack? Actually, there
are two riddles. Who is going to kill whom and will you be in time to
prevent the murder? I look forward to meeting you in two days' time,
17th April, on Sphinx Island.
Yours expectantly,
N. Nygmer

Payne said, 'Anything about that name strike you as a trifle unusual?'

'Of course it does ... I don't believe this. Someone is playing silly games with us. N. Nygmer indeed ... *Enigma* ...'

'That's how the evil Riddler is also known.' Payne helped himself to another piece of toast. 'N. Nygma with an A.'

'The evil riddler? Who's he – she?'

'N. Nygma is Batman's enemy. It's a he. *One* of Batman's enemies according to DC Comics.' Payne raised his cup and took a sip of coffee.

'I wasn't aware that you were such an aficionado of DC comics.'

'I am not. I happen to know all sorts of curious, fascinating and occasionally pointless facts. The only genuine *Liebfraumilch* is really *Liebfrauenmilch*. Facts like that. I also know exactly what Werrity did and *why* he did it.'

'So do I.'

'Only because I told you. What's the mark of true sophistication?'

'Unflappability? Never to demonstrate erudition unless in response to earnest and persistent questioning?'

'What's the character limit on Twitter?'

'You know I hate Twitter. 1666?'

'One hundred and forty. 1666 is the year in which the Great Fire of London took place. Has the Queen got a passport?'

'She has. No, she hasn't.'

'She hasn't. Sovereigns have no need for passports. They are identified by their face on the postage stamps ... Which fictional policeman genially offers to fit a second pair of handcuffs on to an arrested man's wrists in case the first pair feels uncomfortable?'

'Victorian?'

'Yes.'

'Sergeant Cuff?'

'No. Inspector Buckett.'

Antonia looked down at the letter. She took a thoughtful sip of coffee. *'Murder mysteries* ... He doesn't say "mysterious crimes" ... Murder ... He is quite specific ... He's promising us a murder ...'

'The Riddler's crimes are flamboyant and ostentatious. He specialises in death traps. He likes to devise life-and-death intellectual challenges. The Riddler has a fatal weakness for elaborate gimmicks. He is invariably depicted wearing his trade-mark green bowler with a black or purple question mark. Like all of Batman's enemies, the Riddler is a highly warped character. He is described as a "victim of an intense obsessive compulsion".'

Antonia said that perhaps they were dealing with someone who was dangerously stuck in their childhood. 'Or with someone who *wants* us to think they are dangerously stuck in their childhood ... Hugh, what if one of us is the intended victim and it is left to the other to investigate the murder?'

Payne raised his hand in a fist and said he would kill N. Nygmer if he so much as laid a finger on Antonia. 'I'll give him a crack on the nut which will leave him brain-dead. I'll smash his nygmatic nose. And I'll expect you to do the same should it happen the other way round.'

'He clearly knows Sybil has been to see us – but how could he? Sybil insisted no one knew about her suspicions. Apart from your aunt, that is.'

Payne stroked his jawline with his forefinger. 'Could N. Nygmer be Aunt Nellie? Or more precisely, is Aunt Nellie "N. Nygmer"? *Would* an octogenarian baroness play mind games with her favourite nephew and niece-by-marriage with whom she's never had a cross word?' He dabbed at his lips with the linen napkin and poured himself another cup of coffee. 'My answer is, no, she wouldn't.'

'What if this is some variation on the Murder Weekend theme after all? They may be doing it exclusively in our honour, in celebration of our lasting union. This may be your aunt's present to us, Hugh. Your aunt did ask you what we wanted for our anniversary, didn't she? Last month – when you took her for drinks at Harry's Bar?'

'She did ask me, yes. Dear Aunt Nellie. She said she had little patience with the tin or aluminium nonsense, which, apparently, is what people send on tenth wedding anniversaries, but how about eighteenth-century silver or Icelandic crystal or one of her precious medieval tapestries? I said – now what did I say?' Payne tapped his forehead with his forefinger. 'No, I can't remember.'

'I am sure you can. What did you say, Hugh?'

'I said – um – we've got enough silver, darling, we keep breaking things, so crystal would be wasted on us, and nothing in our house really goes with medieval tapestries. But she insisted she must give us *something*. It wouldn't do for her *not* to give us a tenth wedding anniversary present. So I said, if I remember correctly, that dear Antonia and I have been at something of a loose end lately, in fact, we are bored out of our wits, so what we'd like best, darling, is a mysterious murder.'

'You actually said that?'

'OK, I didn't say "dear Antonia".'

'But you did say we'd like a murder?'

'It was all light-hearted badinage.' Payne reached out for his pipe. 'If you want my honest opinion, I don't believe Aunt Nellie's behind it. She is too old to be bothered. A Murder Weekend is an elaborate thing, the devil to organise and get going, and it involves one too many people and "staying in character" and so on … And would Sybil de Coverley have placed her island at Aunt Nellie's disposal?'

'She might have done.'

He couldn't imagine his aunt staging amateur theatricals on an island in the middle of the sea. *Not* at her age. Out of the question.

'Perhaps someone else is doing the staging?' Antonia insisted. 'They may have employed the services of a professional?'

'Too far-fetched,' Payne said.

'Somebody whose metier is Murder Weekends, perhaps?'

'Too far-fetched.'

'Perhaps it's all Sybil's doing. She may be planning to commit a murder with the sole object of having her brother blamed for it?'

Payne nodded. 'She certainly managed to create the impression that brother John is of a hopelessly loony cast of mind if not dangerously unhinged … The kind of chap who *would* get obsessed with Batman comics … Yes, that's perfectly possible.'

'She went out of her way to poison our minds against him … I'm sure I've seen a letter like this somewhere,' Antonia said suddenly. '*In a book.* An Agatha Christie or somewhere.'

'It occurs to me, my love, that we may have been presented with a rag-bag of disparate ideas from various detective stories,' Payne said. 'The gentlewoman who knows too much but is reluctant to let on … Ten people on an island … A letter whose signature reads "enigma" and whose purpose is to taunt and provoke the detective … I wouldn't be at all surprised if, on arriving at Sphinx Island, we were greeted with a body in the library. What a bore *that* would be.'

'Clichés … Yes … All clichés … You are absolutely right …' Something was stirring at the back of Antonia's mind – what was that name Sybil de Coverley had mentioned and then looked as though she wished she hadn't?

'Hate clichés … But perhaps these are deliberate clichés?'

'Not necessarily. We may be dealing with someone who is incapable of original thought.'

'A general lack of definition is at the moment the keynote to the Sphinx Island affair … Why do you keep looking at the clock?'

'I need to go and buy some millinery … Care to come? Or will you think it a bore?'

'No, not at all. Splendid idea. As you know,' said Payne, 'I am awfully good at hats.'

8

A MIND
TO MURDER

It was at the hat shop, one of her regular haunts in Beauchamp Place, that Antonia remembered. 'I believe Sybil referred to a woman called Garrison-Gore. *Mrs Garrison-Gore*. Earlier on, when you talked about clichés something seemed to click. I can't swear to it, but I believe I've heard someone mention a Romany Garrison-Gore. Unless I dreamt it. No, I didn't. It was my copy editor who mentioned her.'

'Your copy editor? Are you sure?'

'I am.'

'Are you telling me Mrs Garrison-Gore is one of you? I mean one of the crime-writing sorority. Romany Garrison-Gore. I am most certainly not familiar with the name. It doesn't ring the faintest bell.' Payne shook his head. 'Perhaps she is one of those obscure ones that are strictly for library distribution? It's ages since I've been to the library.'

Antonia was in the process of adjusting a French straw confection on her head. 'She is "one of us", yes ... Unless it's a different Mrs Garrison-Gore altogether. Her sister or her cousin.'

'No, not her sister – they can't both be "Mrs Garrison-Gore" – unless both women married men called Garrison-Gore ... And no two sisters can ever be called "Romany" ... Didn't they make you study Titles and Forms of Address at your finishing school?'

'I thought Sybil looked furtive when she mentioned Mrs Garrsion-Gore's name.' Antonia's eyes narrowed. 'As though she regretted letting it slip out. Perhaps I imagined it.'

Payne said that a detective story writer who was *already* on Sphinx Island was a damned suspicious thing. 'Yes, it all makes perfect sense now … Sybil was perturbed that you – a detective-story writer yourself – might recognise Mrs Garrison-Gore's name and draw certain conclusions from it. The obvious conclusion of course is that they are putting on some murder show in our honour and that they have hired the services of a professional to stage-manage it.'

'You thought the idea far-fetched.'

'No, not far-fetched at all. Of course Mrs Garrison-Gore's presence on Sphinx Island may prove to be purely fortuitous – she may be John de Coverley's latest mistress – or Sybil's oldest and dearest school chum. Or she may turn out to be a loony ufologist who's writing a thesis on the alien invasion of Sphinx Island in the fifties. That's possible, isn't it?'

'Sybil wouldn't refer to her as "Mrs Garrison-Gore" if they'd been at school together,' Antonia pointed out.

'That may be some kind of a private joke between them. A chap I was at school with was called Puckler-Muskau, but he became generally known as "Pickled Mustard". He was an Austrian Prince who could trace his lineage back to the days of the Holy Roman Empire. But we are digressing.'

'It's you who's digressing … Actually, Sybil said Mrs Garrison-Gore was a "friend of a friend", but that was clearly a fib concocted on the spur of the moment. I think she was trying desperately to distance herself from her.'

'What did your copy-editor say about Mrs Garrison-Gore exactly?'

'It was only a passing remark. I don't think it was particularly nice.' Antonia scrunched up her face. 'Something about Romany Garrison-Gore being the ultimate nightmare to edit.'

'Decidedly not nice ... It was that one word, "clichés", that reminded you of her, wasn't it? That's when things clicked?'

'Yes ... How do I look?'

'You look marvellous ... A little to the left ... That's it ... Perfect ... Clichés ... The lady novelist with a penchant for lethal clichés ... Could we assume that Romany's *romans policiers* are little more than hackneyed rag-bags of disparate ideas pinched from other people's books?'

'For some reason I have the impression she writes under an assumed name.'

'"Garrison-Gore" sounds like an assumed name to me. Somehow one *expects* the pen of a murder mystery writer to be dipped in gore. Which ties up with the letter. I said that looked like blood, didn't I? One must never underestimate the power of subliminal suggestion ... Names are funny things ... I believe President Reagan had a spokesman called "Speakes", didn't he?'

'Shall I buy this hat then?' Once more Antonia was looking at her reflection in the mirror.

'I think you should. It has the wow factor.' Payne put his head to one side. '*Yes.* You will be the queen of Sphinx Island. *Facile princeps* and *ne plus ultra* ... Oswald Ramskritt and Doctor Klein will be impelled to fight a duel over you whereas John de Coverley will throw himself at your feet and beg to kiss the hem of your gown.'

'I don't intend to wear the hat on Sphinx Island.'

'I think you should. It would be a mistake not to.'

'Perhaps *you* should wear it,' said Antonia. 'It may deter you from saying one too many silly things?'

'I think you should pump your copy-editor for more details regarding *la* Romany,' Payne said. 'Or would she consider bitching about the authors she is paid to serve unprofessional?'

'I like the hat very much. I am going to buy it,' Antonia turned to the shop assistant. 'I am so terribly sorry. We've been keeping you waiting. We've been exceedingly thoughtless. You've been extremely patient.'

'No, not at all, madam.' The shop assistant gave a little bow and said that it had been a pleasure.

Antonia watched him place the hat in a luxurious box made of jade-green silk. 'Hugh, would you —?'

'Yes, of course, my love.' Payne produced his wallet.

'Thank you, sir.' The shop assistant bowed again and asked whether there would be anything else he could do for them.

'I hope you won't think my question awfully peculiar,' said Payne, 'but are you at all familiar with what goes on at Murder Weekends?'

'I attended a Murder Weekend once,' said the shop assistant. 'It took place at a very pleasant moat hotel in Surrey. It was my wife's idea. We enjoyed the food and the view but not the actual detection.'

Antonia looked at him. 'Oh? Why not?'

'Some of our fellow participants indulged in noisy and frequently ill-natured disagreements. As a matter of fact, two ladies nearly came to blows over a bronze statuette representing a ruminative monkey. One lady insisted the monkey was a red herring, while the other argued that it was a clue.'

'Which one was it?'

'Neither. As it turned out, the bronze monkey played no part in the Murder Game. It was merely part of the hotel *décor*. It had been given to the manager as a present by a Nepalese tourist, as we subsequently discovered. The odd thing was that we'd convinced ourselves the two ladies were actresses and that the fracas was part of the script, which of course they were obliged to follow.' The shop assistant shook his head. 'People are *so* competitive.'

'I don't think we'll have any competition where we are going,' Payne said. 'We believe we'll be the *only* people who will have to guess whodunnit. You see, we strongly suspect the whole thing's being staged for us and us alone as it is our tenth wedding anniversary.'

'Your tenth wedding anniversary? May I offer you my warmest congratulations, sir – madam?' The shop assistant bowed for the third time.

'We may be wrong of course. It may prove to be – um – something completely different altogether.'

'You aren't by any chance contemplating the possibility of a real murder, sir? That ploy has been used in several books already, I believe. A Murder Game ending in real murder. *Not* a particularly original idea – if I may venture an opinion.'

'Don't you sometimes wish that we possessed the kind of temperament that has been described as "sublimely uninquisitive"?' Antonia said as they left the shop and stood looking for a taxi.

'No, never.'

'We'd have been *so* much happier.'

'I rather doubt it.'

'Oh don't let's go, Hugh! *Please*. It's bound to be an awful bore.' She clutched at his arm. 'Some silly Murder Game, which, for your aunt's sake, we'll have to pretend to enjoy!'

'My aunt would be terribly disappointed if we didn't go … Oh there's a taxi.' Payne held up his rolled umbrella. 'Eight people on Sphinx Island,' he went on after they got in. 'There will be ten, when we go.'

'*If* we go,' said Antonia.

'Ten people on an island, one of whom is quite cranky and has murder on the mind.'

'I very much hope it won't be *that* scenario.'

'The cast of *dramatis personae* promises to be an interesting bunch … Who do we imagine will kill whom and why?' Payne asked.

'I don't know and I don't care, though for some reason I see Mrs Garrison-Gore as the victim … While working out the details of the Murder Game, she does research and discovers something discreditable about one of her fellow guests.'

'Ah. The Mystery of the Murdered Muckraker. Excellent … Which fellow guest?'

'It's *got* to be the rich American as he is the one character who is immediately associated with high stakes. Oswald Ramskritt has a skeleton in his cupboard … Behind every great fortune there is a crime …'

'Who said that? Donald Trump? The Duke of Kent?'

'Balzac, actually.'

'Let's decide on the crime … *Bone in mixed byre that goes with corruption.*'

'You sound like the Riddler now.'

'Perhaps I *am* the Riddler,' said Payne. 'Perhaps this is all my doing.'

'How many letters?' Antonia asked.

'Seven.'

'Seven? Rib, I believe, is anagram of "byre", sort of. Am I on the right track?'

'You are.'

'Oh it's easy. Bribery – bribery and corruption?'

'Bribery and corruption it is. Ramskritt was once in jail. He has bribed some person in a high place in return for having his criminal record destroyed. Or records. He may have more than one. An extremely likely contingency since he is an American. He may have been involved in organised crime. Ramskritt's reason for killing Mrs Garrison-Gore will be to prevent her from blurting out his guilty secret.'

9

PSYCHO

That evening, after they had packed their bags and were sitting down to a light supper of roast duck, peas and new potatoes, Payne said, 'What if this whole thing is *not* a product of Mrs Garrison-Gore's diabolically illogical imagination? What if Sybil's story of a would-be murderer on her island is *bona fide* after all? What if N. Nygmer does exist?'

'Then we'll need to proceed with the utmost caution and infinite circumspection,' Antonia said. 'And I will take that hat with me, if you insist.'

'Sybil assured us no one else knew about her suspicions, yet the very next day we receive us a letter signed "N. Nygmer", confirming that there *is* going to be a murder on Sphinx Island. N. Nygmer says he is expecting us.' Payne paused. 'How *did* N. Nygmer know we were going to arrive at the island on 17th April, Friday?'

'N. Nygmer overheard the conversation between Sybil and your aunt?'

'*Yes*. Which means the killer is aware that Sybil knows his secret, also that she has been to consult us about it … The killer is terribly eager to cross swords with us, hence the personal missive and the promise of riddles … You see what the implications for old Sybil are, don't you?'

'Of course I do. As the only person who knows the Riddler's identity, Sybil de Coverley may be in mortal danger.'

'I hope we don't arrive too late,' Major Payne said.

It was Lady Grylls who told Sybil de Coverley what had happened in her absence.

John had entered the library carrying his gun and looking most peculiar indeed and he fired two shots at Oswald Ramskritt. The first bullet had hit the portrait above the fireplace which showed a seventeenth-century de Coverley, a portly gentleman in a powdered wig. The second bullet had whizzed past Oswald Ramskritt's temple and hit one of the library shelves, embedding itself in a 1914 edition of Gibbon's *Decline and Fall of the Roman Empire*.

'I'm so terribly sorry,' Sybil said. 'I do feel responsible. Something's *got* to be done about John … Do go on, Nellie.'

'Oswald remained rooted to the spot, but he turned incredibly pale, which was hardly surprising. The Garrison-Gore woman and Maisie started asking him how he was. They clutched at his arms. They seemed to be checking for bullet holes. He remained completely unresponsive. You wouldn't believe it, my dear, but it was I who managed to disarm John!'

'You disarmed him?'

'Yes! I addressed him by the special name your darling mother had for him, you see. I remembered how it always used to calm him down. It was clever of me, wasn't it? I may even have mimicked her voice a little, I am not sure, but it seemed to do the trick. It had the most extraordinary effect. It brought him to his senses at once. It made me feel like one of those Indian snake charmers.'

'John adored mama. She was the only one who "understood" him and she certainly indulged him. I remember her saying once that he would end up either a Chancellor of the Exchequer or in Colney Hatch … But weren't you at all frightened, Nellie?'

Lady Grylls said that at her age there were very few things that frightened her. 'Actually I didn't stop to think. John stared back at me in a glazed kind of way. I know he might have shot me. He might have let rip. You might have found me lying in cold storage resembling the proverbial sieve. But I didn't stop to think. I ordered him to submit the gun *at once* – which he did – he hung down his head – he suddenly looked confused and terribly sheepish.'

'What did you do with the gun?'

Lady Grylls explained that she had handed it over to Doctor Klein, who had locked it in the tall Chinese cupboard in the library. 'He did it most resolutely and with startling agility. He's got *such* small hands, have you noticed?'

'I have. As dainty as a geisha's. Most peculiar. What happened next?'

'Oswald Ramskritt went on sitting in his chair. Maisie and the Garrison-Gore went on fussing over him. I believe he asked for a bottle of champagne. Feversham got hold of John's arms and marched him off to his room. John went like a lamb. I followed them. I wanted to make sure things were done properly.'

'Did he say anything?'

'Only that he'd seen it as his duty to protect his property. I believe he referred to Oswald Ramskritt as "that blasted interloper" and said something about Oswald being wrong if he imagined he could ever rule over Sphinx. He then said he wanted to wear his father's tartan gloves and would we go and look for them? He said his father's tartan gloves imparted special powers to whoever put them on, or words to that effect.'

'He'll never have papa's gloves, never!' Sybil cried.

'Then Ella suddenly appeared and she was holding a syringe. It seems she's got some nursing qualification or other, which came as another surprise. She gave him an injection, some powerful sedative, and it seemed to take an instant effect as he keeled over and went to sleep. We then locked him in, to be on the safe side, and that, as they say, was that.' Lady Grylls produced the key. 'Here you are, my dear. Now you are in charge.'

Sybil said she really didn't know what was to be done about John.

'Why don't you have him certified and put away?'

'It's a frightfully hard thing to do, apparently. I did consult with a doctor chum of mine. Notions of madness aren't what they used to be.'

'I couldn't agree more. You only have to turn on the box and out pop utterly unstable people with common accents and names like Norton, Russell and Ross. We live in dangerous times.' After a pause Lady Grylls asked if Sybil had been successful in her mission. Were Antonia and Hugh coming?

'I believe so,' Sybil said abstractedly.

'I told you they'd find the prospect irresistible, didn't I? You don't think we should call the whole thing off, do you? I mean – in view of what happened?'

'No. No. So long as we keep John incarcerated, there should be no more problems.'

'There's something else I've been meaning to ask you,' Lady Grylls said. 'Why *is* John's bed in a diagonal position in the middle of the room?'

'That's according to the rules of Jutland. He's always been awfully keen on Jutland. You remember the Jutland paper game, don't you?'

'I most certainly do. Good old Jutland. Such fun. I must say, John looked terribly distinguished in that eyeglass – same as that other chap, Feversham, who also cuts quite a dash.

I haven't seen a man wearing an eyeglass since 1951, I believe, and now suddenly there are two of them. Most extraordinary. John handled that gun with *such* panache. There's a lot to admire in John.'

Sybil said that, as always, Nellie was too kind.

Oswald Ramskritt had said he wanted to be left alone. He'd then opened the bottle of Louis Roederer champagne and started drinking.

He drank thirstily. He might have been drinking water.

He managed to finish the whole bottle in about twenty minutes.

He had had a narrow escape from death and that was his way of dealing with the shock.

Oswald didn't seem to get drunk. He didn't go into a stupor, he didn't throw up, nor did he collapse or go to sleep. Only his face acquired a waxen corpse-like pallor. When at one point Feversham looked in and asked if he was all right, Oswald talked to him about yachting, fishing and how he intended to improve the facilities on Sphinx Island once he had become its owner. He spoke without a hint of a slur.

Eventually he rose to his feet and left the library.

Coming across Ella in the corridor, Oswald barred her way, stood in front of her and slapped her across the face. There had been no obvious reason for the attack. As she staggered back and leant against the wall, he brought his head close to hers and whispered something in her ear, which made her gasp and tremble with revulsion. The moment she turned her head away from him, he drew back. He smiled and told her he wanted to see her do her martyr act – 'I'd like you to walk away from me, with your chin held as high as possible, your hands clenched in fists. I wish to see courageous suffering neatly portrayed in every inch of your body.'

He then went into the small study which had been placed at Mrs Garrison-Gore's disposal. The study walls were covered in Victorian sporting prints. He sat down at the Regency desk and stared at the screen of Mrs Garrison-Gore's laptop, which she had left turned on. He began to read the detective novel she happened to be writing, humming a little tune under his breath and tracing the words with his forefinger. When Mrs Garrison-Gore appeared, he commented on the way she had started changing her protagonists' names as well as the names of places. 'Not bad, not bad, if one likes this sort of thing. Stinking tripe of course. My fellow Americans call them "cozies" and it's women mainly who read them, correct?'

'I'd rather you didn't read my novel,' she said.

'How come this bit sounds old-fashioned and that bit doesn't? Your readers will accuse you of being inconsistent. Are you experimenting with styles or what?'

'I am sorry, Oswald, but I do need my laptop –'

He took no notice. His eyes remained glued to the screen. His hand moved over the keyboard. 'You leave the Internet on while writing? Why is that? The Project Gutenberg? Gutenberg *Lite* … What's so special about the Project Gutenberg?'

'Gutenberg invented the first printing press.'

'You don't say. The printing press, eh? And of what significance might that be to you?'

Mrs Garrison-Gore explained it was for something she was writing. 'I do a lot of research on the Internet.'

'It all seems to be about novels that are out of copyright … You are spoilt, do you know that? Like most hacks nowadays. Spoilt beyond redemption. Spoilt.'

'In what way am I spoilt?'

'You wanna know? You really wanna know? You have all the information you need at your fingertips, literally. You don't have to go to libraries and put in orders for books and wait for ages and ages. That was how it used to be. The Internet practically writes your novels for you, doesn't it?'

'No, not quite.' Romany managed a smile.

'Don't contradict me.' Oswald shook his forefinger at her. 'I hate being contradicted. Do you know what happens to females who contradict me? No, you wouldn't want to know. Ask Ella. Saintly Ella *knows*. I particularly dislike females of the monitor lizard variety. *Varanus komodoensis*.' He eyed Mrs Garrison-Gore fixedly. 'All right, let me explain. In the olden days writers used to go on pilgrimages to public libraries. They used to put in orders for obscure reference books and then went back home and sat on their fat asses and waited to be notified that their book has arrived. Then *another* journey to the library –'

'I am sorry but I need to work,' she said.

'You call this work?' Oswald Ramskritt tapped the laptop screen. 'What is the *point* of making a Cunningham into a Haverstock and Philippa into a Meredith? For some reason I am very interested in these changes. I can't quite say why but I am. There's something about changes that is always interesting.'

'There is nothing special about them,' Mrs Garrison-Gore said lightly. 'Writers make changes all the time.'

She was standing in the doorway, with her back to the corridor. She thought she heard a noise behind her – she heard someone give a little cough – but she didn't turn to look.

'Philippa is a particularly obnoxious character, isn't she? One of those frigid women who turn into indefatigable bullies and make other people's lives hell? I strongly disapprove of bullying of any sort. Why the heck does Grimmold Manor transmogrify into Cedar Court? For what reason, pray, does a "dickey" become a "gleaming shirt front"?' Oswald Ramskritt went on firing questions at her. 'Can't you make up your bloody mind? Nothing irritates me as much as indecision. Are changes essential to your writing? Is it true that the nearest thing to writing a novel is travelling in a strange country?'

He didn't wait for an answer. As he rose to his feet, he seemed to lose his balance for a moment, but managed to pull himself together, then without so much as a glance in Mrs Garrison-Gore's direction, he walked out of the small study.

He stopped outside Maisie Lettering's room and knocked loudly on the door. When she opened and let him in, he asked her to get back into bed. He then insisted on joining her. When she resisted, he pushed her back and slapped her face, the way he had done with Ella earlier on, only more viciously. When the girl started crying, he put his hand across her mouth. She went on struggling. 'Don't, please, oh don't,' she sobbed.

'*Don't, please, oh don't,*' Oswald mimicked. 'Very well. I will let you continue to maintain your precious virginal status, if that indeed is the case, but you must promise to be more amenable next time.'

'Please, Oswald, go to your room. *Please.* You are not well.'

'I never felt better.' He then asked her if he could come later. 'Some time after midnight, perhaps? Was that a no?'

Suddenly he relaxed his grip and stood up.

She was crying. 'Shut up,' he said. 'Haven't you heard of girls who drown in their own tears?' He then told her she was fired. He would make sure she became unemployable, he added. 'As you know, I have many contacts. People listen to me. In some quarters my word is Law. So don't be surprised when you start finding doors refusing to open for you.' She could take the next boat to the mainland – unless someone was willing to give her a lift?

He laughed as he said this and then he walked out of her room.

Out in the corridor Oswald lit a cigar. He then strolled leisurely to his room, humming a little tune under his breath.

10

THE LIVES
OF OTHERS

Major Payne was to point out later that without John de Coverley firing his gun at Oswald Ramskritt, the murder wouldn't have taken place. In his not-so-humble opinion, the shooting incident in the library was cardinal to the whole affair.

Antonia agreed. She thought of it as a kind of a butterfly effect.

'I am all right. I really am. It was a shock. It was quite awful, but I am – I am used to it. He's done it before, it's happened before, yes, but perhaps he's getting worse. That's the kind of thing he does when he is upset or rather when he gets drunk *after* he's been upset by something. It's happened before. He shows his true nature.' She tried to smile. 'Please don't look so concerned. He cannot cope with crises.'

It was later that same night and Ella was talking to Doctor Klein, who had come to her room to see how she was. He insisted that she should have some brandy.

She wiped the tears from her eyes with a determined gesture. 'When he gets upset, he needs a woman to take it out on. It *has* to be a woman. That's his idea of a catharsis. I've reached the conclusion he hates women.'

'I believe you are right,' Doctor Klein said in his detached way.

'It's perhaps something to do with the fact he had a terrible childhood. Sometimes I am convinced he is possessed. Or else it's some ineradicable psychological quirk. I am sure you can come up with the exact definition of what is wrong with him.'

'I do not intend to come up with an exact definition.'

'He is completely insensitive. I don't suppose he would have been able to do what he did in the early 1980s if he had had normal human feelings,' Ella said thoughtfully. 'He wouldn't have been able to do the job properly if he had been sensitive …'

'What job? What did he do in the early 1980s?'

'Oh. I thought you knew. Oswald used to work for the CIA. He was a spy. One of those "unofficial" ones. I am surprised he hasn't told you anything about it. I thought he told you everything.'

'I thought so too, but he hasn't said a word about his spying work in Germany, no.'

'You know he was in Germany then? So he must have told you?'

Doctor Klein shrugged. 'He may have mentioned Germany, yes, though he never said what he did there.'

'Perhaps he felt constrained by the fact you were a German?'

'That is the likeliest explanation.'

'Well, he was a Romeo spy.'

Doctor Klein slowly rose and walked towards the open window. He stood there, looking out. There was a full moon and, where it touched it, the sea resembled molten silver. It was very quiet …

'A Romeo spy … I don't think I have heard the term used before.'

His voice sounded odd – a little – weary?

Her cheek, the spot where Oswald had slapped her, was still throbbing. She thought it might be a little swollen. She had extremely sensitive skin.

'Oswald used to work for the CIA. He was extremely good-looking as a young man. He was in his late twenties or early thirties at the time. Not unlike the young Robert Redford, if photos are anything to go by. Women found him irresistible, went mad over him. He was chosen for his good looks – alongside a number of other young American men. They were called "Romeos" or "Romeo spies". Because of the love element.'

'I see.'

'Of course love has very little to do with it ... Oswald's credentials were impeccable. His father was a fundraiser for the Republican party. His patriotism was never in question. He adored Ronald Reagan. Still does.'

'What was his Berlin mission about?'

'It involved seducing German girls who worked across the wall in the Soviet sector – as well as keeping a "stable" of fillies living in the free sector of the city. The latter he groomed for the purpose of entrapping Soviet officials and getting state or military secrets out of them. The girls were also trained to put out incorrect, misleading information, which they made sure the Soviet enemy would receive, accept as true, act on and blunder. I may have got some of the details wrong, mind, but this is the gist of it. Oswald's front, or cover, was a restaurant in West Berlin, the so-called "free sector".'

'Did Oswald tell you about it in person or do you have other sources of information?' Doctor Klein turned back and resumed his seat opposite her.

'Oswald told me. He was drunk when he did. Not as drunk as tonight but enough to start showing off.' She gave a twisted smile. 'Benevolently inebriated, if one can put it like that. He enjoys talking about his conquests. He likes boasting, as I am sure you have noticed.'

'I have noticed, yes.'

She started telling him about the last German girl Oswald had seduced before returning to the US. The girl's name was Gabriele Hansen and she had a sister called Freddie. The Hansen sisters. That was one of the most shocking stories she had ever heard, Ella said. She still found it incredible that anyone could do a thing like that.

Doctor Klein sat monumentally still. He looked enormous in his old-fashioned double-breasted dinner jacket, stiff collar and black tie. He brought to mind Watts' picture of the Minotaur, Ella thought. Outside, the moon had intensified its glow and it was as light as day.

'Oswald had marked Gabriele down as a suitable target because her sister worked for one of the big Soviet officials in East Germany while Gabriele herself lived in Free Berlin. The two girls were very close. They exchanged letters and spoke on the phone. They hadn't seen each other for several years. It was very hard for Freddie to visit her sister in Free Berlin but she had managed it somehow. Perhaps she and her Soviet boss were having an affair, I don't know. Freddie was very pretty. Both girls were very pretty. Very fair. Beautiful blue eyes.'

'I expect Oswald showed you photographs?'

'Yes … I also saw the home movie, which Oswald shot on the day Freddie arrived, commemorating the occasion, so to speak … The three of them met at his restaurant where they had dinner …' Ella's voice tailed off.

There was a pause. Doctor Klein leant back in his chair. He brought his fingertips together and urged her to continue.

'I am not sure I want to,' Ella whispered. 'I get upset only thinking about it.'

It was good for her to talk. It was therapeutic. Doctor Klein spoke in reassuring tones. It would take her mind off what happened tonight. 'Tell me about the home movie. I am interested in stories about Germany. I still have relatives who live there. Berlin is a fascinating city. I remember a dancing club. I remember the linden trees. *A little on the lonely side.* That was a song I remember. Do forgive me. I am getting soft and sentimental. Tell me what happens exactly in the home movie.'

She shut her eyes. 'It's after closing time. Oswald's restaurant is empty. A festive candle-lit table. Silver and fine porcelain. The windows are bespattered with rain. Oswald is dressed in a white dinner jacket and crimson cummerbund. He looks very dashing. He is holding the camera in his right hand. He is waving – it is his reflection in a tall gilded mirror we see. There is Gabriele in a long, pale green dress –'

'You have very good visual memory.'

'Freddie looks preoccupied but she smiles bravely. She is painfully thin and pale, cheaply dressed. Gabriele has put her arm around her sister's shoulders. They are about to sit down to dinner. The camera swirls. Close ups of the girls' faces. Although Freddie looks haggard, she is prettier than her sister. She has brought a "socialist" chess set, as a present to her sister.'

'Ach, yes.' Doctor Klein nodded reminiscently. 'I know exactly the kind of chessboard you mean. I used to have a socialist chessboard. They were very funny. They were not meant to be funny. I gave one such set to my sister. That was a long time ago.'

'They set it up and laugh at the unusual-looking pieces. Freddie has a little scar above the right eye. It is in the shape of a horseshoe. Oswald asks about it and she explains that she got it when a boy threw a stone at her. She says she must be very lucky. She could have been killed! She takes a sip of wine, then another. The scar is oddly becoming –' Ella broke off. For some reason she shivered. Something – she couldn't say what – brought an icy chill to her bones and a tingle to the hairs on the nape of her neck.

'What is the matter, Ella?'

'I don't know. Someone walking on my grave.'

'Would you like me to shut the window?' Doctor Klein sounded concerned.

'Yes, please. Just for a moment I imagined that – I don't know what I imagined. No, it's nothing. I feel light-headed – a little giddy – a little sick –'

'I do apologise, Ella. I am keeping you up. You have had a terrible experience. You should go to bed. I must leave you alone –'

'No, don't go yet. I haven't finished. Where was I? Oh yes. The home movie. Freddie picks up and eats a sausage. She laughs. She looks happy and excited. She bares her teeth in a mock snarl. She displays a strong set of teeth. She says she likes to fight with her teeth. She laughs again. Gabriele says she used to be covered in bites when they were children. Freddie starts singing a song – *Wenn Der Sommer Wiede Einzieht* – is there such a song?'

'I believe there is. I congratulate you on your superb memory.'

'Freddie remembers how she danced with a sailor once, at some club, and how he then tried to seduce her … The two girls get quite silly … They hug and kiss and laugh … Oswald laughs with them … They sing and they dance with Oswald … He puts his arms round them … He kisses them … The camera swirls … Blackout … Well, that's the end of the film. It only lasts about seven or eight minutes.'

'What else did they talk about? Did Oswald tell you?'

'Freddie got a bit drunk and became voluble. She said she hated her Soviet job. She hated her Soviet masters. She was terrified of the Stasi. She also said how much she wanted to be with her sister, how much she'd like to live in the "West", though she couldn't quite see how that could happen. Oswald told her that that wasn't as impossible as she seemed to think …'

'He raised her hopes …'

'He gave her presents – a brand new handbag, a cashmere sweater, a warm winter coat, bars of Swiss chocolate, Nivea soap and some nylons … Apparently poor Freddie started crying … She insisted on kissing his hand, which pleased him … He then overheard Gabriele and Freddie talk about him … *My boyfriend is rich and he likes you very much. He can get you out. You can trust him. Look at this gold bracelet he gave me. And these earrings – do you know how much they cost? He can do anything.*'

'He didn't suggest he might be able to smuggle her sister out of the East sector into Free Berlin, did he?'

'That's exactly what he suggested.'

'But couldn't Freddie simply have stayed on, given that she was already in West Berlin?'

'She couldn't. There was an old friend of their late father who was in a hospice in East Berlin. *Onkel* Wolf. She couldn't leave him. *Onkel* Wolf was an old man and mortally ill. He wasn't expected to last long. She had promised to go back. It had to be done at some later date. Oswald said it was tricky but not impossible. He promised her a new identity and protection in case the Stasi sent a hitman after her. There was only one thing he wanted Freddie to do in return. One very tiny thing. So tiny it was hardly worth mentioning. There was a particular file, which he wanted Freddie to leave on a bus in East Berlin.'

'It does sound tiny, yes.'

'It was a bus chiefly used by Soviet officials – to which she had access. The file contained information concerning US military plans. Seemingly accurate but in fact entirely bogus. Freddie agreed. She did as instructed and the operation was a success. Then Oswald asked her to do it again, only this time she had to leave the file in the lobby of a hotel which catered for Soviet officials. Then she was asked to do it a *third* time … Oswald told her she would be able to join her sister soon, very soon. He assured her that everything was in place. She was to wait for instructions. But these particular instructions never came.'

'He lied to her …'

'He'd never had any intention of reuniting Freddie with her sister. Meanwhile, Gabriele had discovered she was pregnant. Oswald told her they'd get married and then they would go and live in America – or in South Africa. One day Gabriele arrived at Oswald's restaurant and found the place closed. She was told the restaurant was under new management. No one knew where Oswald was. He was not in his flat. She became frantic. She went to the police. She was in floods of tears. She sat and waited. She seemed convinced something terrible had happened to him. Eventually she was told that Oswald had left Germany and gone back to the US. Then she had another shock –'

'Yes?'

'She learnt that her sister Freddie had been arrested by the Stasi, tried for spying and summarily executed. Gabriele had a miscarriage.' Ella's voice shook. 'Soon after she committed suicide. She poisoned herself. She took cyanide.'

'Cyanide? Very fast and very efficient,' Doctor Klein said. 'You choke, then you die. You know the two deaths to be an established fact?'

'Oswald told me they were. I don't think he lied about *that*. He said he had seen a photo of Gabriele's dead body. It was his bosses who informed him. His bosses knew the exact sequence of events. His bosses knew *everything*. He said he'd only been doing his job. He said he couldn't very well have foreseen that Freddie would be caught, but that was the kind of thing that sometimes happened. He had *told* her to be careful.'

'Wasn't he sorry for the baby?'

'He said he was but he didn't sound it. He said Gabriele should have taken precautions. He said Gabriele had got pregnant on purpose. She had done her best to "get" him. She had been manipulative and deceitful. He had never been in love with her. He didn't believe the baby had been his anyway. Gabriele had had other boyfriends. They had both been rather stupid girls, he said. Mentally undeveloped. He called them "featherbrains". They were "trashy". He'd found them and their lives incomprehensible, alien.'

'But he regards his Berlin mission as a success?'

'Oh yes. He said it had given him a great sense of achievement. His bosses had been extremely happy with him. He was generously rewarded for his efforts ... After his return to the US, he prospered. He invested his money wisely and made a fortune, which he managed to double, treble and quadruple when he got married. He made a good marriage. He married an heiress.'

There was a pause.

11

AN AFFAIR
TO REMEMBER

'Martita Stanhouse? That was her name, wasn't it? I remember the day I saw photos of the two of them in a newspaper. That, I believe, was the hand of destiny. Perhaps as a man of science I should avoid such fanciful language.' Doctor Klein gave a little smile. 'It would most certainly not endear me to my patients who are frequently highly strung individuals and delusional to boot. The moment I saw those photographs I knew what I needed to do. I knew, yes.' He nodded. 'I didn't stop to consider the pros and cons of the matter. I knew I had to do it. Isn't that strange? I *knew*.'

'Do what? Sorry – I don't understand …' Ella looked at him in some confusion.

'One day you will. The time has not yet come. They had been snapped entering the Metropolitan Opera House. Oswald had his public face on. He looked like a senator, I thought. Suave, respectable, confident, relaxed, faintly amused. He might have been on his way to the Congress. I spent an hour studying those photographs, you see. Martita looked extremely unwell. Her mouth was twisted to one side. Her eyes were wild and staring.'

'Martita looked ghastly, yes,' Ella agreed. 'Hardly human. By then she was very ill. Those photographs should never have been taken. I believe that was her last outing. We had gone to see *Don Giovanni* … Appropriate, in a way … Ironic … Don Juan – the serial philanderer!'

'You were there too? You were with them at the opera?'

'I was. I am not in any of the photographs, but I was there all right. I was always with them. Faithful Ella. Always a couple of steps behind. Oswald wanted it that way. He needed me to take care of Martita. Martita was getting extremely difficult. Well, I was Martita's companion and nurse maid till – till he decided to replace me with a younger and prettier woman.'

'Maisie.'

'Maisie, yes. Sweet, innocent Maisie … Sorry, I mustn't be catty. Oswald and I had an affair. It went on for a couple of years but then it came to an end. I stayed on. He made me stay on.' Suddenly Ella sounded breathless. 'I am ashamed to admit it but I was in love with him once, very much in love, that's what makes the whole thing so awful. I've been doing my best to forget that I was in love with Oswald. I've tried to put it in the bottom drawer of my mind. I wince each time I remember the feelings I had for him. I can't help thinking there is something wrong with me. Something abnormal – freakish –'

'No. You should never think that, Ella.'

'I can't help it. I seem to be one of those natural victims one reads about. Fated from birth to frustration and despair. It couldn't have been love, could it?' Ella's eyes filled with tears. 'I mean – not *love*. I couldn't really have loved a man like Oswald – it seems impossible, when I think about it now. It's obscene – grotesque. What *kind* of love could it have been? I don't understand myself.'

'Wittgenstein says somewhere that love which can't be classified is the best.'

'Apollo and Marsyas.' She was staring before her. 'Do you remember what Apollo did to Marsyas?'

'Apollo flayed Marsyas.'

'The agony of Marsyas is said to be the inevitable agony of the human soul in its desire to achieve God. Nonsense, all nonsense. I am afraid I've lost my faith in God.' She shook her head. 'I don't even know if Marsyas was male or female!'

'You don't? Male or female? Male or female?' Doctor Klein reiterated in an odd voice. Suddenly he laughed. He clapped his hands. 'You really don't know?'

'I am sure you've been wondering why I never left Oswald – why I am still with him? You have been wondering, haven't you? It must strike you as terribly twisted, this whole situation.'

The tall lamp beside the fireplace shed a diffused light upon Doctor Klein's face, which had retained its detached expression.

'I have been wondering, yes. So what is the answer? Why haven't you left him? Why are you still with him?'

'I can't leave him because I am afraid of him,' she said. 'This sounds like the first sentence of an Iris Murdoch novel, doesn't it? *Ella Gales stayed with her former lover because she was afraid of him.* I am afraid of what he might do to me. I really am. It's a complicated story. He threatens to destroy me if I leave. He wants me to stay with him.'

'How could he possibly destroy you?'

There was a pause.

'Years ago he promised to marry me, only he didn't. At first he told me it had to wait, that I needed to be patient. Then suddenly he said he'd never promised anything and that I'd imagined it. He suggested that I was prone to fantasies, that I was delusional. In the very first year of our affair I became pregnant with his child. He said it wasn't his child. He said I was trying to entrap him.'

'He said the same thing about Gabriele.'

'Yes. Certain patterns seem to repeat themselves, don't they? He said he had evidence I'd been seeing someone behind his back. He said he was damned if he would become father to someone else's child. He told me to have an abortion. I didn't want to, but he bullied me into it. I was in a fragile state. You mustn't think I am trying to justify what I did –'

'You had the abortion?'

'I did. Yes. It was terrible. I cried my eyes out. After that I couldn't imagine myself being under the same roof as him a moment longer but when I told him I was leaving, he said he still needed me, if anything more than ever before. I knew then I was dealing with a madman. I went up to my room and started packing. He followed me. He told me that if I left him, I would be sorry. I said I didn't care. I went on packing. He then told me exactly what he proposed to do. To me and to my brother.'

'You have a brother? You have never mentioned a brother before.'

'No. I told you it was a complicated story. I have a brother, yes. I do my best to keep my life separate from his. My brother works at the Vatican. He holds a high office. He is very close to the Holy Pontiff.'

'I see.'

'I care a lot about my brother. I don't want to hurt him in any way. I don't want him to know about the abortion. I would never forgive myself if he came to any harm. My brother is a truly holy man. He is a saint. I am not worthy of him. He is one of the most wonderful human beings who ever lived. Oswald said that if I did leave him, a couple of stories would appear in the newspapers in England, on the Continent, as well as in America. He said the stories had already been written.'

'What kind of stories?'

'He described them as "lurid, shocking and full of all kinds of repulsive details". I am represented as a slut – a professional slut.' She took a deep breath. 'I have had as many abortions as I have had clients – I am immoral as well as amoral – I am hypocritical, insatiable, a nymphomaniac, highly manipulative and heaven knows what else. He also says there are pictures.'

'What pictures?'

'I don't know what pictures. Compromising pictures. Nasty pictures. Shocking pictures. Something twisted and abominable. It makes me sick just thinking about it, wondering. Fear is the worst counsel, I know. There are no pictures. I've had no clients!' She gave a hysterical laugh. 'It's probably something he's fabricated or someone has done at his behest! You can do all sorts of things with a computer, can't you? You can doctor photographs really cleverly. Oswald can have anything he asks for. *Anything*. I can't bear the idea of any publicity, of having to explain myself, of being hounded. I can't take any risks. I can't.'

'I don't think he'd do it, Ella,' Doctor Klein said gently. 'He wouldn't dare, but if he did, you could take him to court.'

'I couldn't. I haven't got the guts. I am a coward, I keep telling you. I wish I were possessed of dauntless courage, but I am not … Two of the stories apparently concern my brother. Oswald hinted he knew things about my brother – vile, disgusting, unspeakable things. He never specified what exactly, but he says he's got *evidence*.' Ella's voice shook. 'That would be worse than anything that might be written about me – *much worse*. I can't bear the thought of my brother being caused pain … He is very sensitive … It would destroy him … And it would all be my fault … Oswald gets a kick out of intimidating people – of making people afraid – of humiliating people – No, not people – *women* – he does it only to women.'

'He seems to enjoy degrading women, yes.'

'He is mad,' Ella whispered.

'*Not clinically insane, only transcendentally wicked.* That, in case you wonder, was said about Adolph Hitler. I admit Oswald is an interesting case. But does he *really* want you to stay with him? I find this very curious. He has made it abundantly clear that he has a *schwarm* for Maisie.'

'His *schwarm* for Maisie is simply a new element in the game he has been playing with me,' Ella said. 'Oswald wants me to stay and watch him being adored. It's all so pathetic, but that's the kind of person he is. He warned me not to discuss him with Maisie. *If you so much as open your mouth, Ella, if I hear that you've been trying to win her over to your side, you and your brother are finished.*'

'Ach. He relishes playing the bogeyman. Fear can be a powerful weapon in the hands of someone like Oswald. Because he is so rich and powerful, you have convinced yourself he can do anything he says ... I think you should call his bluff.'

She shook her head violently. She couldn't do it. She was not brave enough. 'That's why I am still with him —' She broke off. 'You don't think Feversham is spying on us, do you? I keep seeing him creeping about each time we are together.'

'Does Feversham creep about? I haven't noticed.'

'I don't know. I may have imagined it. I've been sleeping badly ... I really don't know what to do ... Perhaps I am doomed to spend the rest of my life with Oswald. What else *could* I possibly do? Kill myself? Kill Oswald? Fake my own death and disappear under a new identity? Pay someone to kill Oswald? Sometimes I get the craziest ideas. Do forgive me! I really don't know what to do.'

'Sometimes the craziest ideas are the best,' Doctor Klein said gravely. 'But materially Oswald is good to you, yes? You said he was a generous employer?'

'Oh he is extremely generous. I can't fault Oswald on *that* count. He pays me a very good salary. He makes sure I have everything I want. I have an unlimited access to cash. He gives me expensive presents. He never forgets my birthday. I am the proverbial bird in a gilded cage. Is my cheek still red?'

'Not any more.'

'Oswald seems to like the idea of a triangle … Before it was Martita, me and him. Now it is Maisie, me and him … I am sorry for that girl. She is the perfect innocent, isn't she? What a night … full moon.' Ella's eyes remained fixed on the open window. There was a pause. 'To think – to think that Oswald was nearly killed! That bullet might so easily have got him in the head. Have you thought of that?'

'The thought did occur to me, yes,' Doctor Klein said.

12

AU COEUR DE LA NUIT

John de Coverley lay in bed. He kept slipping in and out of sleep but he wasn't dreaming, not exactly, rather his mind was behaving in a manner not dissimilar to that of an ancient television set in an advanced stage of an electronic disease. He saw images that flickered and dissolved in monochrome chaos, then formed again indecisively as if behind some undulating flood.

One image slowly came into focus. Why, it was a seagull — a giant seagull! He would have loved to be able to shoot it but he had no gun — the gun had been taken away from him — but he saw he wore his thick leather gloves. If only he could catch up with it, he'd wring its neck. The creature kept flapping its wings and emitting worried squawking noises. Really it was most provoking. It was a new breed of seagull, John could see. The head looked quite human — a woman's head — the same eyes as —

He woke up with a start. So he'd been dreaming after all.

What they did to me was outrageous, John thought. Unpardonable. They — his impossible sister's houseguests — had put him under house arrest.

It was his impossible sister who was to blame for the whole thing.

What he felt like doing was wringing Sybil's neck.

Sybil de Coverley couldn't sleep either.

How *did* one make one's warring brain raise the white flag? Reaching out, she turned on the bedside table light. She wondered if she should get up and make herself a cup of China tea and take a couple Neurophen Plus tablets, to which she had to admit she was becoming quite addicted. Or perhaps she could start reading some really boring book.

She had the feeling things were getting out of hand somewhat. She didn't mean only her brother and the shooting in the library. Since her arrival she had been aware of tensions – she had seen conspiratorial looks pass between Ella and Doctor Klein and between Oswald and Feversham. Sybil wasn't exactly *anxious* – she was never anxious – it was just a funny feeling she had, that something was about to happen.

Thank God there'd been no serious damage done to the library. No one read Gibbon anyway and in her opinion the portrait of Charles de Coverley had been greatly improved by the bullet hole. Charles de Coverley was one of her great-great-great uncles. He had been a High Court Judge, something of the sort. A stuffed shirt if there was one, if the portrait was anything to go by. The bullet had got him in the eye and now it looked as though he wore a piratical patch. It gave him a deliciously dissolute air. She'd always hated that portrait anyhow.

She found herself thinking about the new man, Feversham, whom she had accommodated in the room called 'Charlotte Russe'.

She had taken a fancy to him. The moment she had seen him, she'd felt a small secret thrill creeping down her spine. He looked nothing like her brother, but he brought to mind papa. The same raffish charm. She had always had a thing about papa, when she was a girl. Oh dear! Sybil laughed at the memory. She sat up, opened her bedside table drawer and took out a cigarette. She didn't smoke often, but she felt like it now.

She recalled how she had always compared papa to her beaux, or rather the other way round – those poor chaps who used to take her out dancing! She had been beastly to them. Far from nice. She had been impossibly imperious and made them do silly things, like pretend they were a polar bear or Harold Macmillan or the Sultan of Zanzibar. When they hesitated or didn't do it properly, she'd stomped her foot and told them to go away and never come back.

She'd been terribly picky. Papa had been at his wits' end. He'd wanted her safely married off to someone suitable. But each time a possible husband was paraded for her inspection, she said no. She'd been terrible! Sometimes she'd said it in French: *Non*.

Sybil struck a match and held it to her cigarette. Her hair was in a net and her face covered in cold cream. Most actors were fey violets, but Feversham seemed to be – well, quite the opposite. He was certainly susceptible to feminine charms. Feversham had taken to her in a big way, she did believe. She didn't think he was after her money or after the island. She could always tell when people were mercenary in their intentions.

He told her he felt seasick the moment he had boarded Oswald Ramskritt's yacht, which was a terribly good sign. He then told her she looked like Deborah Kerr, which was a jolly nice thing to say to a lady. Had she seen *From Here to Eternity*? What about *An Affair to Remember*? That, as it happened, was one of her favourite films! Coincidence? She didn't think so! Feversham was a dream that had fallen from Paradise.

When Sybil was eleven, a witch, or a woman who'd pretended to be a witch, told her that in the last thirty-three years of her life she would find unparalleled happiness with a man whose initial was F. or E. Sybil firmly believed in prophecies. On an earlier occasion the very same woman had told papa that an alien spaceship would land on his island, and it had happened! It had been the year of the Coronation – papa claimed he had seen the saucer's reflection on the TV screen, as the Archbishop of Canterbury had placed the crown on Princess Elizabeth's head. The saucer had moved in a gyratory fashion and there had been a sound resembling an organ that was in desperate need of tuning, papa said. Some five minutes later papa had seen the saucer's reflection again as it had taken off.

Years later, when papa got caught in the hinge of the door between life and death and had only days left on this earth, he asked Sybil to help him down to the cellar and he showed her the strange piece of alien equipment, which, he claimed, the aliens had left behind, a most peculiar-looking object, a cross between a toaster and a giant pencil sharpener. Well, it was still there, on a shelf, gathering dust.

Sybil recalled how she had always wished that *her* prophecy didn't come true too soon – she'd have hated it if it had happened when she turned thirty, say, for it would have meant she would die at sixty-three. On the other hand, she wouldn't have been at all pleased if it had come to her at seventy – the idea of living to be a centenarian-plus filled her with horror. But now – *now* – was the right time.

Papa's tartan gloves. She must give them to Feversham. A long time ago she'd decided she would make a present of papa's tartan gloves to the man whom she intended to marry.

Sybil blew out smoke. A woman needed to be given every chance to fulfil herself through those two finest and most honourable of states: matrimony and motherhood. She wasn't too old for the latter, she didn't think. It was, after all, the twenty-first century; scientific miracles happened practically every day.

How old was Feversham? Her age, she imagined, or thereabout. He was divorced, he had informed her apropos of nothing in particular. He'd referred to his former wife as 'quite the wrong kind of person'. As Sybil had handed him a cup of coffee after dinner, their hands had brushed. He'd also told her he'd sniffed cocaine on a couple of occasions – again, for no apparent reason. It was all terribly promising, to say the least.

She'd nearly confided in him her penchant for Neurophen Plus – that if one chewed five tablets, say, one felt like – well, like heaven, really – only one had to do it when one did *not* have a headache.

Feversham also told her he'd always believed the stage was his vocation, despite the fact he'd been to Gordonstoun and might have had a jolly successful army career.

Sybil frowned. She remembered that Oswald Ramskritt had sat not far away and that he appeared to be listening to their exchanges. There had been a curious expression on Oswald's face, one she couldn't quite make out … Knowing?

Mrs Garrison-Gore sat fully dressed beside her open window, glaring at the full moon. She was greatly perturbed. In fact, she was in quite a state. She was frightened. She had a sense of impending disaster. *She felt threatened.* Things had happened, which should never have been allowed to happen. Her life was already full of uncertainties and now a new one had been added. She had been, as she wrote in one of her books, 'plunged into a tormented conundrum'.

She tried to pull her mind away from her worries. She thought of Doctor Klein, of what she had seen him do earlier in the day. Doctor Klein's room was next to hers and they shared a balcony. His side was separated from her side by a low partition. By means of a small mirror which she held in her hand she had managed to spy on him. She was curious about him, extremely curious. Doctor Klein had no idea he was being watched. He had been inside his room, sitting on his bed.

She had seen him put his hand in his pocket and produce a round object. The next moment she had realised what it was. It was most curious – the last thing she'd expected him to produce – she had watched him, mesmerised – the matter-of-fact way in which he had done it – she didn't believe *beauty* came into it – no, a bit late for *that* – the poor fellow was destined to die a monster – it was something he was eager to *conceal*.

She had known at that moment that Doctor Klein had a secret – that there was more to Doctor Klein than met the eye – it was her gypsy blood whispering in her ear – what secret *exactly*, though?

Perhaps she could search his room? She didn't know what she was hoping to find, but she felt sure there would be *something*. She stood up. She told herself she needed distraction, – the kind of thrills only some risk-involving activity could provide – otherwise she'd go mad with anxiety.

She had seen Doctor Klein go into Ella's room and she didn't think he was back yet; she would have heard him. It was now getting late. It was the small hours of the morning. What *did* those two find to talk about? Anything in the nature of a romance between Ella and Doctor Klein seemed extremely unlikely, but of course some women had rather unusual tastes, so perhaps she shouldn't discount the possibility entirely.

The door of Doctor Klein's room was locked, but he had left his balcony door ajar, she'd noticed. All she needed to do was climb over the partition and enter his room …

Raffles in a frock. She was Raffles in a frock. She suppressed a hysterical giggle. She must remember to write this down. Perhaps she could use the phrase in a book? The idea had cheered her up a bit but not an awful lot.

She opened her balcony door. Perverse and foolish oft I strayed, eh? This must come under the heading of 'reckless decisions', she reflected. Well, the *last* reckless decision she made had paid off, actually. She had hunches, which more often than not proved to be correct. She was aware that her behaviour wasn't entirely rational, but she knew in her bones that her search would, as they say, *bear fruit*.

And it did.

A couple of minutes later she stood transfixed beside the chest of drawers in Doctor Klein's room, her skin crawling, her hand clapped over her mouth to prevent herself from crying out, staring down at her discovery ...

13

DEAD CALM

On Friday morning Sphinx Island woke up enshrouded in swirls of milky-white mist, at first no more than a delicate translucent veil that kept dissolving, but then it gradually started thickening into a damp impenetrable fog, which rendered the sea invisible. Nor could the sea be heard. The seagulls were quiet too. It was all a little eerie.

Once more Lady Grylls and Maisie were sitting in the drawing room.

The clock on the mantelpiece chimed ten-thirty.

'You are an awfully brave gel, my dear. If I'd been you, I'd have screamed the house down. I'd have picked up the phone and called the police right away, though I don't think that would have been much good, would it?'

'No.'

'It would have taken them *ages* to arrive – in the middle of the night – we are, after all, in the middle of the *sea* – I suppose they have their own boats and things – *is* there such a thing as coastal police? If that's what they are called. Must ask Sybil. They must hate it, I am sure they hate it, I mean the police, whenever they get an emergency call from an island. You are looking terribly pale, my dear.'

Maisie gave a little smile. 'I didn't sleep very well.'

'I am not at all surprised. What did you do after he left?'

'I cried a little. I was upset, I guess.'

'I bet you were. You poor thing.'

'I am OK now. I really am.'

'Miss Havisham — that's who Oswald reminds me of. Remember Miss Havisham? *Sometimes I have sick fancies.* Trying to get into your bed indeed. You should have screamed the house down. Would you be an angel and pour me another cup of coffee? So cosy sitting here, so *quiet* — looks as though we are among the clouds — we might be up in Valhalla — one of those places.' Lady Grylls gestured towards the window. 'It is jolly sporting of you to have forgiven him. I don't think he deserves your forgiveness.'

'He was extremely drunk. He couldn't have known what he was doing, could he? Actually, it wasn't so very dreadful, apart from the things he said to me.'

'I wish I had your generosity of spirit! My life may not have been a dedicated pursuit of virtue, but there are certain things I draw the line at.'

'OK. It *was* dreadful but — I mean — *nothing happened.*'

'I should think not! I would have refused to stay under the same roof with him if it had.'

'He doesn't seem to remember what he said or what he did. You saw him this morning at breakfast, didn't you? He acted as though nothing had happened. Smiling and talking about the weather and giving me my instructions for the day!'

'Having threatened to throw you out on your ear and make you unemployable!' Lady Grylls shook her head. 'I believe he also asked you if you'd heard from your sister in Oregon and how her baby was doing? He sounded genuinely interested, as though he really cared about you. I couldn't imagine anything creepier.'

Maisie smiled happily. 'My sister gave birth last week. Her first baby! I am an aunt!'

'That's splendid news … Has Oswald ever done anything like that before? *Never*? How perfectly extraordinary. Sybil says that's the way some chaps react after they get their heads nearly blown off. Perhaps she is right.'

'I was so frightened … The way Mr de Coverley appeared at the door with that gun!'

'It was the stuff of nightmares, I quite agree.'

'It looked as though he really meant to kill Oswald!'

'I believe he did mean to kill Oswald. John seems to resent his intentions of taking over the island.'

'I thought Mr de Coverley was quite pleasant when I first talked to him. He never used to open his door. Oh it was so funny. He'd ask for something on the house phone and I'd take it to his door, then we'd talk through the keyhole. He said he liked the sound of my voice.'

'Like Pyramus and Thisbe, eh? Could be the start of a romance, you never know. Maybe all John needs is the love of a good woman and then he'll be right as rain? Or would the age difference be a problem?'

'I saw him watch me through field-glasses from his window.'

'Well, I think that clinches it. Sybil says John's never been violent before, with people, that is, but then Sybil is the queen of understatement. I do honestly believe he needs to have his head properly examined. Some may say he is ready for the men in white coats. Incidentally, how do you clean those solid silver candelabras?' Lady Grylls pointed. 'They become so badly clogged after use, don't they; it must take *hours* to get rid of the wax.'

'Oh, it's not too bad. Ella and I blast them with our hairdryers till the wax runs off on to blotting paper. It only takes a couple of minutes,' the girl explained cheerfully.

'Perhaps they could be fitted with cardboard "collars" – what they use on dogs' necks, to stop them scratching?' Lady Grylls took a sip of coffee. 'We seem to have not one but *two* dangerous men on the island,' she went on in a thoughtful voice. 'I personally believe Oswald is more dangerous than John, but you will probably disagree ... So quiet, isn't it? Or have I gone completely deaf? My doctor keeps telling me I should get a hearing aid.'

'It *is* quiet.'

'Not sure I care much for such dead calm ... Like the hush before the proverbial storm ... Goodness, what was that? Sounds like someone being skinned alive.'

'It's Mrs Garrison-Gore. She wants us in the library. Today's Friday, remember? Last instructions, I think.'

'Last rites more like. What a bore that woman is. To tell you the truth, I've been having second thoughts. I am not sure we are doing the right thing at all. Poor Hugh and poor Antonia. They'll probably never forgive me. Wouldn't be surprised if they stopped speaking to me altogether. I *may* have miscalculated. Oh well. Too late now. *Iacta alea est.*'

'Are you all right, Lady Grylls?'

'Never felt better, my dear. The sea air agrees with me. The die is cast. That's what it means, in case you wonder. Latin, you know. I heard Hugh say it once. I seem to resemble my nephew more and more as I get older. I find the Garrison-Gore a perfect pest. She sets my teeth on edge. Goodness, is that her again? Let's go, shall we?' Lady Grylls put down her coffee cup. 'Where's my stick? Blasted thing!'

'Lean on my arm, if you like.'

'Thank you, my dear, I shall ... I am not as young as I was ... If Mrs G-G makes her quip about putting one's best foot forward and not in it, I shall scream ... All that horrible heartiness must be a cover for something, wouldn't you say?'

'I guess she is worried the murder may not be a success.'

'I don't think all crime writers are like her,' Lady Grylls said resolutely. 'My niece-by-marriage is *quite* different.'

Mrs Garrison-Gore cleared her throat, 'There is a change I would like to make, in view of what happened yesterday ...' Her eyes strayed significantly to the portrait above the fireplace. 'We *must* take the shooting into account ... They are bound to notice the bullet holes and they'll ask questions. We could always have the picture taken down and replaced with another one and remove the book altogether, I suppose, but I have a better idea ... I'll explain exactly how it'll work, so please listen very carefully. This is a corporate effort, don't let's forget. So all hands to the mast, as they say. Do let's put our best foot forward, *not in it*, shall we?'

14

THE PLAYERS AND THE GAME

Oswald Ramskritt met us as arranged and led us to his yacht. He wore what Sybil had called 'his rather superior yachting cap'. (Antonia wrote in her diary.) *He is a pleasant enough chap with an open, weather-beaten face and intensely blue eyes. I imagine he is in his late fifties, but it is clear he must have been a handsome man in his youth. His eyes, I noticed, were a little bloodshot and at one point he popped an Alka-Seltzer into a glass of water and drank it without waiting for the fizz to subside. (Nights of revelry on Sphinx Island?)*

He rhapsodized about the island. He said he'd always dreamt of possessing an island. He said everybody was enjoying themselves very much indeed and was looking forward to our joining the 'gang'. Everyone was having a whale of a time. And wonder of wonders, John de Coverley had at last made an appearance! Must be in our honour, Oswald said with a laugh.

So far John had kept to his room but this morning he apparently surprised everybody by turning up at breakfast, something he'd never done before. John's demeanour was what one would have expected from an old-world English gentleman. With his eyeglass and spats, he might have stepped out of the pages of a 1930s 'Society' novel. John had done something 'very silly' the day before and that seemed to be his way of saying sorry to everybody.

Oswald went on to tell us how much he loved England. One of his remaining ambitions was to become an honorary Englishman. This is what his brother, or rather half-brother, had done. His half-brother was his only living relative and he was more English than the English. His half-brother had suffered a back injury, but that didn't stop him from treading the boards and chasing the ladies. Oswald gave a knowing look and laughed as though at the best of jokes.

Hugh pressed him to tell us what John had done exactly, but Oswald only shook his head and smiled. It was nothing serious, he insisted. Nothing at all.

Oddly enough, Oswald didn't mind informing us how he had made his fortune. Everybody seemed to think it was extremely difficult, but it wasn't. He became quite voluble on the subject. He said he had done it by the simple expedient of combining the haphazard methods of the gambler with the less spectacular techniques of the investor. If we ever decided to become millionaires, that was the way to go about it.

The island has a sinister enough air about it, though, personally, I couldn't see the Sphinx it is supposed to resemble. It is essentially a grey and bare configuration of rocks. The house is white as a bone and it looks forlorn and empty. It brings to mind a painting by Edward Hopper, that master-blender of loneliness, nostalgia and shadowy foreboding.

As we got nearer, I was filled with curious sadness. Despite myself, I felt something resembling a sense of loss …

I mentioned Hopper and the talk turned to painting. Oswald Ramskritt's favourite artist is Norman Rockwell – such a sunny painter, he said – it is always summertime in Rockwell – smiling moms making apple-pie, healthy-looking boys playing baseball, friendly dogs chasing after them. Simple happiness, old-fashioned charm and self-effacing dignity – those were the kind of things Oswald valued most.

I may be tempted to use the house and the island as a setting for a novel one day. Setting establishes atmosphere and it can influence plot and character. An island like that would certainly enhance the horror of a murder, especially if the heinous act were to be committed during a storm. The turbulence of the sea would parallel the turbulence of human emotions. Though this is a terrible cliché, it could still be effective, if properly done.

Strangely enough, the moment I thought about clichés, Mrs Garrison-Gore sprung into view. Of course we didn't immediately know that she was Mrs Garrison-Gore, not till Oswald Ramskritt introduced her to us after we'd landed.

Mrs Garrison-Gore had come out of the house and was sitting on a rock, looking out across the sea, incongruously bringing to mind the famous statue of Andersen's mermaid I'd seen in Copenhagen once. If newspaper reports are to be believed the poor little mermaid had been vandalised a great number of times – head hacked off, red paint splashed over it and, on one occasion, the whole statue was blasted from its base with dynamite. Each time it had been restored. In an odd way this is what has been happening to the literary reputation of Mrs Garrison-Gore.

Romany Garrison-Gore, my copy-editor informed me, writes pastiches of 1930s whodunnits. Her first novel was moderately successful in terms of sales; though that was mainly thanks to a clever Art Deco cover the book had been given. Her second novel did not sell at all well, neither did her number three. The critical reception she received was scant as it was scathing.

One critic castigated her novel Mad About Murder *for its 'complete lack of narrative drive, a storyline that is inconsequential, derivative and painfully predictable … its sole dependence on melodrama and coincidence wince-making … characters who seem to have experienced a kind of pre-frontal lobotomy … a mishmash of ominous and cheap thrills … blunders on like a flat-footed dancer … a ludicrous damp-squib of a climax … entire paragraphs held together by comma splices … eminently put-downable'.*

Mrs Garrison-Gore was dropped by Collins and, as a result, seemed to become slightly unhinged. According to one apocryphal story, she started performing conjuring tricks at children's parties in Kensington and was much admired for her sleight of hand. After an eight-month hiatus, she resumed her literary career. She was taken up by The Severed Head, a much smaller publishing house.

Then a miracle happened. Her book number five was a hit. It was considered 'diabolically ingenious'; it might have been written, according to one critic, in the heyday of the Golden Age of the English detective story and The Severed Head managed to sell the television rights for a decent sum of money.

Mrs Garrison-Gore is probably in her late forties or early fifties. She is short and a little dumpy. Her face is round. Her eyebrows have been carefully, if unwisely, plucked and pencilled and she wears pancake make-up of the peachy variety and cyclamen lipstick. She was dressed in an Irish tweed jacket and skirt in fuchsia hues and she sported a profusion of oriental jewellery. On her head she wore a pork-pie hat.

Mrs Garrison-Gore had a preoccupied air about her. I imagined she cast one or two wary glances at Oswald Ramskritt, but she assumed a hearty manner the moment she started talking to us. She said she was delighted to meet me. She had heard so much about me from dear Lady Grylls. She didn't indicate in any way that she was a fellow crime writer.

It was John de Coverley himself who greeted us at the front door. He has the sly pointed face of an amused lizard. He sported a smoking jacket with silk lapels and a monocle. He is perhaps the only man living in the twenty-first century who wears a monocle that is not part of some fancy-dress. Chaps with monocles invariably project an attitude of contemptuous aloofness, but that is not the case with John de Coverley. He seems to have a problem keeping his monocle in his eye; it makes him scowl ferociously and contort his face.

'And what in faith make you from Wittenberg?' John de Coverley said. 'Terribly glad you managed to come after all. We are going to give you tea. You had a pleasant journey, I trust? It's ages since I've been to London. Does the Royal Overseas League in St James' still stand? Used to meet up with an old girlfriend there quite often. She was involved in charity work. One of those dull but worthy women. I was

experimenting at the time. Your aunt has told us so much about your exploits. Come and meet the others. Everybody's longing to meet you. Everybody is agog.'

From what Sybil had told us, I had expected her brother to brandish a gun, not quote from Hamlet.

He led us through a panelled hall into a spacious drawing room. The white and gold Louis Seize chairs were more agreeable to the eye than to the posterior, as I discovered, and had been designed, one might think, to enforce an alertness of posture in an age when it would have been considered a breach of good manners to relax either physically or mentally. The windows are high and open on to a balcony. The curtains are of striped magenta and cream brocade. There is a grey marble mantel-piece with a somewhat mottled mirror over it, an Empire clock and crystal candelabra. The Aubusson carpet is sun-bleached and in places torn. Two of the pictures on the wall are seascapes and seem to be genuine Turners.

Sybil and a rather striking tall woman dressed in pearly white were presiding over the teatable. The woman was introduced to us as 'Ella'. Sybil wore a loose embroidered garment of a vaguely Byzantine motif, what I imagine to be a tea-gown, 1920s style.

'Would you like to try the Parma ham sandwiches? Or would you rather have good old-fashioned cucumber?'

'Could I have an egg-and-cress sandwich, Syb? These are seagull eggs,' John de Coverley explained. 'Awfully good. I hope everybody agrees. Ridiculous to be squeamish. Awfully good. Taste like no other. Plenty of seagulls around. A positive colony.'

'I would like a fish-paste sandwich,' Oswald Ramskritt said. 'I love fishing.'

'The number of things one can do on a minuscule island is a little limited,' Sybil said. She beamed at her brother. Her face was quite flushed. I thought she looked positively girlish.

'Assam, Earl Grey or Russian tchai?' Ella asked. There were three silver tea-urns. I had the impression Ella was avoiding looking at Oswald Ramskritt.

'I wouldn't touch anything Russian with a barge pole. I have had dealings with Russians. I have always found Russians unreliable,' Ramskritt said.

'Ah, there you are! At long last!' Aunt Nellie greeted us. 'I feared you might have got shipwrecked – or been abducted by pirates. Pirates seem to be all the rage these day, isn't that extraordinary?' She wore a silk dress in dove grey, a single row of pearls and two brooches pinned to her left shoulder.

When I kissed her, she whispered in my ear that something damned odd was going on.

Maisie is a stunningly beautiful girl with a sunny smile who brings to mind Hollywood actress Scarlett Johansson. She was clad in a straw-coloured dress whose design looked – but only looked – simple. He manner was eager and attentive, her face uplifted, her eyes alight.

Doctor Klein is monstrously fat and his skin is of slug-like whiteness. He has sad, wide-spaced eyes and purplish lips. He wore a black suit, white shirt and black tie.

'I understand you are past masters of forensic logistics,' he said tonelessly. 'Your aunt tells us that not even the Prince of Darkness himself could outwit you.'

I found myself wondering if he might be the Riddler.

'I don't know where my aunt gets these ideas.' As usual on such occasions Hugh was breezily dismissive.

'I do believe the Devil is also known as the "Son of the Morning",' John de Coverley's monocle flashed.

'What happens if the electricity decides to go AWOL, Sybil?' Aunt Nellie asked. 'I've been meaning to ask you. Do you use oil lamps or candles?'

'We are much more advanced than that on Sphinx,' Sybil said. 'We have our own electric generator. It's in the cellar.'

'Oil lamps have a charm of their own,' Ella said.

'They can cause a fire, I guess,' said Maisie.

'New lamps for old, eh? Was that in some fairytale or other?'
Oswald Ramskritt looked at Mrs Garrison-Gore. 'Or was it the
other way round? Come on, Mrs G-G, you should know. You are the
expert. Old is always best, isn't it?'

'I believe it's in Aladdin. I heard that there would be a storm.'
Mrs Garrison-Gore spoke in a very loud voice. 'They issued a serious
warning. The news was on the local radio, only some ten minutes ago.'

'We are having Châteneuf-du-Pape at dinner tonight,' Sybil said.

'Du Pape – that means the Pope, doesn't it? But that's amazing!'
Oswald opened his eyes wide in exaggerated surprise. 'Did you hear
that, Ella? The Pope! That's perhaps what your brother drinks? Ella's
brother is the Pope's right-hand man,' he explained, matter-of-factly.

Ella said nothing. I thought she looked very pale.

Oswald started talking to John de Coverley.

'Is old Bonwell still alive then?'

'Oh very much so, very much so, my dear fellow. Ancient as the hills
but self-indulgent as ever.'

'That's swell. I am glad to hear it.'

'Needs constant toning up with gin and Dubonnet – while snack-
ing on warm coddled quail eggs lopped open and dusted with beluga
caviar. Regrettable addiction. Set on a suicidal course. Wouldn't hear of
slowing down.' John sighed. 'One of these days a treacherous aorta will
take him from us, of that I have no doubt.'

'And how is Norah? Does she still maintain I have her eyes?'

'Norah is at a home in Windsor, within a striking distance of the
castle, marvellous view, though she says that's the Reichstag.'

'Forgive me but I have never had a nuanced grasp of European
history. Why the Reichstag?'

'She believes she is in Berlin. She is no longer herself, I fear. Practically
round the bend. Suspects the nurses of trying to poison her and so on.'

Tea cups were replenished. More sandwiches were brought in. There
were no servants, I noticed. The catering was done exclusively by Ella
and Maisie.

'I can never be friends with people whose only redeeming feature is a sort of flaccid amiability,' Sybil said.

'My bêtes-noires are facile enthusiasm and excessive earnestness,' Aunt Nellie said.

'It is fake enthusiasm I abhor,' Oswald Ramskritt said. 'Incidentally, I wouldn't advise anyone to touch the Russian tchai. It is bound to be contaminated by toxic waste. Mismanagement at every level, that's Russia for you. Mismanagement and corruption.'

'I've heard that said about India,' Mrs Garrison-Gore said.

'I've heard that said about Italy,' Sybil said.

'I've heard that said about the continent of Africa,' John de Coverley said. He then turned to Hugh and asked if he could play something called 'slosh' and seemed delighted when Hugh said he could. Perhaps they could have a game after dinner?

It was all rather surreally inconsequential.

Who was Norah and who was Bonwell? Did they exist?

I have no doubt now that we are being set up. I could imagine the instructions Mrs G-G had given them. Extemporise, but try not to lose the sense of artifice, or the role will die on you. Remember you are playing yourselves, your names haven't been changed, but you are not really yourselves.

We seem to be in the kind of story that wears layers of disguises – no sooner does one mask come off, than another is revealed beneath it.

But I was also aware of a tension that felt like an electric current in the air, which I thought was quite genuine. Well, we were warned that there was a storm coming.

15

THE BROKEN THREAD

Later on Sybil gave them a tour of the house, which, she explained, was called Mauldeley (pronounced 'Mudly'), though everybody, without any particular flight of the imagination, insisted on calling it 'Sphinx House'.

On the stairs they caught up with Ella Gales, who was carrying a tray with a silver cover. For some reason, on seeing them, she looked flustered. She went up another flight of stairs and disappeared down a gloomy corridor. A fine-looking woman, Payne thought. He sniffed the air. He had caught the whiff of a fried chicken. There had been something of the automaton about Ella's movements. Something weighing on her mind. As though encumbered with a terrible burden, heavier than a mere tray ...

The library was long and narrow and it had an air of melancholy charm about it. Bookshelves containing a great number of gilt and russet volumes reached up to the ceiling. It seemed to be used chiefly as a repository for things that their owners had not had the heart to throw away. Dilapidated chairs of different styles, a large sofa of the Louis Philippe period, partially disembowelled, with springs and stuffing coming out in places, little tables covered with knick-knacks, pipes, tarnished silver cigarette lighters, candlesticks, bowls full of dry flowers, one or two empty chocolate boxes and a shabby tiger hearthrug. There were some indifferent Edwardian family portraits on the walls. The window curtains were of faded green silk, their pelmets intricate with folds and tassels.

On a side table there lay pre-war copies of *The Field*, *Cineworld* and *The Tatler* and an off volume of the *Revue Hebdomadaire*. There was also a batch of *Batman* comics, at the sight of which Hugh and Antonia exchanged glances.

'My God, what a dump,' Sybil said with a sigh. 'Too embarrassing for words.'

Payne picked up a book that had been left on the sofa and glanced at the title. *Return to the Stars*. Von Daniken.

'One of papa's. It goes back a terribly long time, beyond the flames of Troy and Carthage,' Sybil said. 'At least thirty years. Isn't it odd that people who believe in aliens are never called "alienists"? Mama, on the other hand, was a Socialist. You'd never believe this, but her favourite book was *On the Condition of the Working Classes in England*. Porcelain socialism, papa used to tease her.'

'The female version of champagne socialism, eh?'

'That's mama over there.' Sybil pointed to the portrait on one of the walls. It showed a placid-looking woman swathed in several dead foxes and wearing lace mittens, her hair an immaculate white halo around her head. 'Mama went on two expeditions to Tibet but she never changed the way she did her hair. It's the same periwigged style so beloved by our own dear Queen, as I am sure you've noticed.'

'A bit more cumulo-nimbus than HM's Ionic capital, surely?'

'Mama was the worst cheat at solitaire who ever lived.'

'Whose are those *Batmans*,' Payne asked casually.

'Oh my brother's.' Sybil waved a dismissive hand. 'Batman used to be John's hero. No, sorry – it was one of Batman's *enemies* John used to adore, forget which. The Joker?'

'Not the Riddler?'

'Isn't that the same character?'

'No, not really,' said Payne. He started leafing through one of the comics. 'I don't think many people know that Patricia Highsmith used to write copy for *Batman* before becoming a proper writer.'

'Did she? I wonder if Batman was an influence on Tom Ripley,' Antonia said thoughtfully. 'Duality is central to both characters. Batman leads a double life: dapper man about town by day, vigilante by night.'

She walked up to the fireplace and stood peering at the portrait above the fireplace. 'Is that a bullet hole?'

'How clever of you to notice. Apparently John got carried away with his gun and he fired two shots,' Sybil explained. 'No one was hurt. Happened while I was in London. John seemed to have had a delusional episode or something. He's apologised to everyone now.'

Antonia pointed to the bookshelves on the right of the fireplace. 'I don't think those books are one hundred per cent authentic, are they?'

'*Trompe d'oeil* – yes! If you push *Sodom and Gomorrah* slightly, the panel will open and you will see a secret staircase that leads upstairs, straight to John's dressing room. No, don't touch it! We've got the other matter to discuss first. The reason why you are here. Remember?' Sybil looked round, as though making sure there was no one around who could overhear them and asked in a low voice, 'Well, what do you think? Now you've met *everybody*. Any ideas?'

'I can't say we suspect anyone at this juncture, if that's what you mean,' Payne said.

'None of your guests looks like a homicidal maniac,' Antonia said. 'Unless it's your brother. He is the only one who seems vaguely implicated.'

'Because of the shooting incident? Oh but that's got nothing to do with it, nothing at all.' Sybil shook her head vehemently. 'It isn't John. I'd have told you if it was John. Besides, I never said "homicidal maniac". The killer – I mean the person who is planning to commit the murder – has a very rational reason for wanting to do it. He is *not* a nutcase.'

'So it's a man,' Payne said.

'No, it's not. I believe you are trying to catch me out.'

'You said "he".'

'Did I?' Sybil sighed. 'I knew I'd slip up sooner or later. I might as well tell you the whole story. Wouldn't be at all fair otherwise. But I must show you the object first. To my way of thinking it is the object that proves without any shadow of a doubt that –' Sybil broke off and put her finger across her lips. Her eyes were fixed on the door. 'I thought I heard a noise. No, it's nothing.'

After a moment's pause she walked up to a small desk in the corner. She took out a key, inserted it in the lock but she didn't turn it at once – she glanced over her shoulder –

As though on cue, the door opened and Oswald Ramskritt came into the library.

Sybil took out the key and turned round. She leant against the desk. She smiled. 'Oh Oswald! It's you!'

'It's me, yes. Did you expect somebody else?'

'No, of course not. I am sorry. I'm a little jumpy, I don't know why. Is anything the matter?'

'I would like to talk to you for a moment, Sybil. *If* I may.'

'Of course you may, Oswald, but I am a little busy at the moment. In about twenty minutes perhaps?'

'I need to talk to you *now*. It really is rather urgent.' Oswald Ramskritt looked towards Antonia, then towards Payne. 'Sorry, folks. Do you mind? It's very important. Oh and it's private.' He laughed.

Payne said it was all right, they didn't mind. They watched Oswald Ramskritt put his hand at Sybil's back and pilot her out of the library.

'He practically dragged her out,' said Payne.

'They were acting,' Antonia said firmly. 'The whole thing was staged.'

'You think so? I am not sure.'

As it turned out, they never got another chance to be alone with Sybil de Coverley again.

16

ENTER A MURDERER?

It was five minutes to nine and dinner was over.

Sybil de Coverley led the way to the drawing room where Maisie and Ella served the coffee. Sybil said that although she was awfully fond of the game, she wasn't going to pester anybody into forming a four for bridge. She believed in having things *ad hoc*, in leaving people to their own devices. There were jigsaw puzzles and books and papers and magazines and Scrabble and crosswords and, of course, Cluedo. The box didn't seem to be working for some reason, but then she'd never found television had much to offer in terms of entertainment these days, so terribly vulgar, strictly for the delectation of the half-witted. Thank God there were more than enough drinks – brandy and scotch and several kinds of liqueurs, some rather unusual ones.

'Do help yourselves,' she urged them.

Picking up a small silver hand-bell she gave a prolonged tinkle. 'Sorry. I keep forgetting we haven't got maids or a butler. This place is getting harder to manage by the minute. The roof leaks, windows rattle, pipes burst, floors collapse, cisterns overflow, doors jam – now it's the phone.'

'I'll see to all that. Once we've signed our agreement, things will move very fast, I promise you,' Oswald said.

'What's the matter with the phone?' Antonia asked. She wondered if they were getting closer to the murder.

'I have no idea. It's gone dead,' Sybil said. 'Something wrong with the line.'

'We've all got mobile phones, haven't we?' Maisie looked round.

'I haven't got a mobile phone,' Lady Grylls said.

Payne produced his mobile. 'Still no network, so our mobiles won't be much use.'

'Are we completely cut off then?' Doctor Klein said.

'I believe the wind's rising. Would you excuse me? I need to see to something.' With a vague gesture, Sybil left the room.

'Do let's play some game, shall we?' Lady Grylls said. 'Cluedo can be fun.'

'I hate Cluedo. I absolutely detest it,' Mrs Garrison-Gore said in her alarmingly loud voice.

'There's a frightfully clever game called The Game,' John de Coverley said. 'It goes like this. Everybody writes the names of famous people on sticky labels, which are then put into a hat. Names like Marshall Pétain, Justin Bieber, Nurse Cavell, Pippa Middleton and so on. Each player then draws out a label without looking, sticks it on their forehead and tries to work out who they are by asking questions to which the others can answer only yes or no. It's all frightfully clever. What do you think? Shall we play it?'

'Drinks, let's have drinks. I could do with a stiff brandy. Nothing like a Mind Number followed by a Liver Paralyser when things start flagging!' Mrs Garrison-Gore laughed.

'There was a game we used to play when I was young. It was called Who Can Bring Home the Awfullest Thing.' Lady Grylls looked at Mrs Garrison-Gore fixedly.

'First-class coffee,' Major Payne said.

Oswald Ramskritt had taken Maisie's hand in his. 'My enemies have called me hyperactive and hyper-acquisitive.

You don't believe that, do you? Tell me you don't. You know how much your opinion matters to me.'

'I don't.' Maisie looked very nervous.

'You are a sweet child, but I notice you always smile in the same way at everybody, why is that? I'd have preferred the occasional special smile. Is that such an unreasonable request?'

Antonia was unpleasantly reminded of the murderous Duke in 'My Last Duchess'.

'It will soon be May,' Ella said to Doctor Klein. 'A time of lilacs and shooting stars. I believe there was a poem about it.'

'Summer's practically knocking on the door. For me, buying summer clothes is the ultimate nightmare. It always puts me in mind of Sisyphus.' Mrs Garrsion-Gore raised her brandy glass to her lips.

John de Coverley said that summer was etched in his psyche as the time for girls. 'I think of it as the most magical time of the year. The acrid tang of heat emanating from the sidewalks, the breezes of late afternoon, the whiff of perfume of a passing beauty – eh, Major Payne?'

'One certainly falls in love quicker in summer,' Payne agreed.

'I miss summers in Germany,' Doctor Klein said. 'I remember walking in the Black Forest and thinking, but I haven't yet started to live! One of your English poets, I believe, describes summer as a "dress rehearsal of coming manhood".'

'Am I right in thinking magnolias go into bloom in May?' Antonia asked Ella. 'I love magnolias.'

John was talking to Lady Grylls, ' … the realisation that sooner or later one would fall desperately, knuckle-bitingly in love and lie drugged with pleasure on the grass with the girl of one's dreams … There is nothing that quite compares to the pure poignancy of first love – nothing at all!'

'*Particularly when accentuated by several prodigious dollops of gin.* That's what one of my beaux used to say. He was described as "lovably louche" by his aunt of all people. He was known for spiking girls' lemonades at dances. Do men still do that sort of thing?' Lady Grylls glanced round.

'Girls used to be notoriously broad-minded, but not any longer, it seems. Now they are bound to file for erotic coercion.' Mrs Garrison-Gore boomed with laughter.

'Talking about illicit love, we saw a production of *Romeo and Juliet* last month, but we didn't think it terribly convincing.' Payne said. 'Romeo took the news of Juliet's supposed demise as though it were a disappointing cricket score.'

'Juliet came across as a pert blue stocking, which isn't exactly as Shakespeare intended,' Antonia said with a smile.

'I thought I heard thunder – very distant thunder,' Maisie said with an anxious glance towards the window.

'Do you know how they used to create the illusion of distant thunder in old-fashioned plays?' John de Coverley looked round. '*By rubbing two coconuts together.*'

'The sea sounds furious. There's a storm coming, that's what the forecast said,' Mrs Garrison-Gore reminded them.

'Last time we had a storm on the island, the roof leaked like Alpine streams in springtime,' John de Coverley said. 'Like Alpine streams. Then the waves came – fuming and foaming. Looked as though the Kraken had awoken. Maybe that's why we can't get servants for long. Not that I mind awfully. This place practically runs itself. Practically runs itself.'

'An island is an acquired taste,' Lady Grylls said.

'I hope you will forgive my impertinence, but haven't you ever yearned for a son, Mr de Coverley?' Doctor Klein asked. 'I read somewhere that scions of old dynastic families preserved an ancestral nostalgia for the dignity and ceremonial of kinship.'

'As it happens, I have been thinking about it. Yes, most certainly.' John held up his monocle in a didactic fashion. 'I believe

in asserting the honourable lineage of the de Coverleys …
Where the hell has Sybil vanished to?'

'I think I will go to my room now,' Doctor Klein said. 'Don't
look so alarmed, Ella. Sometimes I am overpowered by a
general sense of worthlessness, that's all.'

None of this is real, Antonia thought. How long had it
taken them to learn their speeches? Had there been any clues
for her and Hugh to pick up? And how closer were they to
the murder?

It was five minutes later.

Doctor Klein stood in front of the chest of drawers in his
room. He had discovered that the bottom drawer had been
opened and that someone had rummaged inside it. The file
hadn't been replaced properly. And they must have seen what
was *under* the file. Not very careful, were they? How very
curious. Someone now knew his secret …

No, not 'someone'. Only Mrs Garrison-Gore from the
room next door could have done it. She was the Nosey
Parker type. He had noticed her shooting curious glances at
him. She *knew*. Did she have any intention of telling anyone?
Would she tell Oswald? Or would she perhaps use the idea in
her next book?

Oh well, it was bound to come out sooner or later.

He sat on his bed. He felt an odd fuzziness in his head.
Perhaps he needed to change his medication?

He thought of Oswald. He found Oswald a fascinating
study. Oswald enjoyed having what the English called the
'whip-hand' on women. Could a man be so unselfcon-
sciously bad – so thoroughly evil? Was that possible? Doctor
Klein had decided that he would continue observing Oswald
and if he found that Oswald had but *one* redeeming feature,

then Oswald might be given another chance – then he might be – well, spared.

Sybil de Coverley had entered the library and was preparing for her murder. She went round flicking an old-fashioned feather duster across the rows of books. She didn't want anyone to start sneezing at what was to be the culmination of the Murder Game. She turned off all the table lamps barring one. She walked up to the desk and pulled out the diaries that had belonged to one of her uncles, perhaps the most a-typical de Coverley – morocco-bound and written in multi-coloured inks – amethyst-purple, blood-red, chrome-yellow, jet-black, sapphire-green.

The diaries contained arcane clues to her forthcoming death – no they didn't, she suddenly remembered. Mrs Garrison-Gore had ruled against using the diaries.

Sybil felt tired and a little confused. She went on leafing through the diaries. Not diaries *exactly*. They contained *pensees*, the odd observation on the predictability of life as well as beauty tips. 'Bathe the eyelashes in moon-water ... When photographed, place tapering hands on cheeks as if supporting a Greek vase.'

How lovely the calligraphy had been seventy years ago, as stern and frivolous as her uncle's pure profile and floating fair ... In his prime her uncle had been known as the 'last professional beauty' ...

She put the diaries back in the desk. 'Tonight is as good a night to be killed as any,' she said aloud.

Turning round she gave an awkward laugh. She'd been startled by her ghostly reflection in the mirror. She felt an odd reluctance to apply the horror make-up they had decided on. For some reason she found herself in the grip of sudden panic – panic, as it had been defined by the ancient Greeks – as a 'conviction that some malignant supernatural power was coming'.

Nonsense, all nonsense, she told herself. It's this bloody island – it's sapping my energy – the sooner I get rid of it, the better –

She gasped and her hand flew up to her throat as she heard the door open.

She gave a sigh of relief.

'Oh, it's you,' she said with a smile. 'Why the solemn look?'

I incline towards overdoing things, Feversham thought. I tend to *become* the part. Like Perkin Warbeck, or was it Lambert Simnel, who had really believed himself to be one of the Princes of the Tower?

He must be careful. By no means must he *become* the part. It wouldn't do for him to edge into something like a play by Pirandello. Pretending to be someone else was rather fun and he believed he could do it really well, but convincing himself to *be* someone else was quite a different matter.

That way madness lay.

17

TRUTH TRIUMPHANT

Antonia and Hugh and Lady Grylls were now the only people in the drawing room.

'What in heaven's name is "slosh"?' Antonia asked.

'A game one plays with billiard balls,' Payne explained.

'This sofa is big enough to hold ten,' Lady Grylls said. 'What period is it, Hughie? It's the sort of thing you'd know.'

'No particular period. Manufactured round the First World War, I imagine.'

'Suggests people had much bigger behinds then. No slimming aids and I don't suppose anyone really *cared*. I read somewhere that a chap was in a shipwreck and was saved from drowning by a sofa. Older women who constantly diet and exercise end up with the asexual body of a young boy, I can't help noticing. Quite extraordinary. Look at that actress – the Barbarella girl – what was her name? In my day people were mad about something called Dexedrine. It was all the rage. It was known as the "go pill". It killed appetite but it made you terribly alert and focused, which was all very well if you were a pilot on a mission, but what if you weren't? Now then, did Sybil manage to talk to you?'

'No. She meant to, but we were interrupted. She was about to show us some object, which was of some special importance, but then Ramskritt barged in and monopolised her. He practically dragged her out of the library.'

'Really? What did he want? That fellow's getting quite impossible. Poor Sybil looked *distraite* at dinner, did you notice? She hasn't been herself for some time. I do hope she is wrong.'

'Wrong about what?'

'She's been imagining things. She said she felt thoroughly jinxed. I'm sorry, but I don't know the precise details. She believes someone is getting ready to kill someone else.'

'That's what she told us,' Antonia said.

'I wish she weren't so annoyingly vague.' Payne produced his pipe. 'I wonder if we could have some fresh coffee? Where's that damned bell? Or maybe not.' He glanced at his watch. 'It would be jolly embarrassing if Ella and Maisie had already gone to bed.'

'So Sybil was interrupted by Ramskritt? I hope that doesn't mean Ramskritt is the man Sybil suspects. It would be a little difficult for her to sell him the island if he tried to silence her or something, wouldn't you say?'

There was a pause. Payne regarded his aunt levelly. 'I believe the time's come for us to put our cards on the table, darling. We actually think this whole thing's getting a trifle tedious. None of you has been particularly subtle, you know. It's all a bit like something out of a novel by Mrs Garrison-Gore.'

'I don't know what you mean, Hughie. I have never read any of that woman's books and I don't propose to do so in the foreseeable future. Life is too short. Why are you looking at me like that?'

'Come *on*, Aunt Nellie, out with it. This is all your doing, why don't you admit it? I wouldn't go so far as to claim you were N. Nygmer, but you initiated the game, didn't you?'

'What game?'

'It's your anniversary present to us,' Payne said patiently. 'We worked it out, so do stop pretending. Sybil decided to humour you. She employed Mrs Garrison-Gore's services. She managed to persuade her guests to take part.'

'What services? I really don't know what you mean, Hughie.' Two bright spots had appeared on Lady Grylls' cheeks.

'I am sure you do, darling. Ten little sailor boys. The Riddler's letter. *The Murder Game.* You thought it was the sort of thing we'd enjoy. Challenge to the famous sleuths and so on – all orchestrated and choreographed by Mrs Garrison-Gore, who is a detective story writer specialising in this sort of nonsense.'

'You might as well tell us who is going to be murdered and by whom,' Antonia said with a smile. 'We won't be cross. I personally believe Oswald Ramskritt is only a red herring, but Sybil *is* going to be the victim, isn't she?'

Lady Grylls scowled. 'However did you discover Mrs Garrison-Gore wrote detective stories? I am told she employs a pseudonym, though I have no idea what it is. You couldn't have *recognised* her. She assured us her photo had never appeared anywhere. So how did you know?'

'Nothing remains hidden from us for long,' Payne said.

'Oh very well. I must admit I was getting fed up with the whole bloody thing. I am glad it's over.' Lady Grylls sat up. 'I meant well I thought it was the kind of set-up you'd find entertaining.'

'Actually it *is* entertaining,' Antonia said. 'I find the *dramatis personae* quite interesting.'

'Do you, my dear? I am terribly glad. So you don't think you've been wasting your time?'

'No, not in the least,' Payne said.

'Then you must go on pretending you know nothing about it. You must. Mrs Garrison-Gore seems to suffer from the most alarming mood swings and heaven knows what she might do if she starts thinking she's been made to look a fool. Hang herself or something, which would be terribly unsettling. Promise you will go on pretending.' She clutched at her nephew's hand. 'Just get on with the investigation, which you will be asked to conduct when Sybil's dead body is found in the library. She won't be dead, merely pretending of course. I believe it's John who will ask you to investigate.'

'The police won't be called?'

'No, the police won't be called. It would be impossible,' Lady Grylls whispered. 'The phone wires have been cut, you see. And as you discovered, there is no "network" on the island, so you won't be able to use those pocket phones of yours either. The G–G checked it all. I must say she's been terribly thorough.'

'The phone wires have been cut? You mean, for real?' Payne's brows went up. 'Wasn't that overdoing it a bit?'

'John did it himself. He hates it when the phone rings. He is a little mad, you see. I must say, everybody's been terribly coop-erative. Ramskritt and those poor girls and the odd doctor –'

'What poor girls? Do you mean Ella and Maisie? Why poor?'

'Well, Ramskritt's been treating them quite appallingly. He keeps upsetting them. The other night he tried to get into Maisie's bed and said some awful things to her. Then Sybil heard him say something vile to Ella, happened just before dinner, apparently.' Lady Grylls shook her head. 'I knew he was a wrong 'un the moment I saw him. He talks as though he owns the Bank of England, but his manners would be better suited to a street bazaar in Cairo.'

'Why do Maisie and Ella stick to him?'

'Heaven knows – it's one of those things – unless he has some hold over them? Can't fathom it myself. He's simply asking to be killed … What was that? Sounded like twenty French horns doing the prelude to *Die Valkyrie*. Not the Garrison-Gore woman again, is it?'

Payne smiled slyly. 'I expect the body has been found.'

Lady Grylls pushed her glasses up her nose. She peered at the Empire clock on the mantelpiece and said that it was all a bit too early for that. 'The body is not supposed to be found till quarter-to-eleven. Mrs Garrison-Gore is not supposed to scream either. I am sure I'd have been told if there'd been any changes.' Her expression was puzzled.

There was a pause. Payne and Antonia exchanged glances. Neither of them believed Lady Grylls was acting. Or maybe she was?

The next moment the door opened and Maisie Lettering appeared. She held her hand at her mouth and her eyes were brimming with tears. 'Oh please – *please* – come at once – there's been a murder!'

18

THE BODY IN
THE LIBRARY

As they entered the library, the windows creaked ominously and the lights flickered. Everybody was already there – no, not everybody – Doctor Klein was missing, Antonia noticed.

Semi-darkness, dark wallpaper, dark drapes. Only the gold script on the crowded book spines glimmered.

The body lay on its back on the shabby tiger hearthrug. There was someone kneeling beside it, John de Coverley, the victim's brother.

A rather theatrical kind of tableau, Antonia thought.

'I am not sure, but I believe she is dead,' John de Coverley said in a hoarse voice. 'Where's that doctor? We need a doctor. Why isn't he here when he is needed?'

'Will someone kindly inform me what's going on? Have we all stepped through the looking glass? It isn't supposed to happen like this at all, you know that perfectly well,' Lady Grylls spoke in an imperious voice.

'Sybil is dead,' John de Coverley said.

'She can't be. It's too early.'

'Don't touch anything,' Major Payne said automatically, though he knew it was a bit too late for that.

'She seems to have been strangled with the curtain cord.' John de Coverley's right hand flew up to his eyes and a sob escaped his lips. He rose. He winced. He clutched at his side. 'Sorry – my back – old injury – always gets bad each time there's a crisis. Sorry – I need to sit down. Old injury.' He collapsed into one of the fraying tapestry-covered armchairs.

Payne eyed him speculatively. Where was it he had he heard something about backache? He asked for more light, then walked up to the body and bent over it.

The curtain cord was deeply embedded into the folds of Sybil's neck. The flesh around it was swollen, reddish-blue – so was the face – distorted, almost unrecognisable – the mouth was gaping open – the tongue protruded from between the teeth. He touched her wrist, then his hand went up to her neck. The skin felt rubbery under his fingers.

'Where the heck is Klein?' he heard Oswald Ramskritt say to Ella. 'He's your buddy, you should know.'

'He is in his room. I believe he is ill.'

'Oh how convenient!'

'I think it's serious.'

'I knew it would end in tears,' Lady Grylls said. 'Something told me it would end in tears.'

Payne took his time. He was taking no chances. He still couldn't quite believe that this wasn't all part of the Murder Game that was being staged in their honour ...

The body was still warm but it was limp and no pulse could be detected.

Payne then noticed that Sybil's left hand was clenched in a fist. Something was protruding from between the fingers. Black silk cord – thinner and finer than the curtain cord –

With some effort Payne managed to open the fingers. There was something clutched between them – something round and flat –

He looked up. His eyes fixed on the desk.

'My love, would you –?'

Antonia seemed to know exactly what he wanted her to do. Silently she walked up to the desk and examined the drawer.

'Forced open. Badly splintered,' she said. She wrapped her hand with her handkerchief, stooped over and picked up a bronze paper knife from the floor. One or two wood fibres still clung to it. She held it up within Payne's view.

'I see.' He nodded. 'Someone was in an awful hurry.'

Sybil de Coverley had been about to unlock the drawer which, she said, contained what she imagined was vital evidence. Sybil had been about to reveal to them the identity of the would-be killer. But hadn't that been part of the murder mystery they were expected to solve? Where did the game end and the real murder begin?

'Is my sister dead? *Really* dead?' John spoke from the armchair, his hand covering his eyes.

'I am afraid she is.'

'But why – why would anyone want to kill Miss de Coverley?' Mrs Garrison-Gore spoke in a choked voice.

Payne cocked an eyebrow. 'You don't know?'

She reeled back. She might have been struck by a bullet. 'Of course not! This has nothing to do with me. Nothing at all.'

'It was you who organised the Murder Game. You wrote the script, didn't you? It was you who decided where and when Sybil's body was to be discovered. In the Murder Game you have been playing,' Payne went on slowly, 'Sybil was going to be killed because she knew the identity of a would-be killer. That's correct, isn't it? No point denying it. We know all about it.'

'Don't look at me! I didn't tell them. I am not a snitch,' Lady Grylls wheezed. 'They worked it out. They are awfully clever, I keep telling you.'

'But maybe this has nothing to do with the Murder Game,' said Payne. 'Sybil was killed for real, brutally strangled. We must call the police at once.'

'That could be a little difficult,' Oswald Ramskritt said. Antonia had the impression he was suppressing a smile. 'The phone is not working. There's no network, so our mobiles are no good either. And it would be impossible to navigate the mainland. The sea's like a seething cauldron – can't you hear it?'

Major Payne locked the library door and put the key in his pocket. 'No, impossible. Out of the question,' he said.

John de Coverley went on pleading with him in an urgent whisper. 'I know this kind of thing doesn't often happen in real life, maybe not at all, but I beg you to investigate my sister's murder. I beg you.'

'Impossible.'

'Please.'

'Out of the question,' Payne said again. 'This is not a game. Not any longer. This is a matter for the police.'

'Can't call the police. Landline not working. No network either.'

'Ramskritt could go to the mainland in his yacht.'

'He said he couldn't. You heard him – the sea's like a seething cauldron and so on. Besides,' John de Coverley said, 'I am damned if I'll let that fellow out of my sight. He'd probably skedaddle.'

'Why should he?' Payne cocked an eyebrow. 'Are you suggesting it was he who strangled your sister?'

'No, of course not. Sorry. I don't care much for him, that's all. Sometimes a chap takes against a fellow for no apparent reason.'

'Couldn't *you* brave the waves? We were given to understand you were a first-class sailor.'

'Were you? Good heavens. Someone must have got hold of the wrong end of the stick. I am afraid I know nothing about boats – complete wash-out as a sailor – get most awfully seasick.

So you see, you've *got* to investigate. You are our only hope. You and your charming wife. You've had experience in matters of violent death. You know exactly what's to be done. Your aunt told us all about it.'

'My aunt often gets frightfully muddled –'

'She said you knew the kind of questions that should be asked,' John de Coverley persisted. 'She said you knew what to look out for. How to set about things. I am sure you can find the killer before the police come. You can begin by checking everybody's alibi –'

'That would be highly irregular.'

'The killer is clearly one of us – well, it isn't me, but it's one of the people staying under this roof.' John de Coverley counted on his fingers. 'Ramskritt, Ella, Maisie, Doctor Klein, Mrs Garrison-Gore. No one seems to have any idea where Doctor Klein has disappeared to.' He frowned. 'What's the point of having a doctor in the house when he vanishes into thin air just when his services are most in demand? Perhaps you should consider Doctor Klein with extra care.'

'You think I should?'

They were still standing in the corridor outside the library door. Payne had crossed his arms. He had asked everybody else, including Antonia, to go to the drawing room.

'I'd hate to prejudice you in one way or another, but there's something damned peculiar about Doctor Klein. I can't quite say what, though ... I think we could eliminate your aunt from the list of suspects.'

'Indeed we could. Jolly decent of you to say so.' I am giving stock responses, Payne thought. Part of me continues to treat this as a game. My mind seems unable to grasp the fact that there has been a murder in the house.

'I believe your aunt was with you, wasn't she? I mean at the crucial time?'

'That is correct. We were in the drawing room. We never for a moment lost sight of my aunt. My aunt is as innocent as the sacrificial lamb.' I shouldn't be flippant, Payne reminded himself. 'Are you sure there is no one else in the house?'

'Positive. No one but us ten – no, *nine* – keep forgetting poor Sybil's gone. You don't suppose someone is hiding somewhere? We could conduct a search, of course, should you insist, but it would be a waste of time. There are no priests' holes anywhere in the house, if that's what you're thinking. Wrong period. No underground tunnels connecting the island with the mainland either, though, during the war, papa seriously considered the possibility. I am sure it would have cost him a pretty penny.'

Payne said that neither his wife nor he had any legal right to ask anyone any questions.

'But it could be *days* before we manage to inform the police!' John de Coverley cried in tones of despair. 'We are cut off. Completely cut off. And one of us is a killer!'

There was a pause. Payne watched him thoughtfully as he tried to fix his monocle in his eye.

'Why do you bother?' Payne's voice suddenly sounded weary. 'It is only plain glass. Unlike *this* one –'

With the air of a magician who is performing a well-known and rather tedious trick which he wants to finish fast before moving on to something of more general interest, Major Payne produced an almost identical-looking eyeglass attached to a piece of black silk ribbon. 'This,' he said, 'is the real thing.'

His host's face, he noticed with interest, became utterly blank, not merely expressionless but *deserted* – as if there was no one behind it. And when he spoke, it was in a voice that was a little different from the one he had been employing so far. 'Where did you find it?'

'It was clutched in her hand.'

'In my sister's hand?'

'Yes,' Payne said. 'Even though she is not your sister. Let's go to the drawing room, shall we? What I want to know is where exactly the Murder Game ends and the real murder starts – or could the two be in some way bizarrely entangled?'

19

THE ACTOR
AND THE ALIBI

'Very well. Perhaps you will allow me to introduce myself. My name is Feversham. As the poet put it so aptly, the loathsome mask has finally fallen. Or was the mask merely tiresome?'

'I think it was merely tiresome,' Payne said as he watched him try to fix his monocle once more.

'I am sure it was "loathsome". In a way I am glad. Terribly glad. It's a relief. It's dangerous remaining "in character" for too long. One could remain trapped. I know it sounds terribly unlikely but it's known to happen. Psychiatrists have a word for it, though at the moment the precise technical term escapes me.' Feversham seemed to be speaking out of a kind of daze. 'Being found out is the common fate of fraudsters and impostors, but it isn't quite that in my case. Not quite the case.'

'Are you a professional actor?'

'Indeed I am, Major Payne. Indeed I am. For my sins. *As an unperfect actor on the stage, who with his fear is put beside his part.* I should stop saying things twice. Have you noticed how I tend to say things twice? That's a mannerism I decided "John de Coverley" would have. Once I get my teeth into a part, I find it frightfully hard to get out of it. So you noticed that the blasted monocle was made of plain glass, what?'

'That – and the fact that you are right-handed whereas the real John de Coverley is left-handed. His sister told us.'

'She did? What else?'

'We saw Ella taking a plate of fried chicken to a room upstairs. Sybil had told us that chicken was John's favourite dish. Ella looked a trifle furtive. John is supposed to bear everybody under this roof a terrible grudge. Besides, he nearly blew off Ramskritt's head. You have been too tame and too amiable. A completely different character altogether. The real John is a good sailor – while you, in your own admission, are a complete wash-out.'

'Did I say "wash-out"? How observant of you.'

'Besides, you kept flirting with Sybil and she blushed girlishly and clearly welcomed your advances in a singularly un-sisterly manner.'

'Was that so obvious?'

'Well, yes.'

Feversham said that forbidden passion between siblings was not that uncommon. It happened more often than people imagined, especially among the upper echelons of society.

'You may be right. Not between these particular siblings, though. Sybil warned us that relations between her and her brother were extremely strained.'

'Are you always so uncannily accurate in your deductions?'

'Not always,' said Payne. 'Most of the time, perhaps.'

'Well, I was asked to play the part of Sybil's brother John de Coverley. Romany – Mrs G-G – knows me. I've already taken part in a couple of Murder Weekends she's organised in the past. Various moat hotels, you know. The grub is awfully good and they let you have drinks on the house, as many as you wish.'

'I believe you are a character actor?'

'Indeed I am. I specialise in middle-aged buffers with a diplomatic background. Once I played a former royal aide, to great acclaim. I was "Holbrook" in *The Sleeping Prince*. Rattigan, you know. I was also "Sir Rowland Delahaye" in Agatha Christie's *The Spider's Web*. This time, I was told, it would be different since the party was taking place at a private house on an island and everybody would be themselves, more or less. Romany encouraged us to perform prodigies of improvisation, invent whole loops of dialogue. Though of course the central situation was carefully thought through. It was to be staged with the minutest attention to detail.'

'By "the central situation" you mean the murder,' Payne said.

'Yes, I do mean the murder.' Feversham gave a little bow. 'I was going to impersonate someone who was in the house, but who was not going to appear at all. Sybil's brother. The real John de Coverley is an eccentric recluse who never leaves his room – unless it is late at night – and whose prowling presence is generally viewed as an irksome if innocuous pastime.'

'John was never approached and asked to play himself?'

'No. They knew he would never have agreed to it. But Romany thought he was too good a character to omit. Well, according to Romany's script, it was John who was to be unmasked as the Sphinx Island killer in the end. John, that is, as impersonated by me.' Feversham paused. 'Acting on Romany's instructions, Sybil paid you a visit and told you she suspected one of her guests was planning to kill another. Meanwhile a letter was sent to you, purporting to be from the mad killer.'

'So the Riddler was part of the game too,' said Payne. 'That was overegging the pudding a bit, wasn't it?'

'Romany wouldn't have it any other way. She wrote the letter personally. She found some ancient bottle of ink the colour of old blood – used to belong to one of Sybil's uncles, apparently. Romany said she wanted to make absolutely sure your curiosity was sufficiently aroused. She was keen on introducing a fantastical element into the story. Something *recherché*. I believe she came across a pile of old Batman comics in the library – that gave her the N. Nygmer idea. The murder was to take place on your very first night on the island. The body was to be found in the library.'

'It was going to be Sybil's body?'

'Sybil would have been "strangled" with the cord of a gentleman's dressing gown. *Not* with the curtain cord.' Feversham held up his eyeglass. 'Later the dressing gown cord would have be traced back to me – I mean to "John de Coverley". You'd have been told that Sybil was heard talking to someone in the library – some ten minutes before her body was found.'

'There would have been a witness to Sybil's last words?'

'Yes. That would have been Ella, or was it Maisie? Can't remember exactly which. Sorry – it's suddenly hit me that Sybil is dead, *really* dead. I liked her an awful lot, you know.' Feversham's hand went up to his eyes. 'Ella – I believe it was Ella, yes – was going to report to you what she had overheard Sybil say.'

'What was that?'

'*Why did you make me go to the Paynes with this rigmarole? I insist on an explanation for the cock-and-bull tale you asked me to feed them. Why did you want me to say I suspected one of my guests was a murderer? I am fed up with humouring you. I do think you should see a doctor.* Words to that effect. Meant to suggest that the idea of a killer preparing to kill someone was John's, that it was some kind of crazy amusement he had dreamt up, with which Sybil had agreed to collaborate.'

'And we would have deduced that she had been talking to "John". The *fake* John. *You*. This is all terribly complicated but I believe I see.'

'There would have been an additional trail of clues leading to "John". His motive would have been the island. He would have killed his sister after learning of her decision to sell the island to Oswald Ramskritt. Sybil had left the island to her brother in her will.'

'Oh yes. She told us about it.'

'Romany wanted to keep as close as possible to the real-life circumstances of her main characters,' Feversham went on. 'Or rather the circumstances of her actors. You would have discovered "John" made Sybil go to you with a cock-and-bull story about a killer. Sybil's murder would have been made to look as though she had been silenced.'

'I see. Or I believe I see … While all along there'd have been no earthly reason for her to have been silenced. I *see*. That would have been a mere "strategy of deception". The desk drawer then contained no real evidence?'

'No.'

'And you cut the telephone wires as part of the game?'

'I didn't. I was only to *say* it, but not actually do it. Someone else must have cut the wires – the *real* killer – unless it was the wind – do phone wires go under the sea? I was meant to make Sybil look dead by applying make-up – blue for bruises – a rubber band around the neck, little rubber bands round the wrists, so that you couldn't feel any pulse … A cruel trick, I know, but we wouldn't have kept you in the dark for long, I promise you.'

'Someone strangled Sybil for real,' Payne said. 'Any idea who that might be?'

'I haven't the foggiest.' Feversham sniffed. 'I can't believe I won't see her again. I miss her already. I miss her dreadfully. We'd been getting on like a house on fire. She loved my impersonations, you know. She said I reminded her of her father who'd been endowed with charm, a fineness of spirit and notable intelligence. I feel pole-axed.' Feversham dabbed at his eyes with a silk handkerchief. 'Positively pole-axed.'

'I examined the body at twenty past ten. She was still warm. I imagine she had been dead for no more than ten or fifteen minutes. Where were you between ten and quarter past ten?'

'I was in the dining room. I was looking for one of my cufflinks. Here it is.' Feversham held up his left hand. 'It was still there, under my chair. Did anyone see me? As it happens, Ramskritt did – he looked in and there I was on all fours. He said hallo. He and I chatted for a bit and then Mrs G-G appeared and – um – said she wondered whether poor Sybil was ready for the corpse make-up.'

20

WOMAN ON THE VERGE OF A NERVOUS BREAKDOWN

To start with Mrs Garrison-Gore's voice was steady. 'I was only following your aunt's instructions. *Make it as complicated as you can – remember they are awfully clever.* Your aunt said that you have *le gout du policier.* She said you believed that murder followed you wherever you went. She said you'd been feeling jaded and that what you needed was an intellectual challenge to get you out of the doldrums.'

'Jaded? *Jaded?*' Payne turned towards Antonia. 'Have we ever felt jaded?'

Mrs Garrison-Gore said she had decided on a plot involving a conglomerate of recognisable clichés. She had done it quite deliberately. 'The clichés were meant to amuse you – to make you feel superior – but also to intrigue you.'

'You will be pleased to know that you succeeded. We were intrigued all right,' Payne said. Actually, she is by no means a fool, he reflected.

'It was the Riddler's letter that decided us,' said Antonia. She had an idea her presence might be making Mrs Garrison-Gore a little self-conscious.

'Ten people on a peculiarly shaped island. A house with a mysterious history. Warring siblings. A provocative epistle. The woman who knows too much. Bluffs and counter-bluffs.

A plot which was to be as artificial as anything *commedia dell'Arte* has produced –'The next moment, without any warning, tears sprang from Mrs Garrison-Gore's eyes and coursed down her cheeks.

Payne rose and asked if she would care for a drink. Some brandy? Mrs Garrison-Gore declined.

'I spent *ages* getting every little detail right, absolute ages! And for what? Sleepless night after sleepless night, scribbling away. I believed I was doing something worthwhile but I was deluding myself. I was doing it for the money, of course.' Mrs Garrison-Gore sobbed. 'Smoke and mirrors, that's what detective stories are – ephemeral piffle – nothing to do with literature – all so *pointless*. I have been wasting my time, my mind, my energies! I have achieved nothing in my life, nothing at all!'

'People love reading murder mysteries,' Payne tried to reassure her.

Mrs Garrison-Gore went on to claim that she could have done better things. She could have helped mankind. She could have tried to improve the human condition. She could have become a teacher or a missionary. Or a nurse! She could have been a nurse at some leper colony in Honolulu or Honduras. She could have been primping the curls and buffing the cheeks of black babies. Instead of which she had been writing detective stories! She spat out the words with infinite disgust. 'Edmund Wilson was right!' She shook her forefinger. 'Edmund Wilson couldn't have put it better!'

'You don't mean the notorious Roger Ackroyd quip, do you?'

'That's exactly what I mean. Nobody should care who killed Roger Ackroyd!' Mrs Garrison-Gore cried. 'Why should they? Readers should start boycotting these so-called "entertainments". Bookshops should refuse to stock detective stories. Detective stories are bad for public health!'

'This strikes me as a somewhat extreme view …'

'It's a perfectly balanced view!'

'Detective stories have been with us for more than a hundred years and have always been vastly popular.'

'They give unbalanced individuals ideas. The world is full of unbalanced individuals. Look at the people at this house, I mean at *us*. Look at us, just look at us! Are we all perfectly balanced? *Are* we? I mean us – not *you* – us! Look at us! We set you up! We played a game with you! Is that responsible adult behaviour?'

'You were accomplices in a conspiracy of histrionics,' Payne murmured.

Mrs Garrison-Gore beat at her ample bosom with her fist. Her costume jewellery rattled. 'I killed Sybil de Coverley! As good as! It was my idea that she should be the victim. Poor Sybil! I killed her! I am a killer! I *must* be arrested!'

Oh dear. Antonia bit her lip. She remembered something else her copy-editor had told her, namely that Romany Garrison-Gore was a past mistress of the unexpected and extravagant emotional response.

'You are clearly upset,' Payne said. 'Perhaps we should have a break?'

Mrs Garrison-Gore shook her head. 'No, no breaks. That's all right. I am fine. Hysterical reaction, that's all. I do apologise. Hate myself when it happens. Nerves torn to shreds. Overworked, that's the trouble. Not enough sleep. Living in a world of my own. You can ask me any questions you like. The least I can do is answer your questions.' She produced a handkerchief and blew her nose rather noisily. 'Shoot.'

'Are you sure?'

'Shoot.'

There was a pause. Payne held his chin between his thumb and forefinger. 'Where were you between ten and quarter past? Do you remember?'

'Of course I remember. That's when I popped up to see how Doctor Klein was,' she said promptly. 'He was lying on his bed, poor man. He said he was OK, though he looked far from OK. Terrible colour and so *limp*. Put me in mind of a beached whale. Then I went downstairs looking for Feversham. Wanted a word about Sybil's make-up. I found Feversham in the dining room talking to Oswald. Then I went looking for Sybil. That was a couple of minutes later …' She sniffed.

'Do go on, please.'

'It was time for her make-up, you see. I was getting nervous. Feversham was going to apply it. Feversham knew how, being an old pro. He'd brought his make-up kit from London. I went into the library and I saw Sybil lying there. At first I thought he had already applied the make-up. I remember looking at my watch and thinking Sybil had got the time wrong since it was too early for her to take her position in front of the fireplace … I called out to her … I thought she was shamming … Only she wasn't … I touched her hand … She was dead … I believe I screamed. I screamed, didn't I? I have the uncanny feeling she'll walk in any minute and say it was all a joke!'

'Any idea as to who might have strangled her?' Payne asked.

'No, no idea at all,' Mrs Garrison-Gore said. 'I really wouldn't want to speculate. I can but I won't. It would be wrong. I've done enough harm as it is.'

Ella Gales had the clearest ice-blue gaze which Antonia had ever seen. It was like glass.

'Yes, that's correct. My story would have been that I'd been passing by the library door. I was to say that the library door was closed but I'd heard Sybil's voice and that she was talking to someone.' Ella held her hands clasped on her lap. 'I was to tell you that Sybil had sounded agitated. That's why I'd stopped and listened since it wasn't at all characteristic of Sybil to show emotion of any kind. As it happens, I never left the kitchen.

I only came out when I heard Mrs Garrison-Gore screaming … Between ten and quarter past? In the kitchen, I told you. I was with Maisie. There was so much to do –'

'I was *meant* to interrupt you in the library. That was according to the script. I was to barge in just as Sybil was about to show you the "evidence",' Oswald Ramskritt explained. 'My manner was to be brusque and jarring. Sybil was to allow herself to be led away like the proverbial lamb to the slaughter. Mrs G-G asked us to rehearse the scene several times. She kept cracking the whip. I felt like a circus animal being put through his paces. I can't say I enjoyed it, but I believe I managed to shepherd Sybil out in suspicious enough manner, didn't I?'

'That was in fact only a red herring …'

'The "lead-up to the murder", that's what Mrs G-G called it. Mrs G-G's purpose was to exercise your little grey cells.' He tapped his forehead, then twirled an imaginary moustache. 'Shouldn't joke, really. Sorry. This is a terrible business.' There was an odd expression on his face. He didn't really look sorry, Antonia thought.

'The breaking open of the desk drawer then was also part of the plot?'

'Yes. I did that myself. Sybil said the desk was only an imitation Sheraton. There was nothing in the drawer – only old theatre programmes, dinner party menus, odds and ends, one of those pens fashioned out of a silver bullet, which, as it happens, Sybil gave to Mrs G-G as a present. To protect her against evil.'

'A real silver bullet?'

'I believe it is, yes. Sybil said one of her ancestors went vampire hunting in Transylvania. It happened at the time of

139

the Boer War. He was meant to go to Tans*vaal*, but apparently got on the wrong train. I don't know if any of it is true. Sybil was in a skittish mood last night and no mistake. She probably made it up. She seemed to be in an odd state altogether.'

Antonia spoke. 'What sort of state?' She told herself she didn't really trust this man.

'There's a word for it, I think.' Ramskritt frowned. 'A feeling of exalted happiness that precedes disaster –'

'*Fey?*'

He slapped his knee. '*That's* the one! She was all flushed – girlish – positively girlish – laughing – giving people presents – she gave me a Victorian antimacassar – she gave Doctor Klein an ivory cigarette holder – she gave Feversham a pair of tartan gloves that had belonged to her late father. I do believe she was sweet on the actor, Feversham. That might explain it; yes … She was acting like a girl in love … As though she was standing on the very threshold of ecstasy.'

21

THE DOOR
IN THE WALL

Lady Grylls shook her head. 'I still can't believe it. Poor Sybil. Lying dead in an ugly heap in the library. Thank God her dear mother is no longer with us. I can't help feeling guilty. The police could take ages, couldn't they? Goodness, one o'clock – can that clock be right? It seems it's already tomorrow.'

'Yes, it's already Saturday,' Antonia said.

'*Tomorrow and tomorrow and tomorrow*,' Payne said. 'Shakespeare meant this line to convey the relentless heat of time.'

'You poor things! So much for your wedding anniversary!'

'The murder of Sybil de Coverley has nothing to do with the Murder Game,' said Payne in a thoughtful voice. 'We don't think the killer was inspired by it or anything of that sort, do we, my love?'

'No. He would probably have done it anyway,' Antonia said grimly.

Lady Grylls pushed her glasses up her nose. '*He?* Do you mean you know who killed Sybil?'

'We believe we do.' Payne produced his pipe. 'All of Sybil's guests seem to have alibis. Feversham was in the dining room looking for a cufflink and he was joined by Oswald Ramskritt who confirmed it. Mrs Garrison-Gore looked in on Doctor Klein – we managed to have a brief word with him – then she went to the dining room and found Feversham and Ramskritt there, so that's alibis for all three – Ella and Maisie confirmed they were in the kitchen till they heard Mrs G-G scream. Unless they are all in it, everybody seems to have an alibi for the time during which we believe Sybil was killed.'

'People walked up and down the corridor past the library door, so the killer couldn't have got to Sybil that way without being observed,' said Antonia.

'But how *did* he get to her? Who *is* the killer?'

There was a pause.

'Sybil was clutching a monocle on a torn ribbon,' Payne said. 'She appeared to have ripped it off, which suggests a struggle. Sybil seemed to have tried to fight her killer back. Monocles are usually attached to the lapel or are worn round the neck –'

'Feversham!' Lady Grylls cried. 'It was Feversham, wasn't it?'

'Feversham's monocle is intact.'

'He may have had a spare.'

'That's certainly possible, but, as it happens, we have a some-what different theory,' Antonia said. She wished she didn't keep thinking it was all too easy. 'Apart from Feversham, there is one other person in this house who wears a monocle. John de Coverley.'

'The *real* John de Coverley,' Payne said. 'Earlier on I paid him a visit, you see. I went up to his room. *His hands are bandaged.* I may be wrong, but I think the bandages are suggestive –'

'Oh but it can't be John. A virtual impossibility. He's been kept under lock and key.' Lady Grylls spoke dismissively. 'John is under house arrest. He couldn't have got out of his room and gone to the library.'

'As a matter of fact he could have. There is a concealed door in the library wall which leads to John de Coverley's room.'

It was all too easy. Too easy, too soon. But then wasn't that how things happened in real life? Antonia knew she was being irrational but she couldn't help an acute sense of an anti-climax. She kept thinking something was not right. She blamed her mindset, which was that of a crime writer first and a normal human being second. How tedious that made her sound.

She found it hard to accept it was all over. Her sense of structure and pacing, if she had to be perfectly honest, were offended. Denouements, she reflected, do not happen as early as that. Not so soon after the finding of the body. If she ended a story at this point, it would be sent back to her with a request to make it longer. It wouldn't have been the right length.

She was dismayed to find she felt close to tears. I am as bad as Mrs Garrison-Gore, Antonia thought. I write the same kind of rubbish. They say I give it a post-modern twist, they say it's a 'clever take', they say that I tease both the detective story genre and its audiences, but it's the same kind of rubbish. The normal recreation of noble minds indeed. Guedalla didn't know what he was talking about. It's nothing of the sort.

I keep thinking it can't be John. We are *meant* to think it's John. But it isn't him. Too simple, too obvious. So easy to frame someone like John, to create a trail of clues that lead to him ...

'A secret door?' Lady Grylls said.

'Yes. A door camouflaged as bookshelves. Sybil pointed it out to us while she was showing us round the library. All you have to do is push in Proust's *Sodom and Gomorrah*,' Payne explained. 'The door opens onto a staircase – a jolly narrow one, the precipitous, corkscrew variety – which winds up to John de Coverley's room, or rather his dressing room. I checked. About twenty minutes ago I went up. On his side the door opens into his wardrobe, Narnia-fashion. The wardrobe is in his dressing room. I found John de Coverley in his room. He was sitting at his desk chewing blotting paper.'

'He didn't try to shoot you, did he?'

'I don't think he cared for the sight of me emerging from his dressing room, but he remained quite calm. He said he had no idea there was a door at the back of his wardrobe; his bloody sister had never told him about it. I was struck by the fact that his hands were bandaged. When I asked him what had happened, he said he'd been pecked by a seagull. A seagull had perched on his window sill and he tried to catch it. He managed to get hold of one of its legs and the gull pecked him ... As he wasn't wearing his special gloves, it was really bad. It drew blood ... He let the seagull go ...'

'You don't believe his story? What do you think happened?'

'I don't know.' Payne stroked his jaw with his forefinger. 'Sybil seemed to have struggled as he was strangling her. She might have scratched him. I couldn't possibly make him show me his hands. I have no right. That's for the police to do ... He said he had no idea what had happened with his blasted eyeglass. His blasted eyeglass had vanished.'

'Did he look guilty?'

'He looked put out. If John is as potty as everybody believes him to be,' Payne explained, 'he wouldn't feel any guilt. In his mind he's done nothing wrong. He killed his sister because he wanted the island to himself. She had left the island to him in her will ... Exactly the way it happens in the Murder Game.'

22

METAMORPHOSIS

Ten minutes later they announced the results of their 'investigation' to the rest of the house party.

Everyone was there with the exception of Doctor Klein. Doctor Klein, Ella informed them, had gone to bed.

'It is of course for the police to conduct a proper investigation. This,' Payne said in conclusion, 'is what we *believe* happened.'

Feversham rose solemnly to his feet, put up his eyeglass and shook Major Payne and Antonia by the hand. He thanked them for their efforts. Nothing could ever bring Sybil back, but the fact that her killer had been apprehended provided him with some comfort.

'This is only what we *believe* happened,' Payne repeated.

Feversham did his ambassadorial trick; he bent his body from the waist ceremoniously and held his well-tended hand at an angle. All he needed was a plumed hat, Antonia thought. He might have been greeting the President of the French Republic or the King of Siam. Feversham seemed to have slipped unconsciously into his John de Coverley persona.

Once more Payne had the uneasy feeling they were still playing the Murder Game – but Mrs Garrison-Gore's distress struck him as genuine.

'It was all my fault,' he heard her whisper. She was holding her handkerchief pressed against her lips.

They had already made sure John de Coverley – the *real* John de Coverley – was under proper house arrest. No more loopholes. They had removed from his room anything remotely rope-like, including his dressing gown cord and shoelaces. The secret door was carefully locked.

They didn't go to bed till two in the morning.

Antonia lay on her back and stared at the curtained window. The wind was howling. Rain had started pummelling the house. The sea made a sound like the apocalyptic thundering of hooves.

Though she felt extremely tired, sleep refused to come. She was surprised and a little annoyed that Hugh should have fallen asleep the moment his head hit the pillow.

Tomorrow we'll get up and if the wind has subsided, we'll go and fetch the police, Antonia thought. Or rather Oswald will, in *Cutwater*. Hugh will go with him …

John de Coverley had told Hugh he had not been aware of the secret door in the library wall. Nothing John de Coverley said could be regarded as reliable, but what if he was telling the truth about the secret door? The secret door was the only access he had had to the library. What if it hadn't been him after all? What if someone else killed Sybil – that person could easily have cut off John de Coverley's monocle without him realising it –

Saintly self-composed Ella could have given John an injection and sent him to sleep. She had done it before. Or Doctor Klein could have given him an injection …

Ella … or Doctor Klein? Sybil had used the word 'cabal' in connection with those two …

Antonia's eyes closed. She had started feeling sleepy.

There was something about Doctor Klein. Some indefiniteness or ambiguity which was hard to place ... An incident had taken place earlier in the day, at tea. No, not an incident exactly. Why did she think it important?

They had been talking about cloning, about scientists playing God. Hugh had mentioned an interesting article he had read that morning, something about the possibility of cloning babies in the near future. Doctor Klein had taken part in the conversation and had propounded some very curious ideas. Then he suddenly seemed to lose interest in the discussion. He asked for *The Times*. Doctor Klein had been sitting in an armchair beside the window. Ella had folded the paper and tossed it at him. The paper had fallen on the floor. Doctor Klein didn't seem to mind. Ella's relaxed, rather informal attitude suggested she and Klein might indeed be rather close.

Doctor Klein had done something which had struck Antonia as odd. Now, what *was* it?

No, she couldn't think. She was tired – oh so tired ...

The sea seemed to be getting closer ...

Suddenly she remembered something else.

She had seen Oswald Ramskritt trying to catch someone's eye – it had happened in the drawing room, in the course of their last gathering – as Hugh had stood explaining why they believed it was John de Coverley who'd done it ...

Oswald had winked at someone. As though to say – what? *Well done, we pulled it off?* Oswald's lips had twitched into a smile. That, Antonia reflected, was what people did after pulling a successful prank or a hoax – only Sybil de Coverley had been killed for real.

Antonia had seen Feversham and Ramskritt looking conspiratorial together – they had been walking round the terrace before dinner – talking in low voices – she had the feeling Feversham was *reporting* to Ramskritt … They seemed engaged in arranging some carefully thought out scheme … She could not rid herself of the impression … But perhaps it was her imagination?

No. There *was* something. She was sure of it.

Were they accomplices? Not a terribly likely combination. Feversham was absurdly English, Ramskritt so very American. And why *would* they want to kill Sybil? Not for the fun of it, surely?

Antonia stirred restlessly. She turned to the left, then to the right.

Feversham and Ramskritt … Ella and Doctor Klein …

Ella had been aiming at Doctor Klein's lap – *but the newspaper had fallen on the floor.* That was it. That was the odd thing. Doctor Klein had had to bend over and pick up the newspaper. Which he had done with some difficulty, puffing, due to his girth. His face had became mottled with the effort. But why *did* she believe that was important?

Eventually Antonia fell into an uneasy sleep.

He was an outcast on a cold star, enclosed in a wall of glass. He was unable to feel anything but an awful helpless numbness. He was looking down on the warm earth, into the nest of lovers' beds, baby cribs, meal tables, all the solid commerce of life, of which he knew he would never be a part …

Doctor Klein decided to think of something funny, to relieve the gloom. He had been such a happy creature once, but these days he didn't laugh often, not at all in fact …

Something funny. That socialist chess set? Yes. Why not? The socialist chess set had been funny. *Very* funny. It had not been meant to be funny, which only made it funnier.

The socialist chess set contained no king. The king's place had been taken by a worker holding the economic plan in his hands. The rooks had become figures in the uniform of East German factory defence squads and the bishops were athletes. The pawns were workers of different trades, one carrying a hammer, the other a sickle. All that had been left of the original chess figures were the two knights, called 'horses' in German. The queen remained a woman, but she was intended to depict 'the progressive intelligentsia'.

Doctor Klein laughed.

Major Payne was dreaming.

He had got out of bed and gone down to the library, unlocked the door and found the room empty. There was nothing on the hearthrug in front of the fireplace. Where *was* the body? It would be so easy to get rid of a body on a small island, he thought. One had simply to drag it to the rocks and drop it into the sea …

Smoke and mirrors, he heard Mrs Garrison-Gore's voice whisper in his ear. *Smoke and mirrors.*

A girl had entered Ella's room and was standing by her bed. She was thin, with a pale face and large feverish eyes. She was attractive in a haggard kind of way. She held out her hand towards Ella, in an imploring gesture.

'Who are you?' Ella asked.

'Now you see me, now you don't,' the girl whispered. '*Watch.*'

She then started changing shape – expanding – she became bigger and bigger, rounder and rounder, till she was transformed into a grotesque blob. The only thing that stayed the same throughout the transformation was the mark above the left eyebrow –

Ella cried out and woke up.

23

DAWN OF
THE DEAD

It was quarter past nine in the morning. The house was very quiet. There seemed to be a lull in the storm. They couldn't hear the sea. No squawking gulls either.

Thanks to the Teasmade, a 1950s model, which stood on Antonia's part of the bed, they sat drinking their second cup of Darjeeling.

'I am ravenous,' Payne said. 'Despite everything that has happened, I am ravenous. Do you think the good Ella has managed to rustle something up? Bacon and eggs would be just the ticket. What about you?'

'I'm not hungry,' Antonia said. 'I didn't sleep too well. I'd rather sit here for a bit.'

Their room was pleasantly spacious, furnished in cherry wood, with narrow windows.

They were fully dressed now.

'Today we have been married for ten years,' Antonia said. She raised her cup of tea to her lips. She was sitting in the window seat.

'Good lord. I completely forgot. What with the murder and everything. Awfully sorry. Happy anniversary, darling.' He put down his cup and saucer. He went up to her and kissed her. 'Ten wonderful years. Do you remember my wooing you at the old Military club?'

'I most certainly do. I can't believe it's been ten years. It feels like yesterday. And here we are ten years and I don't know how many murders later.' She sighed. 'Not counting this one.'

'I suppose it's hard not to feel morbid when there is a dead body lying in the library,' Payne said.

'I can't believe it. Our hostess is dead and her brother is locked in his room, suspected of her murder.'

'This is for you.' He dropped a little onyx box in her lap. 'Happy anniversary, darling.' He kissed her again.

Antonia opened the box. 'Oh Hugh — it's *lovely*. Thank you! I've also got something for you — it's in the suitcase.'

'What is it?'

'It's a surprise.'

'Let me guess — as you know, I am terribly good at guessing ... A silver hip flask with *Per Aspera* engraved on it?'

'It isn't a flask.'

'A folding Malacca cane with a silver handle?'

'No.'

'A frock coat and knee breeches which are an exact replica of the ones worn by George III?'

'No.'

'A Masonic tie-pin — topped by a topaz as large as a gull's egg?'

'No! You will never guess —' She broke off. 'Oh.'

She had suddenly remembered what it was about Doctor Klein that had been bothering her.

She sat very still.

'*What lent thee, child, this meditative guise?*' Payne said. 'What on earth is the matter? Why the owlish expression all of a sudden? I'd rather you didn't make yourself look like my aunt, you know.'

'I thought you adored your aunt,' Antonia said absently.

'Yes, but not quite in the same way. It would have been terribly peculiar if I did adore my aunt in the same way.'

'Hugh, I have had an idea. It concerns Doctor Klein … You'll probably think me mad …'

He waved his hand. 'Everything is permissible today. Fire away.'

'Doctor Klein did something yesterday, which led me to think –' She went on to explain exactly what she meant.

There was a pause. He stared back at her. 'Golly … You may be right … Could it have anything to do with Sybil's murder?'

'If there is a connection, I don't see it.'

Payne glanced at his watch. 'Shall we go downstairs or would you rather have breakfast here? Shall I ask Ella to have a tray sent to you?'

Antonia had a faraway look on her face. 'It was all *too easy*. What if John did tell you the truth? What if he had no idea the secret door existed? What if those scratches on his hands *were* made by a seagull and not by a struggling Sybil? Sorry. Did you say a tray? No, no. We'll go downstairs together.' Antonia rose. 'I am damned if I am staying here all by myself.'

'It's so quiet, Hugh … *Too* quiet … Don't you think? Where *is* everybody?' Antonia whispered, unnerved.

'*And then there were none*. Sorry, shouldn't be saying things like that. Maybe they have all chosen to stay in their rooms? To catch up on their sleep?'

'A moment ago I thought I heard someone singing – it sounded very peculiar – maybe the pipes? Or am I losing my mind?'

'Couldn't have been the pipes. The pipes are cold as ice,' Payne said. 'Could have been sirens, you know. We are in the middle of the sea, remember. Gosh, I'm freezing. This place is a bloody morgue … What kind of singing was it? Can you describe it?'

'Sounded unbearably sad, like a lament. Odd kind of voice. Neither male nor female.'

'So it was a siren after all.' Payne nodded. 'Sirens are notoriously androgynous.'

'No, they are not. Sirens are ultra-feminine … Maybe I imagined it.'

'Maybe you did.'

They walked down the stairs and made for the dining room.

The dining room was empty and looked uninviting in the bleak morning light. There was no sign of breakfast.

Outside the windows the sea looked black.

The dawn of the dead, Payne thought though he didn't say it.

'Where *is* everyone?' Antonia stood looking round.

They retraced their steps to the corridor. 'No smell of cooking, why is that? I am ravenous. I'd kill for some kedgeree,' said Payne. 'I'd been hoping for some freshly brewed coffee.'

'When I am worried,' Antonia said, 'I can't eat a thing.'

'*Are* you worried? You poor thing! Where *is* Ella? It isn't like her to abandon her duties. Shall we go to the kitchen – or shall we start knocking on our fellow guests' bedroom doors? Let's go and rouse Aunt Nellie, shall we? No,' Payne suddenly said. 'Let's go to the library.'

'Why the library?'

'I want to check if the body is still there.' Payne patted his pocket. 'I've got the key.'

She looked at him sharply. 'Why? What's the idea?'

'Last night I dreamt that the body had disappeared. It was a damned unsettling dream. It isn't often that I fall prey to silly fancies, as you know, but I'd like to go and check anyway. All bloody nonsense.'

'*Case Without a Corpse*. That's the title of an obscure detective novel by the rather dubious Rupert Croft-Cooke.' Antonia spoke with a nonchalance she didn't feel. 'Pen-name: Leo Bruce.'

'Why dubious? Oh – there was something he was involved in – a scandal of some sort – young girls, was it? Or was it choirboys?

How interesting. One always imagined detective story writers to be the cleanest-living of all writers.'

'I believe most of us are,' Antonia said.

'Let's check if the corpse is still there, shall we?'

The library door was ajar. They halted. Antonia pulled at her husband's arm.

'Yes. I see it too,' Payne said in a low voice. 'I don't think we are having a joint hallucination. This suggests the existence of another key.'

Light seeped through the door. Antonia didn't think it was a lamp. The light flickered – unless her eyes were deceiving her – not *candles*? What kind of devilry was that? Not a *wake*, surely?

Angels and Ministers of grace defend us, Antonia thought.

Payne had also seen the light and he stiffened. He glanced round – he needed a weapon – just in case. A table lamp with a heavy bronze base on a side table drew his attention – he picked it up, winding the flex round his wrist.

'Keep behind me,' he whispered.

He pushed the door open.

He felt Antonia grip his elbow.

The sight that met their eyes made them stop and stare.

Antonia gave a little cry.

Gott is tot …

Doctor Klein was in his room and he was singing. It was an old and rather obscure German song with an untranslatable title. Something about the death of hope, the death of love, the death of God …

Tears as large as pearls ran down his white face. A cinema buff might have been put in mind of Cocteau's *La Belle et La Bête*:

Belle's teardrops turning into glittering diamonds, much to her delight.

But in Doctor Klein's heart there was no delight, only darkness.

God, I declare, is dead.

God is dead.

Did you hear the news?

God is dead.

We have killed God.

How shall we comfort ourselves, the murderers of all murderers?

Who will wipe this blood off us?

What water is there for us to clean ourselves?

What festivals of atonement?

What sacred games shall we have to invent?

Is not the greatness of this deed too great for us?

Doctor Klein looked at his reflection in the mirror, at his opening and closing mouth. He waved an imaginary conductor's baton.

He thought of his hostess and fellow guests. They were all — *dead.*

Dead souls ... They were not aware of it of course ...

He too was dead

There hadn't been a sound, then suddenly some kind of peculiar chant. Damned annoying, John de Coverley thought. It was clear what they were up to. *They were trying to drive him mad.*

They had taken his gun away, then his eyeglass had vanished and, as though that were not enough, they had locked him in his room. He had no idea how he managed to remain so calm. Could they have been putting something in his food and drink — some drug — some kind of bromide — to induce docility?

The chap who had come out of his wardrobe the night before hadn't given him any explanation. A military-looking sort of chap with quite an air about him. Terribly polite. Hadn't turned a hair. As though emerging from people's wardrobes was the most natural thing in the world. He had just stood there, looking at him in what appeared to be a speculative manner. He seemed to be particularly interested in his hands.

John regarded his bandaged hands with a puzzled frown.

Antonia and Hugh went on staring.

Aeons passed …

The cake was shaped like a giant question mark of the kind favoured by the incorrigible Riddler. The icing was of a virulent green colour. There were ten burning candles sticking out of it.

'Happy anniversary,' Sybil de Coverley said. She gave them a dazzling smile.

She was wearing white lace gloves.

24

TWISTED NERVE

And everybody joined in. Antonia looked round in dismayed disbelief which quickly turned to anger. They were all there: Mrs Garrison-Gore, looking exhausted and self-deprecating; Oswald, grinning broadly, though showing signs of irritation; Ella, with her familiar air of defensive aloofness; Feversham, elegant and debonair; Maisie, a terrified smile on her face; Lady Grylls, looking sheepish …

No, not everybody – Doctor Klein was again absent.

They were all in it …

'There you are! We knew you'd come this way sooner or later! We've been cooped up here since dawn!' Lady Grylls cried in exaggerated glee. 'Hate hiding, unless it is from the Taxman, ha-ha. I beg you not to hate me. The whole thing was all Mrs Garrison-Gore's idea anyhow. I mean this particular scenario. The double bluff and so on. I haven't got the brains for such diabolical twists.'

Oswald Ramskritt said, 'Shall we open the champagne? I think it's time.'

'No, no. Antonia and Hugh will need to blow out the candles first,' Sybil de Coverley said. 'The candles have started dripping. Do blow out the candles, quick, otherwise the cake will taste foul! Poor Ella took so much trouble making this cake.'

Major Payne surveyed the scene with a mirthless smile; thus the ancient satirist must have contemplated the Ship of Fools. 'I'd rather someone explained first. My aunt or Miss de Coverley or Mrs Garrison-Gore, perhaps?' He didn't make any great effort to keep the stiffness out of his voice. His eyes fixed on Mrs Garrison-Gore.

Mrs Garrison-Gore failed to return his look. She appeared to be entranced by the bowl of dry daffodils on a side table. She was wearing what looked like window curtains fashioned out of stately brocade. Her hair gave every appearance of being freshly permed. She must have brought her own electric tongs, Payne reflected inconsequentially. Everybody seemed to be ridiculously over-dressed. Were he and Antonia expected to be impressed by their sense of occasion? Ella was wearing a high-collared dress in silvery-grey. His aunt was clad in a powder-blue cashmere and wore her pearls. Feversham sported an immaculately cut three-piece Prince of Wales check suit, a butterfly collar and a bow tie.

'Shall we open the champagne?' Oswald said again. He sounded impatient. 'I don't know about you folks, but I have a thirst. I had a whisky before I came down. I was feeling tense. I guess it's given me a thirst.' He wore a sharkskin suit with buttons that looked like opals, perhaps *were* opals, which, in Payne's very private opinion, was the most bounderish kind of outfit a chap could ever think of.

'Major Payne is perfectly right. We need to provide an explanation for our seemingly outrageous conduct.' Feversham sounded very much the *grand seigneur*. His monocle flashed. He appeared to have assumed a position of authority. 'We agreed that we should adhere to the rules, didn't we?'

'What rules?' Oswald asked.

'The rules of fair play, my dear fellow.'

'I don't remember any rules.'

THE RIDDLE OF SPHINX ISLAND

'We have been terribly good at it so far, why spoil it at the very end? Major Payne and his charming wife are entitled to an explanation.' Feversham gave a little bow in Antonia's direction.

'I think the storm's starting again.' Ella was gazing out of the window.

'*How tedious is a guilty conscience – methinks –* How did that go on? *Methinks –* something or other? What exactly did the bishop – or was it some mad radical? – see when he looked into his garden pond?' Lady Grylls glanced round. 'I do believe he was a character in one of the bloodiest tragedies ever written, if memory serves me right.'

'*Methinks I see a thing armed with a rake, that seems to strike at me.* It was the mad Cardinal in *The Duchess of Malfi*,' Payne explained in a distant voice. 'Not a mad radical.'

'Hugh always manages to convey his vast knowledge with grace and wit,' Lady Grylls said ingratiatingly.

'I am sorry, but this whole thing's started to get on my nerves. I think I've had enough of this nonsense,' Ramskritt said in a very loud voice. His face was red and a vein pulsed in his temple.

Sybil said again that the candles were dripping.

'No they are not – not any longer!' Stooping over, Feversham blew out all ten candles at once. '*Voilà.* No more dripping.'

'You shouldn't have done that, Fever.' Sybil slapped him playfully across the wrist. 'It's a bad omen when someone else does it. Oh well, too late now.' She beamed at Hugh and Antonia. 'Such fun, having you, as they say, fall into the trap.'

'We did fall into the trap, yes, but I would hesitate to call it fun,' Payne said.

Sybil patted Mrs Garrison-Gore's arm. 'Congrats, Romany. Well done. Jolly good show. You made it work! What do you think, Nellie? Mission accomplished, eh?'

'I am not at all sure. Hugh looks as though he'd like nothing better than to strangle me,' Lady Grylls wailed. 'Perhaps it was a little thoughtless of us. I'll never forgive myself.'

'Good to see you are after all alive, Miss de Coverley,' Payne said.

Ramskritt turned to Ella who was standing on his left and hissed, 'Go and change at once. You are dressed with disfiguring austerity. Why do you insist on making yourself look like a nun? You know how much I hate this dress.'

'But –'

'At once I said. And don't give me murderous looks or the Vatican will hear about it.'

Antonia was standing beside Ella and she could hardly believe her ears.

Ella left the room without a word.

'So that was a hoax,' Antonia said. 'A double bluff.'

'I would like to think we were all involved in an experiment of considerable psychological complexity,' said Feversham.

'It was a hoax. We were summoned on a fool's errand devised around a double bluff,' said Payne firmly.

'Sorry folks, but I am getting bored.' Ramskritt yawned ostentatiously. 'Perhaps Mrs G-G could entertain us? Come on, Mrs G-G, give us some more old lamps for the new.'

'I don't know what you mean,' she said.

'Only that you are a brilliant storyteller. A proper Schehera – you know the one I mean.' He glanced round. 'I managed to read some bits from her latest book and I can tell you it is an awesome achievement. As a man of business, I am particularly impressed by Mrs G-G's *enterprise*. I am thinking of phoning her publishers and telling them, in case they aren't aware, and then they may increase her advance!'

'I wasn't at all sure whether the double bluff would work,' Mrs Garrison-Gore said with a frown. 'Elaborate ruses tend to go wrong. I kept changing the plotline. If I may call it that.

I know you have had double bluffs in some of your novels,' she addressed Antonia.

'I have had characters discuss the *possibility* of a double bluff, but I have never actually employed a double bluff as a plot device.' Antonia hoped she didn't sound too tart.

'Deception within the deception ... What the hell did you have round your throat?' Payne asked Sybil. 'Why didn't I feel any pulse? A rubber band, I suppose?'

'*Yes.* The most horrid thing.' Sybil shuddered histrionically. 'Looked positively indecent. I also had to put on a contraption around my chest, like corsets, to make my heartbeat hard to detect. And I wore flesh-coloured tourniquets around the wrists. Fever had thought of *everything*. Fever managed to outwit you.'

'He most certainly did,' Payne conceded.

'I hit on the concept of the double bluff when Lady Grylls told me you were bound to smell a rat right away. At some point before the "murder",' Mrs Garrison-Gore went on. 'Lady Grylls was to admit to you that it was all a game. Then the "murder" was to take place, but it would seem to come at the *wrong time* – and it would have every appearance of being a *real* murder.'

'I bet Major Payne looks so terribly miffed because he fell for the wheeze,' Sybil said.

'That may indeed be the case, though we were also shocked and upset by what happened last night. In fact we found it a nerve-taxing experience. We felt responsible for your death, you see.' Payne spoke in a tired voice. 'We felt guilty for failing to prevent it. Does anyone actually imagine that we enjoy dabbling in violent death?' He looked round. 'Well, we don't.'

There was an awkward pause.

'I am so sorry, Hughie,' Lady Grylls said in a tremulous voice. 'Can you find it in your heart to forgive an old and foolish woman? It was terribly insensitive of me. I made a big mistake. I can see that now. Can't we kiss and make up?'

'I will have to think about it,' Payne said.

'My dear, do you despise me?' Lady Grylls turned to Antonia.

'Of course not.' Antonia smiled. 'We aren't really cross. It's just that I slept badly –' She broke off. Why make a public spectacle of self-pity?

'Sybil could have stopped me but she didn't. Why didn't you stop me, Sybil?' Lady Grylls chided her friend. 'I can plead galloping senility as an excuse – but there is nothing wrong with *you,* my dear, is there?'

Sybil sighed. 'It's this island. When I am here, I tend to act irresponsibly. The island is to blame.'

'I rather liked the idea of having *two* John de Coverleys on the scene,' Mrs Garrison-Gore went on, addressing herself to Hugh and Antonia. 'You were *meant* to discover that one was a fake and that it was the real one who killed his sister.'

'I don't think my brother is aware of what we have been up to,' Sybil said. 'I mean making him the murderer in the game and so on. He will never know. I don't want anybody to imagine he has been caused any undue distress because he hasn't.'

'Did a seagull peck at his hands?' Antonia asked.

'Yes. That was quite a coincidence, wasn't it? I understand Major Payne jumped to the conclusion I'd scratched John as I'd struggled!'

'You were given some important clues,' Mrs Garrison-Gore said. 'Sybil drew your attention to the hidden door in the library. Then there was the fried chicken, the plain-glass monocle and so on – all of which you succeeded in taking into account. You drew all the right conclusions, which of course were also all the wrong conclusions. Your aunt said you would bring order out of the chaos, like sedulous botanists in a wild garden.'

'Please forgive me, Hughie!' Lady Grylls cried.

'Where the hell is Ella? Why is she taking so long? How long *does* it take to change a dress?' Ramskritt looked at his watch.

'I must say Mrs Garrison-Gore is a first-class manipulator. She did manage to fool us.' Payne seemed to have relented somewhat. 'We should have seen through the ruse, but we didn't. It was all rather cleverly staged, wouldn't you agree, my love?'

'We were completely bamboozled,' Antonia smiled.

'Were you?' Mrs Garrison-Gore said. She sniffed. 'Were you really?'

'Oh yes. It was perfectly done.' Antonia's mood had lightened. Why should they be cross with Mrs Garrison-Gore, anyway? The poor woman had only been doing her job, what Lady Grylls and Sybil de Coverley had ordered her to do.

'I am so sorry about the sleepless night.' Mrs Garrison-Gore touched Antonia's arm. She spoke with genuine compassion.

'I am going to open the champagne now. I don't think we should wait for Ella. Ella's sulking. Ella can go to the blazes. She's doing it to spite me. She hates me. Oh how she hates me.' Ramskritt laughed. Once more he reached out for the festive bottle. 'I *must* have a glass of champagne. Otherwise I may not be responsible for my actions. You don't really want to see my eyes go pink, do you?' He smiled. 'Only kidding.'

'Now we can. *Yes.*' Feversham gave a magisterial nod. 'Let's have champers. Jolly good show. I will certainly have a glass m'self. Even if it's a trifle early in the day. Jolly good show.'

Sybil produced a tray with elegant flute glasses. 'Perhaps we should all get gloriously drunk. Nothing much else to do, on a horrid day like this. I'm afraid there's something wrong with the central heating. The thermostat's being temperamental.' She peered out of the window. 'Goodness, look, the sea seems to be getting higher and higher! *Rearing with a roar.* Poets always think they know best, don't they?'

They heard a sound like that of a train approaching from a long way down a tube.

'I find it jolly curious that nature should be so keen on building up such portentous threats instead of getting on with whatever release of forces it has in mind,' said Feversham.

'Sometimes I find myself wondering what it would be like if the house got swept away by a giant wave,' Sybil said dreamily, hooking her arm through Feversham's.

'I used to dream of treasures long lost at sea,' said Oswald. 'I imagined ornate chests overflowing with rubies embedded in nacreous green rock, shifted here and there on the sandy floor by shoals of spotted fish … As a young man I was extremely romantic … Still am, I suppose …'

The door opened. Antonia expected it would be Ella wearing a new dress.

But it was Doctor Klein who entered the room.

He was wearing a dress.

25

THE PERFECT STORM

Antonia remembered what had been bothering her.

And, mind you, when a girl tries to catch anything in her lap she throws her knees apart; she doesn't clap them together, the way you did when you caught the lump of lead.

That was how the woman had known that Huck Finn was a boy and not a girl. Well, Doctor Klein had done just the opposite – he had thrown his knees apart – that's why the folded *Times* had fallen to the floor – that's when Antonia had started suspecting he was in fact a woman. Or had been.

The cork popped and at the same time the storm broke. There was an audible hiss and roar as the rain came down on the house. The windows rattled.

Doctor Klein sat in a high-backed chair. He said nothing. His eyes were fixed on Oswald Ramskritt.

Doctor Klein's dress was of the long and loose variety. It was lavishly decorated with artificial flowers and bows around the coy décolletage. Doctor Klein carried an embroidered reticule, which he now placed on his lap.

Payne drew his forefinger across his jaw. The sight they were witnessing was without doubt monstrous, unnatural and quite grotesque. How *should* civilised people react when a male fellow guest of great girth suddenly and without prior warning turns up *en travestie*? There is nothing about it in the etiquette books. Staring, gasping and demanding an explanation was not on, he didn't think. At least that would be the well-bred British attitude.

But Ramskritt wasn't British. Ramskritt laughed.

'What's up, Doc? What's the idea?' Ramskritt had started dispensing champagne, filling flutes and handing them round. 'Getting in touch with your feminine side? Or is that more of what our friend Feversham calls an "experiment of considerable psychological complexity"?'

Doctor Klein sat very still. He had a slightly disoriented air about him. He looked extremely unwell. His pale fat face hung in pouches. His eyes were a little unfocused. His lips were a pale purple colour. He seemed to have a problem breathing.

Had he taken something? Was he under the influence of some drug? Antonia wondered. What did she know about transsexuals? Not much, apart from the fact that it was a long and frequently painful process. Apparently it was easier for a man to become a woman than the other way round. She remembered reading a detective story by the late Patricia Moyes. *Who is Simon Warrick*? The twist at the end hinged on the fact that Simon Warrick had been born a woman, but nobody had had an inkling about it. Antonia had had doubts as to whether a woman could ever make a convincing man. She shuddered as she recalled watching a Channel 4 documentary about a woman who became a man.

Doctor Klein said, 'I don't suppose you remember me, Oswald?'

Ramskritt took a swill from his champagne glass. 'Of course I remember you. I have never forgotten you. You are Doctor Klein. I think your first name is Friedrich. You are my shrink, dermatologist and reflexologist.' He raised the glass to his lips once more, emptied it, then gave himself a refill. 'You did wonders with my rashes. As good as rid me of them. You understand me when I talk to you. Only *you* know the real me. I feel good after I have talked to you. Thanks to you, I am a new man …'

A deafening clap of thunder made all the windows shake and rattle.

Hysterectomy … Mastectomy … Gender reassignment surgery … Psychoanalysis … A course of androgen paves the way to the transformation … Hormone treatment … Depression … Strong drugs can have adverse effect … Reversals … Mood swings … Psychotic episodes … Antonia went on watching Klein …

Something was the matter. Had the drugs stopped taking effect? Would that explain the dress? Was he – *she* – having a reversal, which was also a psychotic episode?

'Don't you recognise me?' Doctor Klein asked.

Ramskritt, glass in hand, went up to where Doctor Klein sat. He walked around him. He took a sip of champagne, then put his glass down on a side table. He stood frowning at Klein, his hands thrust into his pockets. Doctor Klein might have been something displayed in a glass tank.

'I don't know what you mean. It couldn't matter less,' Ramskritt said, 'but are you actually a girl?'

'Would you like a drop of champagne, Doctor Klein?' Sybil said in her best society hostess manner. 'It's deliciously dry.' She carried a full glass to him. When he didn't react and continued clutching at the reticule, she put his glass on the side table, beside Ramskritt's.

Ramskritt brought his face close to Doctor Klein's. 'Why, I believe you *are* a girl … *Yes* … No sign of a stubble and such small hands … Well, I am jiggered.' He straightened himself up. 'I don't think I have ever seen anything like it in my whole life.'

'Freddie Hansen. Do you remember Freddie Hansen?' Doctor Klein asked. His voice, Antonia noted, had become a little slurred. He seemed to find it hard to get the words out.

'Can't say I do. Who's he?'

'She. Freddie was Gabriele's sister. You met them in Berlin. In 1980.'

'Berlin 1980?' Ramskritt echoed. 'Was I in Berlin in 1980? Now, what was *that* about? Berlin 1980 ... .Yes ... *Yes* ... But that's more than thirty-five years ago! An interesting time in my life.' Ramskritt drew back a little. 'Perhaps I should have done things differently. But I am *not* going to apologise to anyone. No sir. Hey, what's the idea? What do you know about Berlin 1980?'

'Gabriele and her sister put their trust in you,' Klein said. 'You took advantage of them. You deceived them. You destroyed them.'

'Freddie and Gabriele. Oh yes. Ghosts from the past. Not the sweetest of memories. I didn't set out to destroy them. That wasn't my intention. I am not a bad man, whatever that bitch Ella may have told you about me. I can't remember all the details now, Doc, but I didn't want them to die.'

'You *destroyed* them,' Doctor Klein repeated.

'I was only doing my job. My duty to my country. To Ronnie. To Western Civilisation. Ronnie *was* our President, wasn't he? It was an important job. Not many men could have done it. Spying is dangerous business.' Oswald picked up his glass and drank off the remaining champagne. 'I was doing my duty to mankind.' He snapped his fingers. 'Maisie, darling, bring over the bottle. I need a refill. My duty to mankind, that's right, that's what I believed in.'

'Here you are, my dear fellow.' It was Feversham who had brought the bottle over to him.

'No, not you, you old fool. I said *Maisie*. Go back and give the bottle to her. These things matter to me. I want a beautiful girl to do the pouring, not an old fool.'

'No call for that kind of talk, Ramskritt.' Feversham bristled. 'This is not on. Most definitely not on. Would you apologise? A public insult deserves a public apology.'

'I honestly believed I was helping the world to become a better place. Thank you, sweetheart,' Ramskritt said as Maisie stood by his side and held up the bottle. '*More*. I want my glass to overflow. Sybil was right. *Let's get drunk*.' He looked at the full glass Maisie had placed on the side table, licked his lips in anticipation, but didn't pick it up. 'I was on a mission. Us against Them. The damned Commies. But who *are* you? Some relative – their father? What were those girls called now? Oh yes, Gabriele and Freddie. No, you can't be their father – are you their mother? I have no idea how old you are. You could be *anything* –'

Doctor Klein gazed up at him out of his odd dolorous eyes. He raised his hand slowly and pointed to his left eyebrow.

'I am Freddie.'

Mrs Garrison-Gore watched fascinated. There was more tragedy in Doctor Klein's eyes than Hamlet watching Little Nell's death on the sinking *Titanic* ...

It was the kind of situation she would love to put in a book!

It was getting darker by the minute. Only a single table lamp of low voltage had been turned on. There was a ghostly pool of light around it. Perhaps it was better that way. More – *dramatic*. The skies outside were the colour of tar now – the wind howled like hounds from hell – the sea roared. The sea gods were angry, no doubt about it.

Something is about to happen, Mrs Garrison-Gore thought.

There was a cracking sound – as though the windows were going to burst out of their frames.

It was a moment of great psychological intensity, of that Mrs Garrison-Gore had no doubt. She was susceptible to atmosphere, even though she didn't always succeed in conjuring it up by the force of her pen. Thinking of which, where *was* her pen? She meant her silver-bullet pen. It would protect you from evil, Sybil had said. Opening her bag she started rummaging in it frantically. I don't believe in superstitions, she thought.

An idea dawned on her. It was so outrageously bold and brilliant, it took her breath away. For a moment she stood very still, not daring to breathe, then closing her bag slowly, she looked across at Doctor Klein once more.

Doctor Klein's face glistened in the dim light. He was deadly pale. His lips were blue. He sat perfectly immobile, like a stuffed thing ... Medication gone wrong?

She had known he was a transsexual since she had seen the photos, which she had found in his drawer. 'Before' and 'after'. 'She' becomes a 'he'. She had gone through his file, which contained a record of the transformation ... He hadn't been so fat to start with ... Why had Klein brought the file to the island? Did he – she – need a constant reminder of the hell he'd been through? Had he experienced some kind of identity crisis? She couldn't help wondering. She was interested in mysteries.

What was it Klein had above his left eyebrow? Unobtrusively she moved nearer and peered. Some mark – an old wound in the shape of a horseshoe. Most distinctive!

So *that's* what he had been trying to conceal. *That's* what he had been dabbing at when she saw him sitting in his room. She had seen him take out a powder compact and dab at his forehead ...

'But you can't be,' Oswald Ramskritt said. 'Freddie's dead.'

'I am Freddie,' Doctor Klein said again.

Oswald's face had a sickly grey tinge to it. He took a step back.

Mrs Garrison-Gore glanced across at the windows, at the darkness outside.

Another crack came. One giant billiard ball might have hit another. A sound like a breaking-up of icebergs. The house shook.

'King Lear in all his madness couldn't have bawled for a more clamorous storm,' she heard Major Payne murmur.

Doctor Klein made as though he was about to rise to his feet. Oswald swore under his breath. All eyes, as far as Mrs Garrison-Gore could see, were on the two of them.

Later she was to say to Antonia that sometimes the purveyor of sensational fiction in her tended to take over. She couldn't help herself. Awful of her, but there it was. People stopped being people and became *characters*. Was that a feeling Antonia Darcy was familiar with? It was terrible, wasn't it?

As the wind intensified, it seemed the house would be torn off its foundations and hurled into the sea.

The sound of glass smashing, when it came, was deafening.

For a wild moment Payne imagined that a bomb had been detonated somewhere close by.

One of the French windows had given up its resistance. The blast of the wind was so powerful, that books, papers, bowls of dried flowers and brick-a-brack as well as bits of glass flew up in the air and swirled round the room in a frenzied dance. The library was filled with rain.

Someone screamed.

The portrait with the bullet hole in Charles de Coverley's eye was swept off the wall and crashed to the floor.

26

SPARKLING CYANIDE

'I hope no one is hurt? Have you all got your drinkies? Make sure the library door is shut, whoever's fetching up the rear. Who *is* fetching up the rear? Is that you, Maisie?' Sybil de Coverley glanced over her shoulder. She was leading the exodus down the corridor and seemed quite unperturbed. '*Well done*. No danger of anyone being sucked into the stratosphere now, Dorothy-fashion. Thank God we have no dogs. A dog is the last thing we'd want. Do let's go into the drawing room, shall we?'

'Why not the dining room? What about brekkers?' Payne asked his aunt *sotto voce*. He smoothed back his damp hair.

'We all had toast and marmalade in the kitchen. That was *before* you put in an appearance. Far from satisfactory but we meant to give you a proper scare.'

'You made it look as though everybody had vanished into thin air, or that you'd been murdered in your beds.' He shook his head.

'That was another of Mrs Garrison-Gore's ideas. *So* glad we are on speakers again.' Lady Grylls beamed. 'Nothing like a crisis to bring people together. I am sure Ella and Maisie can rustle up some bacon and eggs for you. Not the way you envisaged your tenth wedding anniversary, is it?'

'Not quite the way, no.'

They entered the drawing room.

'We can draw the curtains across the windows and turn on all the table lamps,' Sybil said. 'This room can be made to look terribly cosy. We can light the fire. Have you got the champers, Fever? Well done. Goodness, dear boy, you are bleeding!'

'*Ay scratch, ay scratch, tis not as deep as a well, nor so wide as a church door.*' Feversham held up his bleeding hand. 'Some treacherous shard. Not to worry.'

'It looks bad to me! I'll bandage it. It may turn septic. Hope no one else is injured? Well, I must say I've never seen anything like this on Sphinx Island before. Never!'

'Your poor library, Sybil,' Lady Grylls said.

Sybil shrugged. 'Nothing's permanent, nothing endures.'

'I suppose it would be impossible to start boarding up that window right now?'

'I don't see how it could be done and who could possibly do it.'

'I used to do carpentry as a hobby. Not any longer. I'm a martyr to back pain,' Feversham said with a heavy sigh. 'Old back injury.'

'If I have to be perfectly honest, Nellie, I don't care two pins what happens to my "poor" library,' Sybil said. 'It's full of unreadable books. *To swift destruction doomed.* Sometimes the poet gets it *just* right, don't they? No regrets, as *la* Piaf put it. Well, it's begun.'

'What's begun?'

'The demolition process. Oswald said he'd have the house pulled apart and a brand new one built the moment he took over, didn't you, Oswald?'

'Yes, ma'm. That is correct.' Oswald seemed preoccupied.

'We'll sign the papers as soon as possible, shall we? I'm yearning for the lights of London. Can't wait to get out of this hole … I see you managed to save your glass. Well done.'

'My glass, yes.' Oswald put down his glass on a small table beside his chair. He ran his hand across his face.

'Oh, what about the anniversary cake? We left the anniversary cake behind!' Maisie cried. She was standing beside Oswald. 'Couldn't someone go back to the library and fetch it?'

'Too damned dangerous.' Feversham was walking round, turning on lamps. 'I have the feeling the cake wasn't exactly a hit, eh, Payne?'

As the house shook again, Payne observed that in his opinion the anniversary cake's chances of surviving the storm were negligible.

'Doctor Klein is not here,' Mrs Garrison-Gore said. 'Did anyone see where he went?'

'I suppose he went upstairs, to his room, which is perhaps for the best. Oh hallo, my dear,' Sybil said as Ella entered.

Ella looked stunning in a dress of shimmering gold with bare shoulders and elbow-length gloves. She was holding a golden purse. Her outfit was quite inappropriate for this time of day, but perhaps that was the intention, Antonia reflected. It was a gesture of showy defiance. Ella's expression was impossible to fathom.

Even though she passed close by and paused beside the table with his champagne glass, Oswald Ramskritt took no notice of her. He was staring before him.

'I can't believe that Doctor Klein is a woman, is he?' Maisie said, glancing round. 'I think he is very ill.' She turned towards Ramskritt. 'What did he want from you? Who is Freddie?'

There was a pause. Oswald slowly looked up. His eyes were bloodshot. 'Who is Freddie? You really wanna know? It happened such a long time ago. Freddie was a German girl. She lived in East Berlin. She was attractive in a haggard, offbeat kind of way. Nothing like you, my sweet.' He patted Maisie's cheek. 'You look like a young goddess.'

'Was she very young?'

'She was then in her twenties, I reckon. She rather liked me. She took to me. She believed I could help her join her sister in

West Berlin. I recruited her. I was a master spy of sorts. Freddie did a couple of jobs for the free world, but, unfortunately, was arrested and tried for treason. She was executed by the East German authorities. At least that's what I was told. Crucified by the Commies, as our wordsmith here may wish to put it, eh, Mrs G-G? Tragic of course. Very tragic. Not my fault. I told her to be careful.'

'Doctor Klein said he was Freddie.'

'He did, didn't he? Well, he *does* seem to have the same kind of a horse-shoe mark above his eyebrow. I remember the mark. *Kleine Fraulein Horseshoe.* Little Miss Horseshoe. That's what I used to call Freddie. Maybe that's why she chose the name 'Klein'? I mean after she became a he. Unless,' Oswald Ramskritt reasoned, 'that was some kind of faked-up thing intended to unsettle me? What do you think, Major?'

'I really can't say,' Payne said stiffly.

'Perhaps that was the work of my enemies? My enemies would do *anything* to destroy me. Perhaps it was a scheme concocted by our model of efficiency here, eh, Ella? Ella and Klein are buddies. Strange but true. I am sure Ella's been badmouthing me, for which of course there's a price to pay, as she knows perfectly well … A mighty high price … I seem to be a magnet for preposterous and unverifiable stories …' Oswald sighed. 'So unfair, given that I've always done my best to act according to the dictates of my conscience … Let's drink to it, shall we? To truth!'

Picking up his glass of champagne, he drank it off at a gulp.

Too quickly perhaps. He choked – rather badly by the sound of it. His face twisted, turned purple. He coughed – started gasping for breath – he made an awful gurgling sound. The glass fell from his hand. He clutched at his throat, then pitched forward and collapsed on the floor.

As he fell, his toupee detached itself from his head and in death Oswald Ramskritt was revealed to have been almost completely bald.

For a stunned moment they remained still as statues, staring at the crumpled figure on the floor.

'Oswald?' Maisie took a step towards the body. '*Oswald?*'

Sybil said, 'Dear me – his heart, must be – there's so much electricity in the air, can you feel it? Static electricity. We need a doctor – Doctor Klein – it *must* be his heart – he had a terrible shock. Would somebody be an angel and go and fetch Doctor Klein? Fever?'

'Don't think that would be such a good idea, Syb.' Feversham put up his eyeglass.

'I don't think he's breathing!' Maisie cried. 'Please do something!'

Ella did not move. She sat with her hands crossed on her lap, unnervingly still. Her face was completely expressionless. She raised her glass to her lips and took a sip of champagne, then another.

'There's something in his drink,' Mrs Garrison-Gore said in a very loud voice. No sooner were the words out of her mouth than she wished she had kept quiet. Everybody was looking at her now. She was a fool. Suddenly she felt sick. The room swum before her eyes. She hoped she wouldn't disgrace herself by swooning into a dead faint or throwing up.

Sybil said, 'You can't possibly mean poison, Romany, can you?'

No, not again, Antonia was thinking as she watched her husband bend over Oswald Ramskritt's body. Not *again*.

This time Payne was taking no chances. No more tricks. He checked Ramskritt's pulse by holding a forefinger at his neck. He then made sure Ramskritt's neck was his own and not made of rubber. Overcoming his distaste, he pinched some of the flesh between his thumb and forefinger. He tried not to let his eyes linger on Ramskritt's slack mouth –

The next moment something extraordinary happened. Ella sprang to her feet and with a sob she flung herself across Oswald Ramskritt's body. She pushed Payne to one side, causing him to marvel at her strength. She was still holding her golden purse and empty glass but now she let them slip from her hands. She reached out and stroked Oswald's face.

'I loved him once. I loved him very much. For a while I even considered him the very reason for my existence,' she said quietly. 'Now that part of me is dead too.' She laid her head across the dead man's chest.

Sybil and Antonia tried to pull her away but succeeded only after their second effort. Before she allowed herself to be led out of the room, she picked up her purse and her glass. It was Sybil who went with her. Antonia stayed in the room.

Payne bent over the body once more. He sniffed at Ramskritt's lips. He then wrapped his hand with a lightly starched napkin he found on a side table and picked up Ramskritt's glass.

The glass hadn't smashed. It had fallen on the carpet and rolled away from the body.

He dipped his little finger in the dregs and then cautiously licked it.

'There was something in his champagne, wasn't there?' The irrepressible Mrs Garrison-Gore said.

'There isn't.' Payne rose. 'There is nothing wrong with this champagne.'

She stared back. 'Are you sure?'

'Positive.'

'Oswald is not – he is not – dead – is he?' Maisie whispered. She had a dazed air about her.

'I am afraid he is,' Payne said. 'He was poisoned all right. His lips exude the unmistakable whiff of bitter almonds which strongly suggests poisoning by cyanide.'

27

A LITTLE ON
THE LONELY SIDE

'I don't understand. In what other way could he have swallowed the cyanide? He couldn't have popped a lump into his mouth like a pill, could he? We'd have seen it. But maybe it has something to do with the fact that he was a spy once? That's what he said, wasn't it? Spies keep cyanide capsules under their tongue and crack them when faced with imminent capture. At least that's what spies did during the war.' Feversham might have been wrestling with an abstruse mathematical problem. He was holding his handkerchief over his bleeding hand. 'You don't think he committed suicide, do you?'

'I don't know,' Payne said. 'It didn't *look* as though he was committing suicide. He was raising a toast to Truth.'

'Wouldn't that count as suggestive?' Lady Grylls said.

'He wasn't the suicidal type, but then not many people are,' Mrs Garrison-Gore said.

'He can't be dead,' Maisie said. 'Oh my God.' She started crying.

Payne rubbed his nose and looked sideways at his wife. 'No doubt about it this time.'

The gel couldn't really be sorry for that fellow, Lady Grylls thought. Not really. No one could be sorry for him. It was the shock. Or perhaps the gel was doing it for form's sake?

The door opened and Sybil de Coverley re-entered the room.

'Poor Ella. I don't think she is quite herself. I believe her nerves are in tatters. You'd never guess what she did, not in a million years. She did something terribly peculiar. You see, when we reached her room she begged me to leave her alone, which I did, but then I went back to ask her if she would like some brandy. I saw her open the window. For a wild moment I imagined she was about to throw herself out –' Sybil's voice tailed off. She stood looking down at Oswald Ramskritt's body. 'I can't believe any of this is happening. Oswald didn't commit suicide, did he?'

'He was poisoned,' Lady Grylls said.

'He was holding his glass, then – then he put it down – then he picked it up again. Then he drank it off fast. I can see him. I only have to shut my eyes. I think it's all some ghastly mistake but of course it's nothing of the sort. We can't stay here, can we?' Sybil glanced round. '*Not* with the body?'

'Payne? What's the form?' Feversham asked.

'We'll have to move,' Payne said.

'First the library, now the drawing room,' Lady Grylls said. 'It's like playing musical chairs with rooms.'

'Papa used to say I was terribly good in a crisis, but I am not. I am worse than useless. I don't think papa knew me at all well.' Sybil sighed. 'Oswald said he would buy the island but now of course he won't be able to, will he?'

'I am afraid not. Your brother will be in the seventh heaven,' Feversham said. 'Your brother will be holding celebrations with gun salutes.'

'My brother is a fabulous monster. One of those creatures that creep out of the sea and assume human shape.'

The awfully silly things people said when they were in shock, Antonia reflected.

They trooped out of the drawing room and Payne turned the key in the lock.

Maisie was crying.

'The conservatory at the back *used* to be my favourite place,' Sybil said. 'It was my hidey hole when I was a child. There are palms and wicker chairs and things. It looks a bit like a mini Palm Court, I always thought. Memories of the Ritz, you know.'

'How delightful,' Feversham said.

'All it needs is a trio of grey-haired ladies in black silk dresses, playing *Stormy Weather* on their violins and cellos, but the roof leaks horribly.'

'The question is, are we safe?' Lady Grylls said. 'That's the really important question. What if Oswald's death is only the beginning? I am sure I am talking rot, but it's suddenly hit me that this may be only the beginning.'

'*One choked his little self and then there were Nine.* I hope that's not what Lady Grylls means,' Feversham said. 'Sorry. Awfully bad form. Don't know what possessed me.'

'How about the dining room?' Payne suggested, though he no longer felt hungry.

'An excellent idea,' Lady Grylls said. 'There's something solid and immovable about a dining room.'

Some five minutes later they sat around the mahogany table in the dining room.

Antonia turned to Sybil. 'What was the terribly peculiar thing Ella did?'

'Oh, didn't I say? She hurled her empty champagne glass out of the window.'

The telephone was not working and there was no internet. No network either, so their mobiles were useless. Outside, the storm continued raging. Even if it stopped, they had no means of getting to the mainland. There was the launch *Cutwater* and Oswald Ramskritt's yacht, but only Oswald had been able to operate those.

'My brother considers himself a great sailor and he may be right, though I think it would be imprudent to entrust our safety in John's hands,' Sybil de Coverley said.

They used to have a servant whose sole function had been managing the launch but Sybil had dismissed him – together with the other two servants. They hadn't been much good, she said. They either snooped about or drank the sherry or sneered. Besides, Mrs Garrison-Gore had suggested that ten people on the island would be the ideal set-up for the Anniversary Murder Mystery. An echo of that other more famous multiple murder mystery – now, what *was* it called?

'It's like the war all over again,' Lady Grylls said. 'Only then we knew *why* we were sacrificing things.'

Feversham inclined his head. 'We are in deep water and at the mercy of the elements. We are completely cut off.'

They listened as the wind slammed the house with unusual force, making it shake once more.

'We might have to compose ourselves for a protracted haul, without any guarantee of a recompense for the agonies we've been enduring,' Sybil said. 'There is enough food in the house. Tins, mainly.'

'As soon as contact with the outside world has been established, we'll call the police.' Payne looked grim.

'I could do with some coffee,' Feversham said.

'Coffee would be just the ticket,' Mrs Garrison-Gore said.

Maisie rose. 'I'll make it. And I'll go to see if Ella's all right.'

'What a nice child you are,' Lady Grylls said.

'The coffee's Kopi Luwak,' Sybil said with a deep sigh. 'It was a present from poor Oswald. He was telling me about it. It comes from Sumatra and the beans are made of animal droppings, apparently. It's a most wonderful story. The native palm civet, a cat-like creature that eats ripe coffee cherries but can't digest the hard centres and excretes the beans on the forest floor. Only 450lb of the rare beans are harvested per year. It's absolutely marvellous, incredibly frothy. It seems to cost seventy pounds per cup, if you have it at the Savoy and Planet Hollywood and places like that.'

Antonia was thinking.

They had never been *quite* in this kind of situation before. She had stopped wondering why things like this happened to them. It seemed they simply did.

Who *was* the killer? The ingénue who had nearly been ravished by the victim? The tragic former mistress who always spoke with such soft sadness? The bumptious authoress of mysteries? The vague hostess? Feversham, the gentleman actor? Doctor Klein, formerly Fraulein Freddie?

No, not Lady Grylls. The real John de Coverley should also be exempt since he had simply *not been there*.

The most obvious suspect was of course Doctor Klein. Ramskritt had destroyed the lives of the two Hansen sisters, one of which Doctor Klein had been. Doctor Klein's behaviour in the lead–up to the murder had been very strange indeed. At the other end of the spectrum there was Sybil de Coverley, the least likely suspect. Sybil had been eagerly looking forward to selling the island to Ramskritt, which now she wouldn't be able to do. She had everything to lose and nothing to gain from his death.

But how *was* Oswald Ramskritt poisoned? There wasn't any cyanide in his glass. Unless –

What was Feversham doing? He had put on the green and yellow tartan gloves which Sybil had given him as a present. Feversham twiddled his fingers, then executed a couple of boxing moves. He then put up his eyeglass. All too absurd for words. Maybe that was his way of coping with the crisis. Of letting off steam?

Ella Gales also had a good reason for wishing Ramskritt dead. Ramskritt had treated her appallingly, if what Antonia had overheard him say to her was anything to go by.

One couldn't really see Maisie as a cold-blooded poisoner, but the fact remained that Ramskritt had caused her considerable distress and a sleepless night after he had tried to get into her bed and then threatened not only to dismiss her but also make her unemployable.

As for Mrs Garrison-Gore and Feversham, Antonia couldn't think of a rational motive that could be attributed to either of them – at least not at the moment.

But there might be factors of which she was not aware …

Major Payne had started speaking.

'How was he poisoned? Well, that's fairly obvious, I should think. I was puzzled like all the rest of you, but I managed to work it out. Ramskritt's glass contained cyanide all right. No, there's no trick. The glass I examined wasn't his glass. As simple as that, yes. That was Ella's glass. Ella picked up Ramskritt's glass and she managed to carry it out of the room. Did she do it on purpose? Well, yes, I firmly believe so. I can't conceive of any other reason for her performance, for throwing herself across his body, for dropping her glass beside the body and so on, can you? The glass she carried out of the room and disposed of so neatly later on was Ramskritt's glass.'

'I am, as they say, 'reft of speech,' Feversham said.

'She was trying to get rid of the evidence, though of course it wouldn't have been much good,' Mrs Garrsion-Gore said thoughtfully.

'Poor Ella. Does that mean she killed Oswald?' Sybil asked.

'Not necessarily. I have an idea she switched round the glasses because she believed it was Doctor Klein who poisoned

Ramskritt's champagne. I think she wanted to protect Doctor Klein. She was wearing gloves, so there wouldn't have been any fingerprints on her glass.'

'Oswald Ramskritt's fingerprints wouldn't be on the glass either. The police, when they come to examine it, would immediately know that that's the wrong glass,' Mrs Garrsion-Gore said.

'Indeed they would. You are absolutely right.' Payne nodded. 'Ella didn't think it through. She had no time. I think she acted a little too spontaneously. But to go back. Ramskritt drank his champagne and died in the drawing room, though the poisoning of the champagne might already have taken place in the library. He put his glass on a side table, beside Doctor Klein's glass, as it happened. Then the window got smashed and all hell broke loose – everybody's attention was diverted – there was the rain and the wind howling and things flying around.'

Mrs Garrison-Gore said, 'I believe it was only Maisie who went near him in the drawing room, wasn't it? Oh and Ella stood beside him for a moment, didn't she?'

'I think so,' Antonia said.

'Ella carried a purse that matched her dress. Maisie's skirt has pockets. What I mean is that either of them could easily have had cyanide on their person.'

'These two girls are wonderful, simply wonderful,' Sybil said. 'How they do it, I have no idea, but they keep the house in splendid order. They manage to polish everything that needs to be polished to the highest sheen, they launder the curtains, they cook and they arrange all the *objets* with perfect precision. And between them they hoover the rooms. I pay them nothing. It would be wrong to pay them as they happen to be my guests.'

'As a matter of fact,' Mrs Garrison-Gore said, '*anyone* could have poisoned Oswald's glass in the library – and remained completely unnoticed – yours truly included.' She poked her forefinger at her voluminous bosom. 'Or Feversham. I am sure I passed by the table with Oswald's champagne glass – so did you, Sybil, I do believe?'

'Did I, Romany?' Sybil said vaguely.

'Yes. You were holding your bejewelled little box in your left hand, I couldn't help noticing.'

'What's that got to do with anything?'

'The cyanide could have been inside,' Mrs Garrison-Gore explained. 'I'm not saying it was. Merely observing that you had the opportunity, like all the rest of us.'

Feversham held up his monocle. 'I think it was Doctor Klein who did it. He was actually sitting beside the foresaid table. He hardly moved, even after the window got smashed. Ella seems to think it was him, as Payne pointed out so astutely. It would be a waste of time considering other possibilities. It's not as though we are playing the Murder Game. Doctor Klein had both the motive *and* the opportunity.'

In the pause that followed their coffee arrived.

It's over, Doctor Klein thought. He had a feeling of anti-climax. But also of great peace.

Peace at last ... .

He could hear the sea.

A memory floated into his head, which was also her head.

Green smoke coming down steadily from mysterious openings in the ceiling, as if expelled from the mouth of a theatrical dragon. Dancing couples. Music. The club was called Fun Under the Sea. There had been a sailor, clasping at her wasp waist. He had tried to kiss her. At first deep sub-aqueous silence, then a song. *Wenn Der Sommer Wieder Einzieht*. It was known in English as *A Little on the Lonely Side*. She had seen her face reflected in the mirror walls: round, greenish, enigmatic, the face of a mermaid, her mouth black and slit like a wound from a knife, her blonde hair waving like weed in a cold green current. The sailor had become rather urgent in his attentions. How she had laughed!

All a long time ago. A different world.

Doctor Klein sat on his bed. *Wenn Der Sommer Wieder Einzieht*. Humming, he slowly eased himself and lay down on one side. He still wore the dress.

He had no idea what had he had hoped to achieve. He was not sure. The embroidered reticule was beside him. The bottle with the cyanide was inside the reticule. Only he hadn't been able to use it. Too slow, too clumsy, his mind not functioning properly …

Or perhaps he *had* used it – Oswald had been poisoned – perhaps it had been him?

He was getting a little confused.

Ella … Dear Ella … Perhaps he had done it for Ella … Ella was free now, free as a bird, that's all that mattered …

It was some time since he had had proper sleep. He was feeling … a little on the lonely side? He tried to still his thoughts.

He shut his eyes.

The best thing about an island was that once you got there, you couldn't go any farther … You'd come to the end of things …

He couldn't imagine a life *after* the island.

A little on the lonely side?

He didn't want to leave the island – ever.

28

THE HEART HAS ITS REASONS

Ella had reappeared and she and Maisie were now pouring out coffee.

Major Payne's eyes were fixed on Ella, whose face was once more devoid of any expression. He believed that Ramskritt's murder had been that peculiar mixture of the premeditated and the spontaneous. Someone had brought cyanide to the island and had been waiting for their opportunity – which came when the window, overpowered by the wind, smashed into smithereens …

Sybil observed that Fate was famously fickle, its caprices notorious, and that it would be pointless to kick against the kind of cards Fate chose to deal us. 'I've come to believe in pre-destination. Awful things have been happening to members of my family with sinister regularity. Papa's father decamped to Monte Carlo with his mistress. I kept finding fault with my suitors. My brother was attacked by seagulls. Perhaps I am not meant to sell the island after all. Perhaps I will be saddled with it till the Terrible Day of Judgement. Perhaps all I'll ever have is Fool's Gold.'

'You are being unduly morbid, darling,' Feversham said, his cup of coffee poised in mid-air.

Mrs Garrison-Gore deliberated whether to admit that she had been spying on Doctor Klein and decided against it. No one looks kindly on a snooper.

'Where *is* Doctor Klein?' Lady Grylls asked. 'Does anyone know?'

'He is in his room. He is asleep,' Ella said. 'I didn't want to wake him up. I believe he's got a number of ailments, some of them very serious. Heart, liver, blood pressure. He's also got diabetes –'

'So *that's* why he didn't touch the trifle last night,' Sybil said.

'Most seriously, there are the side effects of the special medication he takes. Some hormonal therapy. He is not yet – how shall I put it?'

Feversham regarded her through his eyeglass. 'Fully male?'

Antonia turned to Ella. 'I couldn't help overhearing what Oswald said to you. He told you to go and change your dress. I thought it was quite appalling. We were waiting for you to come back but when the library door opened it was Doctor Klein who appeared – and he was wearing a dress. There was a certain symmetry about it. You told him about the dress, didn't you?'

'I did tell him, yes. I went to his room. As it happens, that was the latest humiliation inflicted on me by Oswald,' Ella said. 'I am afraid I was in tears. Doctor Klein had an odd look on his face. He said – he said –'

'Yes?' Payne put his cup down.

She bit her lip. 'He was very concerned about me. We are friends. He is the only person to whom I have dared unburden my soul. He knows all about me and Oswald. He feels sorry for me. He cares about me. I am worried about him. Extremely worried.'

She thought back to Doctor Klein's exact words.

This has gone on for too long, Ella. An outrage too far. I don't think he should be allowed to go on. Oswald needs to be stopped.

'Is that why you switched round the glasses?' Payne asked.

'Oh that was so silly!' Ella shook her head. 'I wasn't thinking straight. I did think it might have been him, so I did it to protect him. So you noticed!'

'Is he Freddie? I mean, is he *really* Freddie?' Maisie asked. She was gazing at Ella with wide eyes.

'Yes. There is the horseshoe mark above his left eyebrow. This morning, when I went to his room, he told me who he was, though I think I'd guessed it without fully realising it. I had a dream. He said he'd kept dabbing powder over the mark. He told me what happened.'

'Tell us more about it.' Payne leant back in his seat.

It took Ella about three minutes to relate the story of Oswald Ramskritt's spying activities and his involvement with the two young sisters.

'Freddie was reported to have been executed by the East-German authorities, but that story was a fabrication. It had been deliberately spread by the Stasi to demoralise Gabriele. In which they succeeded. When she heard of her sister's death, Gabriele committed suicide. That had been the final straw. Gabriele had been very upset by Oswald's sudden disappearance. She had been expecting his child. She realised Oswald had been deceiving her … Freddie was thrown into jail. It had been a *mixed* jail.' Ella's expression changed.

'Why *did* she have a sex change? Did he say? What reasons could she have had? No woman in her right mind would ever do a thing like that. Something must have gone wrong, very wrong. I mean in her brain. She couldn't have been thinking straight.' Maisie's voice shook.

'In her first week in jail Freddie was raped by three men. Three of the male inmates. What I believe is called a "gang rape". Later that same day she was raped by a prison guard –'

'Oh, no,' Maisie whispered.

'She was left semi-conscious – bruised – bleeding. She told the prison authorities what had happened, but they showed little sympathy for her. They suggested she must have been asking for it. Shortly after she was assaulted again.' Ella paused. 'She had a nervous breakdown. She broke a window and tried to cut her wrists with a piece of glass. She was transferred to a psychiatric hospital. When she recovered, she decided she no longer wanted to be a woman. She decided to have an operation.'

'She couldn't have recovered then,' Feversham said.

'But why – *why*? This is too horrible!' Maisie cried.

'She did it,' Ella said slowly, 'so that she would never be vulnerable to men again. That's the explanation Doctor Klein gave me. He doesn't seem to have any doubts about the rightness of his decision. So perhaps something did go wrong in her brain after all.'

'What happened then?'

'Eventually she was released from the clinic. She managed to leave Germany and go to America. She had already learnt of the suicide of her beloved sister Gabriele ... She underwent the sex change operation a week after arriving in New York. She was warned that the process of recovery would be long and laborious and painful and that there was no absolute guarantee that things would go without a hitch. Despite all the warnings, she chose to go through with it.'

'She must have been desperate,' Maisie said.

'Or unhinged,' said Feversham.

'Freddie's intellectual faculties appear to have remained unimpaired. She – or "Friedrich", as she became – managed to get a degree in psychiatry as well as in several other medical disciplines. She always held Oswald responsible for what happened. She – he – referred to Oswald as a "murderer". Doctor Klein blames Oswald for her sister's death – for the death of Gabriele's unborn baby – for the death of hope – for her own death as well.'

'Does she regard herself as dead?' Payne asked.

'Well, yes. Freddie *is* dead. She is no longer recognisable as Freddie. The only thing she and Doctor Klein have in common is the horseshoe-shaped mark above the left eyebrow. Plastic surgery could easily have removed the horseshoe, but he wanted a reminder, Doctor Klein said. One tiny memento of his former self. He set his sights on Oswald. He kept looking for him and eventually succeeded in tracking him down.'

'How did he manage that?' Antonia asked.

'It was a photograph in a newspaper – Oswald and Martita, that's Oswald's first wife, outside the Metropolitan Opera. That's what put him on the trail. Doctor Klein was by then a famous psychiatrist with an established clientele. Most of his patients were super-rich. He had also acquired a degree in cosmetology – that had helped him to cope with some of the terrible things he had had to go through – the endless procedures – removal of breasts – modifying certain organs – adapting and disciplining parts of the body –'

'Oh no.' Maisie's face twisted squeamishly. 'Poor, poor Freddie!'

'A tragedy too sacred and intimate for human consumption,' Feversham murmured.

'Doctor Klein managed to become friends with a doctor who had been treating Oswald for some rare allergy and got him to recommend him, Klein, to Oswald. Oswald didn't have an inkling as to his true identity and employed his services. Doctor Klein was able to bring great improvement to Oswald's health. After Klein started treating him, Oswald's nervous rashes all but disappeared. Oswald thought Doctor Klein was the best thing that had happened to him, so he made him part of his entourage. He came to regard Doctor Klein as indispensable.'

Sybil de Coverley leant forward. 'While all along Doctor Klein plotted revenge?'

Mrs Garrison-Gore produced a notebook from her handbag. 'I hope I will be allowed to make a note or two. One doesn't know when a story like that might come in useful, eh, Antonia? *Everything exists to end up in a book.* That's how Mallarme or someone put it ... I actually saw Doctor Klein conceal the mark above his eyebrow by dabbing some powder on it – though of course I had no idea at the time he had anything to conceal.' Mrs Garrison-Gore went on rummaging inside her bag. 'My pen's missing. My bullet pen. Has anyone seen it?'

'I think you lent it to Mr Feversham last night.' Maisie was the only member of the house party who called Feversham 'Mr Feversham'.

'So I did! He asked me for it last night. You wanted to write something down'

'Did I? Oh yes, I did, I meant to write down a reminder to myself about something, but I am sure I gave it back to you, Romany.' Feversham patted his pockets. He looked a little flustered. 'Didn't I?'

'No, you didn't. I would hate to lose it. It was a present from Sybil. It's my lucky charm. Hate to make a fuss but I tend to get a trifle obsessive. Perhaps the pen is in my room. Let me go and check. Am I allowed a temporary leave of absence, Major?' Mrs Garrison-Gore rose from her seat. 'I won't make a dash for freedom, I do promise.'

'It would be a bit difficult for anyone to swim one's way to the mainland.'

Payne smiled at the idea.

29

WHAT
MAISIE KNEW

It was half past eleven now, the storm had abated somewhat, though it was still raining. The company had dispersed and Antonia and Hugh Payne were trying to see people individually.

'Can you smell fear?' Sybil de Coverley asked. 'I read somewhere that detectives can smell fear and that can lead them to the guilty party.'

'We are not detectives,' Payne said.

'Of course you are. I am sure you are insanely thorough and exhaustive. *The smell of fear met them, sour as a sickroom miasma.* That was the sentence I came across in a book, though I can't remember which book it was.'

'You mustn't believe everything you read in books.' Antonia gave a little smile.

'I keep thinking of the vagaries of Fate, you know. If the storm hadn't smashed the library window, Oswald might have been alive now. I mean, his champagne was most probably poisoned in the library and it must have happened *after* the French window got smashed – we all looked in the direction of the explosion, didn't we? I can't help thinking that the killer took advantage of the chaos.'

'Is there cyanide in the house?' Payne asked.

'I wouldn't have thought so. We've never had wasps' nests or rodents or anything of that sort. I don't recall my parents ever referring to cyanide. *Cyanide*. Sorry. I am an inveterate Scrabble player, that's all. Comes before cybernation and cyclamen. I mean in the dictionary.'

'What about your brother? Has he never mentioned cyanide?'

'I don't think so. Of course John hated the idea of the island changing hands – but how *could* he have contrived to poison Oswald's champagne given that he never left his room?'

'He couldn't have,' Antonia said.

'I think the two of you are quite terrifying.' Sybil shuddered. 'You bring to mind a pair of surgeons approaching the operating table for a difficult and dangerous operation … Can you think of a motive *I* might have had for killing Oswald?'

'You might have formed a powerful and somewhat irrational attachment to someone who benefits financially from Ramskritt's death. You might have become obsessed with this man – who happens to be in dire straights. He needs money badly – you have marriage on the mind – you are determined to help him – by hook or by crook – so you kill Ramskritt.'

'Most ingenious, but, as it happens, no such man exists!'

'I've been meaning to ask you about your pill box,' Antonia said. 'Where is it? May I see it?'

'My pill box? I seem to have mislaid it. It was so silly of Romany to suggest I might have carried cyanide in it, wasn't it?' Sybil glanced at the clock. 'What about some brunch? I would hate to be caught out in dereliction of my duties as a hostess. I am sue you are feeling peckish. I'll see to it.'

'That's terribly kind of you,' Payne said.

Sybil left the room.

Antonia frowned. 'What *is* cybernation?'

'Control by machines, I think.'

'Sybil said something very interesting, actually. It's given me food for thought …'

'Oh? What's that?'

'One of those "what if" questions,' said Antonia. 'What if Fate hadn't intervened? What if there had been no storm? What if the library window hadn't smashed? What if our attention hadn't been diverted? Would Oswald Ramskritt have lived?'

'Anything, yes. Anything that might be interpreted as out of the ordinary.'

'Well, I did notice something, but I don't think it's of any importance,' said Maisie. She sat on the edge of her chair. She looked very young.

'What was that?'

'I'd hate to waste your time. All right. It was a light. There was a sudden little light in the library. I saw it flash in the middle of the room. It happened for a split second. I immediately forgot about it – so much happened *after* that – only a moment later there came the blast – the window exploding – the wind and the rain – books flying – then we went to the library and Oswald died …' Her voice trailed off.

'A sudden light … How very interesting,' Payne said. 'We could do with a little light right now – we are still labouring in Cimmerian darkness.'

'No one flicked a lighter, did they?' Antonia said. 'Or struck a match?'

'I don't think so. No one lit a cigarette or a candle or anything of the kind.' Payne stroked his jaw with his forefinger. 'Perhaps it was Tinker Bell deciding to put in a sudden appearance? Or was it a stray firefly? Could it have been a signal? But who would have wanted to send a signal to whom and with what?' He shook his head.

At midday they had brunch. Scrambled eggs on buttered toast and tea. Earl Grey for Payne, Lady Grey for Antonia (which Payne thought somewhat twee – apparently it had been Maisie's idea – like His and Her bath towels, which the Paynes most definitely did *not* keep in their bathroom in Hampstead). This was followed by roly-poly pudding with lots and lots of jam, which, as it happened, Payne liked and Antonia didn't.

Mrs Garrison-Gore marched in as the clock was chiming the half hour.

Her eyes were puffy. Her face sagged.

'I feel dog tired. I shouldn't have drunk that champagne. I get high, but then I get terribly low,' Mrs Garrison-Gore said. 'I tried to have a nap in my room, but couldn't. Doctor Klein next door was singing in that padded voice of his. It gave me the horrors.'

'We were given to understand he was asleep,' Payne said.

'Maybe he sings in his sleep? Some people do. There was a certain incantatory repetitiveness to it, which I found jolly disturbing. I was put in mind of some compulsive ritual that was devoid of rational significance. I seem to have lost my silver bullet pen. I am sure Feversham stole it.' Mrs Garrison-Gore started crying quietly into her handkerchief. 'Everything's gone wrong. *Everything.* I wish I didn't feel so *low.* I feel the irrepressible urge to scream.' She blew her nose. 'No, don't worry. I won't do it.'

'Did you by any chance notice a little light flashing in the middle of the library?' Antonia asked. 'Seconds before the window smashed?'

Mrs Garrison-Gore dabbed at her eyes with her handkerchief. 'What kind of light?'

THE RIDDLE OF SPHINX ISLAND

'We have no idea. Maisie believes she saw a light.'

'Only one of the table lamps was on ... There wasn't *lightning*, was there?'

'Everybody would have noticed lightning,' Payne said. 'Apparently this was a very tiny light, or so Maisie claims.'

'No. No. I saw nothing. Is that important?'

'It seems an insignificant little thing but I don't need to tell you how tantalising details like that can be.'

'I know exactly what you mean. Have you ever organised a Murder Game?' Mrs Garrison-Gore asked.

'No, never. We were approached once, I remember, but we said no.' Antonia smiled at the memory.

'The money was good. But we smelled a rat,' Payne said. 'We suspected the whole thing was going to be used as a cover for something sinister, didn't we, my love?'

'The venue was one of the grandest country houses in England,' said Antonia. 'We were sworn to secrecy, so I can't tell you the name ... We were asked to provide the script, act as advisors and generally supervise the whole thing ... Unlike you, we didn't have to provide a single actor. The actors were already there, at the house. All we needed to do was work out the details of the plot.'

Mrs Garrison-Gore sniffed. 'I didn't have to provide any bloody actor either.'

'Didn't you? We thought you did.' Payne's left eyebrow went up. 'What about Feversham? Feversham was your idea, wasn't he? That's what we were given to understand.'

'No, he wasn't. Feversham was Oswald Ramskritt's idea.'

'In *re* Ramskritt – may I ditch the *de mortuis* dictum and speak with a degree of bluntness instead?' Feversham said. 'May I?'

'Please do,' Payne said.

'I wouldn't have called him a decent fellow. It wasn't immediately apparent, but Doctor Jekyll could have taken a leaf out of Ramskritt's book. Perhaps he had something and couldn't help himself? One of those conditions. Tourette's Syndrome? That's not only to do with spontaneous swearing, is it?'

'That's to do with making socially inappropriate and derogatory remarks,' said Antonia. 'Tourette's Syndrome sufferers also twitch, I believe.'

'Ramskritt didn't twitch but when he was shot at, he went mad, quite mad. Got DD. Disgustingly drunk. Didn't look it, which is always a bad sign. I believe he was an alcoholic. Made a total nuisance of himself. Slapped poor Ella's face. How she put up with him, I have no idea.'

'Ramskritt slapped Ella's face?'

'Indeed he did. I saw it with my own eyes. I was at the other end of the corridor. They didn't see me. Gave me quite a turn. Poor Ella – poor Maisie – and for that matter, poor Romany.'

'Why poor Romany?' Antonia asked.

'Ramskritt teased her mercilessly about her books. About the fact that she writes Golden Age pastiches – and the fact she used Gutenberg *Lite*.'

'Oh – all that old lamps for the new business?'

'Yes. He had no sense of proportion. He just went on *and* on. But I have a specific incident in mind. It happened that same day, after he got DD. By an extraordinary coincidence, I happened to be passing by the study Romany had been using. Ramskritt was sitting beside the desk, reading out bits from the book she was writing and making fun of the way she changed names of characters and places. He called her "spoilt" because she had the Internet at her disposal. The Internet practically wrote her books for her, some such thing. I could see that it upset her.'

Antonia said, 'Upset her enough to make her want to poison him?'

'I'd have said no. Poison *is* a woman's weapon, if one believes the popular myth, though I rather doubt Romany is the malefactor in this particular instance. I wouldn't have called her a wonderfully balanced character, but she is by no means a homicidal loon. I believe Ramskritt got a serious kick out of rattling people. He called me an old fool –'

'Who is "old Bonwell"?' Payne asked. 'Or Bonewell?'

'As it happens, my father's name is Bonwell.' For a moment Feversham looked confused.

'And is Norah perhaps your mother?'

'My mother? Is this some game?' The next moment Feversham slapped his forehead with his hand. It was a particularly histrionic gesture. 'Good lord. You probably mean that silly piece of dialogue Ramskritt and I exchanged at tea on the day of your arrival? Oh that was nothing, my dear fellow, nothing at all. Romany instructed us to extemporise. We were all saying silly things at tea that day. Awfully silly things. A positive orgy of silliness, if I remember correctly.' Feversham had started speaking very fast. 'Things like, "I detest people who make helpless gestures" and so on. At the time of course I had no idea what an impossible fellow Ramskritt was, but then he was perfectly amiable to start with ... But what a wonderful memory you have! You should have been an actor, you know.'

'As a matter of fact I did consider the stage at one point. Talking of actors,' Payne said, 'I understand that it was actually Oswald Ramskritt who recommended you to Mrs Garrison-Gore?'

'Ramskritt? No, of course not! Wherever did you get the idea?' Feversham's monocle fell off his eye. Suddenly he looked frightened.

'Mrs Garrison-Gore told us that you were chosen to play the part of John de Coverley on Oswald Ramskritt's recommendation,' Payne said.

'Poor Romany must have got hold of the wrong end of the stick. She hasn't been herself, you know. If I were you, I would take everything she said with a pinch of salt.'

The afternoon was spreading like blood floating in water.

Mrs Garrison-Gore sat hunched over her battery-operated laptop. She was trying to write in the hope it would take her mind off things. Well, *not* bad – as similes went, that is – but was it her own or had she come across that particular simile in somebody else's book?

'Romany, you must cease cannibalising other people's books, or you'll find yourself in hot water.' She spoke the words aloud.

Taking a sip of coffee, she gazed balefully out of the window, at the sea below, glinting in the shadows. The waves crashed rhythmically against the unyielding cliffs. Suddenly another sound came: the disconcertingly human-like shriek of a gull. An angry but ultimately futile lament for the unhealable anguish of the world …

She really felt awful. Her ears reacted to the slightest sound. She longed for oblivion. She remembered how once, while on holiday in France, she'd visited a local museum where she had been shown a peculiar torture arrangement of the Middle Ages – an iron cage wherein prisoners had been confined and in which they could neither lie, stand nor sit. Well, that was the way she felt now. As though she'd been put inside that particular kind of iron cage!

'I am my own prisoner,' she said. 'I am consumed with doubt and dread and vile intentions.'

For some reason her thoughts turned to her former husband. On one memorable occasion he told her she needed to be chastised for her soul's sake –

It occurred to her that self-loathing had been her inseparable companion for some time now.

'Unhealable anguish? You may not realise it, Romany, but you display an incorrigible taste for the bogus. Every word you write ought to be a prize item in any anthology of humbug.'

It was raining again.

Still no network. Major Payne put his mobile phone away. He shook his head. Being penned up on a small island with a devastated library and a dead body must be the ultimate in enervating experiences …

At five minutes past three in the afternoon they had tea brought to them in the dining room, which they now regarded as their 'base'. It was so dark they had to turn on the lights.

Muffins, crumpets, pats of lightly salted butter, Devonshire cream, two kind of jam, strawberry and seedless raspberry, a variety of sandwiches: potted ham, egg-and-cress, cucumber on brown and white bread.

Tea, thank God for afternoon tea. As he picked up the silver knife and cut across a crumpet, Payne was struck yet again by the incongruity of it all.

At six o'clock, he asked Antonia, 'What's the most unusual solution you could think of?'

'If I had to propound a theory, I'd say that the cyanide was intended for Klein. It was Ramskritt who put it into Klein's glass. Ramskritt wanted Klein dead, silenced, because Klein could have created bad publicity for Ramskritt.' Antonia paused. 'Klein could have exposed Ramskritt's spying activities, talked to the papers about Ramskritt's awful treatment of the Hansen girls which led to Gabriele's suicide and Freddie's sex change and so on.'

'But in the chaos that follows the smashing of the window, Ramskritt makes a mistake and picks up Klein's glass?'

'Precisely. Imagining it is his own. He takes a sip and dies. Though why *should* Ramskritt have been carrying cyanide in his pocket? He clearly had no idea as to Klein's real identity, not till Klein told him. So he couldn't have come down this morning, intending to poison Klein.' Antonia sighed. 'Makes no sense.'

'Unless Ramskritt was only *pretending* he didn't know who Doctor Klein was. What if someone had told him?'

It was at seven o'clock that they decided to talk to Doctor Klein. They asked Ella to see if he was awake and well enough.

30

DARKNESS FALLS

Outside the rain was pouring.

'I remember jigsaw puzzles on card tables that never got finished,' Sybil said.

'I remember *not* loving Paris in the springtime,' Lady Grylls said.

'I remember, I remember the house where I was born – the little window –'

'No, no. We can't have poems, Fever. Didn't you hear what Nellie said?'

'Oh sorry, darling. Um. I remember disapproving of order and symmetry.'

'I remember not knowing my catechism, nor understanding what an oath is,' Lady Grylls said.

'I remember my brother describing the sea as a pointillist picture. I remember accepting the anguish of ageing.'

It was the next moment that the lights went out and complete darkness engulfed the island.

'Damn,' Feversham said. 'That rather puts the tin hat on, doesn't it?'

They were sitting in what Sybil had referred to as 'mama's morning room'.

'I've got a torch somewhere. Oh there it is.' Sybil turned on the torch. 'We could run the engine in the cellar, get it going. Perhaps you and Major Payne could do it between you, Fever?'

'I must say, my dear, you are handling this latest crisis with laudable aplomb,' Lady Grylls said.

'May I suggest we leave our expedition to the cellar for tomorrow morning? There are several packets of candles in the kitchen, I noticed,' Feversham said. 'We could use those for tonight, if people don't mind frightfully?'

'You are afraid of the dark, admit it!' Sybil teased him.

'No, not at all. All right, maybe the tiniest bit.'

Lady Grylls pushed her glasses up her nose. 'I was thinking of going to bed, but I can wait till you bring the candles. I doubt I'll be up to navigating the stairs in the dark. I don't suppose you would want an old baroness with a broken neck on top of everything else, would you?'

'We most certainly would not. Are you sure you will be all right, Nellie, sitting alone in the dark?'

'Perfectly sure. At my age, Sybil, there are few things that scare me.'

'According to the Chinese,' said Feversham, 'the years between sixty and seventy are the richest in living and one is then most appreciative of the beauty and delight of life.'

'I am well over eighty, alas. I'd give anything to be sixty-five again,' Lady Grylls said. 'I was in my element at sixty-five … I don't think I will be the next victim somehow … Famous last words!' She laughed.

The door closed behind Feversham and Sybil and the morning room was plunged into impenetrable darkness.

Lady Grylls adjusted the woollen rug across her knees. No, she wasn't afraid of the dark … She mustn't fall asleep in her armchair … Pins and needles in her left leg … Would make getting up later on a bore …

Who *was* the killer? Doctor Klein seemed to be 'indicated', but there were other possibilities … Little Maisie, for example … She and John had talked through the keyhole, like Pyramus and Thisbe, she'd admitted as much … What if John had taken a fancy to Maisie? Lady Grylls had joked about it, but what if John had hit on a scheme to employ Maisie's services? What if they had come to some understanding?

John wanted to be rid of Ramskritt since Ramskritt intended to deprive him of the island … John might have commissioned Maisie to murder Oswald Ramskritt for him – in return for – what? His hand in marriage? *Yes.* The notion was not as laughable as it sounded.

Lady Grylls didn't think Maisie had any illusions about Ramskritt, how could she? To start with, yes. *Not* after her ordeal. Maisie gave every impression of being endearingly naive and refreshingly straightforward, but what if that was only a front? Maisie might have said yes to John's proposal. American gels did fall for mad English aristocrats. So many novels had been written on the subject. Quite a tradition at one time … The Duke of Marlborough had married Consuelo Vanderbilt … Adele Astaire had married the younger son of the Duke of Devonshire … Then there was Mrs Simpson … Then there was the Downton nonsense … As it happened, two of Lady Grylls' cousins had also married Americans …

Lady Grylls yawned. John might have a supply of cyanide – perhaps he'd used it to poison seagulls or something … John was mad as a hatter … He might have given the cyanide to Maisie … Maisie had been the only person who'd stood near Oswald Ramskritt's glass of champagne in the drawing room … How easy it would have been for her to drop a lump of cyanide into the champagne …

Lady Grylls nodded to herself, satisfied with her own logic.

Maisie Lettering sat huddled in a chair in her room, staring at the flickering candlelight, her slender arms hugging her shoulders. She brought to mind a bird that had dashed its head against glass and had been picked up by a human hand. The bird crouches there terrified, unable to move, hoping to save itself by its immobility …

Oswald hadn't been the man she had taken him to be. Her great respect for him had disappeared after he tried to violate her … And he had treated those poor German girls terribly… She had started hating Oswald … She recalled the revulsion she felt when Oswald said he wanted her to stand by his side and how she had tried to hide her true feelings …

John de Coverley said he had as much need for candles as he needed a third leg. The extravagance of it! One could be excused for imagining his sister was attempting to recreate Brompton Oratory. He said he rather liked the idea of sitting in the dark. 'Actually, I've got a torch somewhere as well as my battery-operated lantern. If you are not careful with those candles, you may set the place ablaze, you know. I'd never forgive you if you did. Unlike you, I am attached to Mauldeley.'

'I see you are in good spirits, dear boy,' Sybil said. 'I am so glad.'

'Can I have my gun back, do you think? It is, after all, registered under my name.' John de Coverley peered at his watch. 'I'll need to go out soon, you know.'

'That would be quite impossible, I fear.'

'You don't mean I am still under house arrest?'

'You are not under arrest. All you need is a good rest. It's getting late. Why don't you go to bed?'

'I never heard a proposition I liked the sound of less. I need exercise. You are stopping me from having exercise.'

'I will tell what you could do,' she said. 'Toss a pack of playing cards on the floor and then pick them up one by one. That's one of the most marvellous exercises there is. Apparently our dear Queen and several Cabinet ministers swear by it.'

'Who is that chap lurking behind you?' John de Coverley pointed his forefinger.

'He is not lurking. He is one of my guests.'

'Is he your lover?'

'Don't be ridiculous.'

'You have that complacent secret smile. Your mug is smoother, as if a hand has passed over your skin and conjured away all the etchings of advanced middle age.'

'No, not *advanced*.'

'Your features should be worn with dissipation but they are not. You look repulsively rejuvenated. You positively glow. That's what happens when women start imagining someone's in love with them. I say, that chap looks a bit like papa!'

'He does, doesn't he?'

John grimaced. 'Ugly things really hurt me, you know. You used to be as demure as an early Victorian bride, Sybil, but you look quite different now. I believe you are wearing lipstick. If you are not careful, you will soon start resembling one of those ghastly middle-aged *grandes horizontales*. Painted, powdered and predatory.'

'I do think you should go to bed, John.'

'The trouble with you, Sybil, is that you are too easily steered off course. It is imperative that you should get a proper occupation,' he went on sternly. 'Some sort of a reassuring routine to buttress your inner self that will keep you from getting pernicious ideas. I used to know a woman who found arranging multi-coloured skeins of silk in an alabaster box fulfilling.'

'Shall I make you a cup of camomile tea? It will calm you down.'

'That chap looks a frightful cad. All through my life I have been governed by one golden rule – and I am perfectly prepared to tell you – or anyone else who happens to be interested – what it is. *Give the cad the bum-rush.*'

'He is not a cad. His name is Feversham.'

'I heard you and your so-called guests smashing up the library this morning. Something happened this morning, didn't it? One of your degraded orgies, no doubt.'

'Nothing happened. Nothing at all.'

'You and your so-called guests should be shut up in a dungeon and fed with the tails of haddocks, two a day, till you all perish of pure indigestion. I do think it's time for the troupe, as they say, to be disbanded.'

'I think it's time you went to bed, dear boy.'

'Where is the American girl? I need to talk to the American girl. I intend to ask her a very specific kind of question. It's frightfully important,' John de Coverley said. 'Would you be kind enough to take time off your dalliance and tell her I want to see her? It's terribly urgent.'

All the candles had now been distributed, two to three for each room.

While admitting that it was a filthy habit, Major Payne claimed that smoking helped him to concentrate. Indeed a pipe could prove a source of the subtlest inspiration. But his pipe needed cleaning. He produced the spear-shaped metal implement he used for scraping out dead ashes from the bowl.

The 'spear' caught the flickering light of his candle and flashed it back. Payne blinked.

'What was that?' Antonia sat up. 'A metal object catching the light. Perhaps that was the light Maisie saw a moment before the window was broken. That's possible, isn't it?'

'It is perfectly possible, yes. She saw it in the middle of the library, though … What was it doing in the middle of the library?'

There was a pause.

'Somebody must have thrown a metal object across the room,' Antonia said slowly.

'Why would anyone want to do that? What metal object?'

'I am not sure, but I think I can guess…'

'No, don't tell me.' Payne held up his hand. 'Let me think … Good lord,' he said quietly. 'I believe I know … Not the –?'

'Yes.'

'But then that means –'

'Yes.'

'She lent it to Feversham but he never gave it back to her,' said Antonia.

Enlightenment had come when least expected. The time was now half past seven.

31

COLD HAND
IN MINE

There was a knock, the door opened and Ella Gales entered. In her hand she held a candlestick. Although they couldn't see her face properly, they knew at once something had happened.

'What's the matter?' Payne asked sharply.

'It's Doctor Klein. I don't seem able to wake him up. He is a bad colour. He doesn't seem to be breathing.'

The Paynes were quick and efficient. They asked no more questions. They got up and followed Ella. Each one of them held a burning candle.

The staircase creaked.

Back in the 1930s, when it was first built, Mauldeley, had been considered the very essence of modernity. It had been new and bright and shining. There had been no 'atmosphere' about it. But things had changed. More than eighty years on, the house had become old and eerie, at the moment, quite terrifying. It seemed to be pervaded by a faint smell which suggested seaweed that had been left drying in the sun.

No one said a word. As Ella led the way into Doctor Klein's room and they filed in after her, there was a sudden draught and their candles flickered.

Doctor Klein – it was difficult to think of him as a 'Freddie' – was lying on his right side. His bulging body threw grotesque shadows on the walls.

Payne put his candle down on the bedside table. He then bent over the bed. Antonia and Ella stood close by and held up their candles, so that he could see better.

Payne lifted the cold hand, noticing how small and soft it was, dainty, even. He raised the eyelid, then placed his forefinger at Doctor Klein's neck. Rigor Mortis not set in yet. Doctor Klein's eyes were open, frozen in what Payne imagined was a ferocious expression. The lips were parted. The teeth were clenched in what looked like a snarling grimace. Or was he imagining it? The light was very poor.

The lips appeared slightly bruised. A minuscule crystal sparked on the corner of the mouth. And there was another one on the lower lip. With extreme care Payne detached the crystals and placed them on his handkerchief. Then he noticed a tiny cloth fibre sticking to Doctor Klein's teeth. He held it up and gazed at it thoughtfully. Green … and yellow?

Should have been wearing gloves, he thought. Damn. Too late.

He frowned. Something stirring at the back of his mind … No, gone.

He closed Klein's eyes, then straightened up. His expression was difficult to read.

Ella said, 'He is dead, isn't he?'

'Yes, he's gone.'

They heard the patter of raindrops against the window-panes …

Payne's eyes travelled to the bedside. No glass. No Bible. No, of course not. Doctor Klein had clearly cocked a snook at God's divine right of determining who should be male and who female. There was a book sticking out of the drawer. *Thus Spake Zarathustra*. How very interesting. Payne picked it up. The central irony of the book was the fact that Nietsche had consciously mimicked the style of the Bible to present his defiantly anti-Christian ideas. Had Doctor Klein been fascinated by Nietsche's *super-mensch*? That would be another irony.

Payne leafed through the book. His German was a little rusty …

Despisers of life, decaying and poisoned themselves, of whom the earth is weary, so let them go!

Putting down the book, Payne raised the handkerchief to his nose and sniffed at it delicately.

'What's that?' Antonia asked.

'Cyanide crystals. He seemed to have swallowed a lump of cyanide.' Payne lifted Klein's right hand and examined it carefully by the light of the candles. There were several crystals stuck to it. What kind of despair compels a man to pop a lump of cyanide into his mouth as though it were some luxurious bon-bon?

'There doesn't seem to be a suicide note,' Antonia said. 'He's still wearing the dress.'

'He killed himself. Perhaps it's for the best. In fact, I am sure it's for the best,' Ella said quietly. Her voice was expressionless, as though coming from far away. 'I will miss him,' she added.

Payne picked up the reticule from where it lay beside the body – from inside it he extracted a phial, which he held against the candlelight, squinting at it. He unscrewed it. His nose twitched.

'Bitter almonds,' he murmured.

The next moment Payne remembered. *Gloves.* Where *had* he seen a pair of green and yellow tartan gloves?

The door burst open and Mrs Garrison-Gore appeared. She was wearing a flowered dressing gown, a blanket around her shoulders, her pork-pie hat and gloves. Payne's eyes fixed on the gloves. No – these were black.

Mrs Garrison-Gore was holding a candle. She had a wild air about her. She brought to mind Grace Pool in *Jane Eyre*, Antonia thought.

'So sorry, didn't mean to barge in, but I heard voices.' Her teeth chattered.

'I am freezing. It's impossible to do *anything*. What's happened?' Her eyes fixed on the body on the bed.

'Doctor Klein is dead,' Payne said.

'What? When?' She clutched at her bosom. 'How did he die?'

'He was poisoned. Cyanide.'

'My God! Not – not by his own hand?'

'It would appear so, though of course it is for the police to have the final say.'

Mrs Garrison-Gore emitted an inarticulate sound at the back of her throat.

Her hand shook and wax from the candle dripped on the floor.

Her eyes went to the balcony door, then travelled to the chest of drawers.

'Do you think you'll be all right sleeping next door? We could ask Sybil to get you another room.' Payne was watching her carefully.

'No, thank you. I'll be perfectly all right.' Mrs Garrison Gore lingered. She seemed to come to a decision. 'I've got a confession to make. No, I am not the killer!' She guffawed. 'It's about Doctor Klein. I knew he was a transsexual before most of you did. You see, I sneaked into his room and ransacked his drawers. I found papers and photographs.'

'While he slept?'

'No, no. I am not that brave! He was with Ella at the time. Happened the other night. I was curious. I'd been wondering about him. Terrible thing to do, but there you are. I am a snooper. A Nosey Parker. I know I will be in trouble. When the police come, they will find my fingerprints all over that chest of drawers. It didn't occur to me to wear gloves. I only wear gloves when I am cold. I had no idea he would kill himself or be killed or whatever.'

'You think he was killed?'

'It would be idiotic not to consider the possibility.'

'Any idea as to who might have done it?' Antonia asked.

'No. Rather, I wouldn't like to say. Not till I have sorted out my thoughts.'

'So you have an idea?'

'I am not sure. Perhaps.'

'You didn't by any chance tell Oswald Ramskritt about your discovery? I mean about Doctor Klein being Freddie?'

'No, of course not. I told no one. I had no idea he was Freddie, only that he was a transsexual.' Mrs Garrison-Gore's voice was gruff. Her bosom rose and fell. She kept rubbing her right hand with her left. She seemed to be in pain. 'I am going now. I am sure I will survive the night. In fact I am not sure at all but another death on the island would definitely be *de trop*, so I promise to do my best *not* to add to the count of dead bodies!'

The door slammed shut behind her.

Back in her room, Mrs Garrison-Gore lit the spirit lamp Sybil de Coverely had given her and made herself a cup of tea. She put in two spoonfuls of sugar and took a sip. She told herself she was one of those rare fortunate people who actually *know* the difference between good and evil.

She spoke her thoughts aloud. 'He was entirely evil. An unregenerate bully, if there was one. He'd elevated the act of malicious teasing to an art form. But why did you have to draw attention to yourself, Romany? Was that wise? You seem to positively enjoy courting disaster, my girl. And why do you persist in splitting your infinitives? Well,' she went on in a slightly modified voice, 'snooping is not such a heinous crime. Not as bad as murder anyway.'

It occurred to her that 'snooper' just missed being an anagram of 'poisoner'. It would be dreadful if Major Payne and Antonia Darcy started suspected her of murder. Of *double* murder.

Once more she started crying. She couldn't help herself. She was a self-deluding fool. Her nerves were in a poor state. She felt like opening the window and jumping into the sea. She was in the grip of a cold, lifeless despair. Her thoughts were running with the frenzied violence of a rat caught in one of those old-fashioned traps. It was as though some noxious substance had been syringed into her mind, curdling and destroying her peace.

She should never have allowed herself to be led into this quagmire. She cursed the day she said yes to Sybil de Coverley, who, of course, had been acting on behalf of Lady Grylls. She should have said no.

Pampered aristocracy, never done an honest day's work in their entire lives, expecting everybody to be at their beck and call. Romany had bourgeois blood running in her veins and she was proud of it. Well, she had made a wrong decision. She had thought a small island would be rather fun to stage a murder mystery on. She had also felt flattered to have been asked to do the staging. She was a vain fool.

'Bring back the guillotine!' Mrs Garrison-Gore waved an imaginary banner. 'Off with their heads!'

Murder by request. Perhaps she could write a book with a title like that one day?

She had always been aware of the ambiguity within the human condition; the double-sidedness that allows us to exist within ourselves, yet be different …

'Pull yourself together, Romany. You never killed anyone.'

She still felt a little queasy. Deep breathing should do the trick. *Inhale, exhale.*

Mrs Garrison-Gore spoke out loud again. 'You are completely innocent, my girl. You have nothing to fear. Your reputation remains unblemished. You are a good person. Your feet are not clawed, nor do you sport a tail, don't you ever forget that. You need to be strong because it is up to you to nail down the killer.'

'Well, that's that,' Feversham said. He swung his monocle on its black ribbon. 'It's perfectly clear what happened. Doctor Klein killed Ramskritt and then employed the same technique, only this time for purposes of self-extinction. Poetic justice, some may ay. Nothing poetic about it, really. Ghastly business. Poor fellow. Though perhaps "fellow" isn't quite *le mot juste*. Chaps like that are never happy. They lead their lives in limbo. Neither fish nor fowl. Problems with passports, heading for the wrong lavatory and so on. I have heard some *very strange stories*. Neither fish nor fowl.'

'Is that a hunting metaphor, Fever? Papa *loved* hunting metaphors,' Sybil said. 'Does your encyclopaedic knowledge extend to any hunting metaphors, Major Payne?'

'To hunt with the hounds and run with the hares? That's the only one I can think of.'

'I know a good one. *The quick brown fox jumps over the lazy dog.*'

'That's not a metaphor, Miss de Coverley, it's a pangram.'

'I don't think there is such a word. It would be absolute hell playing Scrabble with you.'

'A pangram contains all twenty-six letters of the English alphabet,' Payne explained. 'It was particularly popular in the benighted pre-computer days when it was used to test typewriters.'

'Quite a Mr Know-all, aren't you? I bet you were frightfully unpopular at school.'

'*Au contraire.*'

'Tragic collisions between the two identities can become a daily occurrence. A fragile sense of self and a general feeling of futility and pointlessness. Chaps like that never feel they are in charge of their own destiny,' Feversham went on in a meditative voice. 'Self-pity and self-disgust are constant companions, not to mention the dreadful loneliness that comes with an inability to enjoy real intimacy. I am not talking entirely through my hat, you know. I *nearly* played a transvestite once.'

'That's not the same thing, Fever,' Sybil said. 'Different psychology altogether. Transvestites are quite happy, I think. They adore dressing up and putting on wigs and false eye-lashes and sequins and dancing and making risqué jokes and seducing boxers and cage fighters.'

'I considered wearing a girlishly tiered ra-ra skirt of crushed velour,' Feversham said in a reminiscent voice.

'What a coincidence, my first teddy bear was made of crushed velour!'

'I have locked Doctor Klein's room. I will keep the key, if you don't mind. I will hand it over to the police, whenever that may be.' Payne spoke stiffly.

Sybil and Feversham had started getting on his nerves.

'It's a comfort in a way,' Sybil de Coverley said. 'Absolutely ghastly of course, but at least we know the nightmare is over. Poor Doctor Klein. A merciful release, I can't help feeling. I don't think he had any future, really.'

'It's got a lot quieter, hasn't it?' Feversham said. 'Some wind, but no gibbering gulls. They have all been swept to the very bottom of the sea and eaten by giant turtles.'

'In my opinion, it was Doctor Klein who killed Oswald and then took his own life. An open-and-shut case, if there was one. Wouldn't you say?' asked Sybil.

'I wish I had your certainties, Miss de Coverley,' Payne said.

His eyes were on Feversham.

32

THE CLUE OF THE SILVER BULLET

The following morning the rain stopped and the sun showed, pale and watery, from between the clouds.

In the room known as 'Charlotte Russe' Feversham woke up with a start. He hadn't slept at all well. He was cold. No early morning tea. Why wasn't the Teasmade working? No electricity! Of course. He'd forgotten. They would need to go down to the cellar and get the generator going. He and Payne. He didn't relish the prospect at all ...

Seven o'clock. Was that a spirit lamp on the side table? So he would be able to make himself some tea after all. There was a tin of powdered milk as well. The situation wasn't as cataclysmic as it had seemed.

The moment he sat up in bed, he realised what it was that troubled him.

He hadn't told Sybil.

Sooner or later he'd be found out. Payne already suspected there was a connection between him and Oswald, despite Feversham's denials. Feversham had tried to avoid a display of anything that suggested a guilty conscience, but he was far from convinced he had been successful ... Damn Romany. Why couldn't the bloody woman keep her trap shut?

He'd got himself into a flap. He'd acted in a guilty fashion.

Once the story of Oswald's death hit the papers, it would only be a question of time before the connection was made public property. The news would be everywhere, not only in the papers but on TV and the bloody Internet. Oswald was a big fish, a multi-millionaire, an oligarch. He'd had his finger on all manner of pies.

So odd that they should have shared a mother …

Feversham got up and put on his rather sumptuous dressing gown.

His eyes fell on the gloves that lay on his bedside table. He must get rid of them. He didn't care much for them, if he had to be perfectly honest. He'd tell Sybil he'd lost them or something.

The window curtains were an attractive shade of dark green – like the patination of an ancient bronze. He pulled them apart.

He needed to *think*.

The sea appeared calmer. But how black and swollen it looked!

That silly conversation at tea, the day the Paynes had arrived. He had given himself away. It had made Payne wonder. Payne was clearly the noticing kind. He should have steered the conversation into a different direction, Feversham reflected; he could have talked about something else – grouse shooting, the absolute disgrace of wind turbines or the addictive absurdity of *Downton Abbey*. No – he shouldn't blame himself. It had been Oswald's fault. Oswald had led him on. Oswald thought he was being clever and funny.

Feversham wondered what his next line of action should be. Sybil. He should tell Sybil. Yes. That would certainly be the decent thing to do. That was what a *gentleman* would do. These things did matter. He must tell her before his mask – his *second* mask, so to speak – was ripped off …

He took a sip of tea. Masks – his whole life had been a series of masks. Who *was* he? He really had no idea. But one thing he knew: he loved Sybil better than life itself. He meant to marry Sybil, though heaven knew when that would be. The police wouldn't take to him kindly, oh no. Still, he must tell Sybil the truth. Wouldn't be fair otherwise.

He must make a clean breast of things. Tell her exactly *who* he was.

He would become suspect number one right away, he had no doubt about it. Would Sybil come and visit him in jail? He felt certain she would. He must speak to her as soon as possible.

As he dressed, he rehearsed his little speech in his head …

At eight o'clock Major Payne was fully dressed. So was Antonia.

Antonia was talking.

'It was Sybil who started me thinking. She mentioned the vagaries of Fate. If the storm hadn't smashed the library window, she said, Oswald might have been alive now. In her opinion his champagne was most probably poisoned in the library, after the French window got smashed.'

'When we all looked in the direction of the explosion?'

'Yes – in the chaos that followed. She said the killer had taken advantage of the chaos. Then I had my bright idea. *What if it was the killer who caused the chaos?* Do you see what I mean?'

Payne looked at her. 'Clever girl. Of course I see what you mean. I am so proud of you.'

They went on to discuss the situation from every possible angle. Now they believed they knew who the killer was, what they needed was proof. It always boiled down to proof in the end …

'I am going down,' Payne said, glancing at his watch. 'It's the early bird that gets the worm. Gosh, hate clichés.'

'It's the early Christian that gets the fattest lion,' said Antonia. 'Or is it the other way round? You will be careful, Hugh, won't you?'

'You think I may be in danger?'

'Well, unless we've got it all completely wrong, we are dealing with a double murderer.'

'Up and about already? In the grip of "a detective fever", I see.' Lady Grylls nodded.

'Is it so obvious? Who said that? I rather like it.'

'Mr Wilkie Collins, I believe. He came up with the phrase at the height of the Constance Kent murder case.'

'That was a nasty business, wasn't it? One doesn't often come across sisters slitting their brothers' throats.'

She peered at him through her glasses. 'You look like the cat that's got the cream, but you don't seem *entirely* happy.'

'No, not entirely. Well, we believe we know whodunnit, but here is the tricky question of proof.'

'You mean you haven't got proof?'

'No. Not what could stand up in a court of law. That's the fly in the ointment. Anyhow I just wanted to see if you were all right.'

'I am fine. Soldiering on. I am not *comfortable* – not at all – though that's not quite the same thing, is it? Do you think we'll be able to get back home today?'

'I doubt it. Not today.'

'You don't think Doctor Klein killed Ramskritt?'

'No.'

'You don't think then that Klein committed suicide?'

'No.'

'Who *is* the killer?'

He told her.

'Can't say I am particularly surprised,' said Lady Grylls. 'Fed up with this island. Freezing cold – guttering candles – no hot water – no wireless, so I can't listen to the Shipping Forecast – no frilly-aproned, apple-cheeked maids bringing early morning tea.'

'I don't think you will find any frilly-aproned, apple-cheeked maids anywhere these days, darling. Except, I imagine, on certain rather dubious websites.'

'It's my fault. We should never have come here. Thought I was giving you the most original present you were ever likely to get on your wedding anniversary.' Lady Grylls sighed. 'Seemed *such* a good idea at the time.'

Although much overgrown, the terrace outside the library could be distinguished as attractively paved in ancient brick.

Mrs Garrison-Gore was walking about, scowling at the devastation the storm had caused and poking among the broken statuary with the tip of her golf umbrella. Neptune had been split into three pieces. Odysseus had been decapitated – if that indeed was Odysseus – might be Jason, of Argonaut fame, she reflected. Those muscular mythological mariners all looked the same.

She wore a voluminous belted trenchcoat in mud-grey, her green pork-pie hat and gloves.

Where *was* the blasted thing?

Hal Jackson would have found it by now. Hal Jackson never missed a trick. Hal Jackson was Mrs Garrison-Gore's detective. A former First World War naval commando who always managed to sleuth his way to the truth and had done so in her first three novels. Shame she couldn't continue writing about him, but for some reason her number two and three had been deemed 'weak', so she'd had to change gear …

Critics were such vermin! Stoats, snakes and stinking centipedes! She'd have them all hanged or garrotted, if she ever got the chance!

She went on raking the rabble with her umbrella, but it was like looking for a needle in a haystack. If she'd been a character in a novel she would have found it by now. Although the first fictional sleuths had been men, detection was a feminine talent, really. Women were more observant than men. They had a more natural instinct for deciphering what they saw and they put their intuition to good use.

Mrs Garrison-Gore had started feeling light-headed. She took a deep breath. *Inhale, exhale.* If she stood absolutely still for a moment or two, she would be all right. For all her appearance of bluff solidity, she was not emotionally robust. *Your soul is threatened with eternal damnation.* That's what her former husband had told her once.

She had had a bad night. She had listened to the wind blowing in erratic gusts down the chimney, making the lulls between each onslaught less a relief than an ominous spell of unnatural calm. Anxieties and sinister presentiments kept flooding her brain.

And it all culminated in a dream.

Doctor Klein had been buried, but for some reason, the Home Secretary had given orders for the body to be exhumed. Romany was among the small group of people standing reluctantly beside the grave. When the coffin was unscrewed, they were faced with the ghoulish sight of Doctor Klein's corpse, swollen to the point of bursting, a monstrous Michelin man with silver florins placed on his eyes and wearing a ball gown. Then a hissing sound was heard and the body started deflating. Foul gases emanated from the coffin, so powerful, so vile, it made Romany gasp and choke and stagger back. The next moment she had woken up, feeling terribly ill –

She blew her nose. Pull yourself together, Romany, she ordered herself. Snap out of it. Chin up. Put your best foot forward and not in it. But it was difficult getting the details of the nightmare out of her head. The ghastly gases – she could still smell them!

She reminded herself she was on a trail now. She needed to be disciplined. If someone came along at this very moment, she would tell them *exactly* what she was looking for and why. She would be blunt about it. She would say what it was she suspected.

Unless it was Feversham who appeared. Well, if Feversham turned up, she would tell him she was taking the air. She would say she was looking out for a boat.

Hearing a sound behind her, she turned round sharply.

'Good morning, Mrs Garrison-Gore,' Major Payne said with a pleasant smile. 'I wonder if you and I might be looking for the same thing?'

'Lovely morning, isn't it, though there is a decided nip in the air,' he went on. 'The sea looks a lot calmer – and not a single seagull in view … Good lord, the library's gone – completely gutted – what a waste – I thought there were some good books there …'

'Terrible devastation. Brings to mind the worst excesses of a Baghdad or a Tripoli.' Mrs Garrison-Gore harrumphed. 'Shocking, simply shocking.'

'Look at the broken glass … How curious.' Major Payne frowned. 'How terribly curious.'

'What's curious?'

'Most of the glass is on the *outside* of the window. If it had been the wind that broke it, the pieces would have been on the *inside* … You know what that means?'

'I believe I do.' Mrs Garrison-Gore took a deep breath. She looked like a woman who had suddenly found herself free from all doubt and indecision. 'Major Payne, I have no doubt you are someone I can trust. May I talk to you? I mean in confidence?'

'Of course you may. Absolutely. I am the soul of discretion.'

'You wouldn't think it an imposition?'

'Not a bit of it.'

'I think I know who the killer is,' she said after a pause.

'You do?'

'Yes. I have had my suspicions for some time and now I am convinced, though the whole thing is – well, too fantastic for words! I am sure you will laugh at me.'

'I wouldn't dream of it … I also suspect someone,' Payne said. 'Could we, by any chance, be talking about the same man? It is a man, isn't it?'

'It is a man, yes,' she breathed. 'It's all so terribly far-fetched …'

'Shall we compare notes?'

'I would like nothing better. You go first, Major, if you don't mind frightfully. Shoot.'

'Ladies first.'

'Ladies? What ladies?' She gave a loud laugh. 'Shoot!'

Payne cleared his throat. 'You told us something very interesting yesterday afternoon. You said that you didn't have to provide any of the actors in the Murder Game since they were already here, on the island. The only exception was Feversham, who joined the "troupe" later – but he had nothing to do with you either. You said that Feversham had been Oswald Ramskritt's idea. Those, I believe, were your precise words?'

'That is correct.'

'I didn't pursue the subject – you seemed very upset – you said you were dog tired – but I have been meaning to ask you about it. I believe it is important to establish Feversham's credentials. Did you mean Oswald Ramskritt had already contacted Feversham and asked him to join you on the island?' Payne scanned the terrace as he talked. He kicked a stone.

'Yes. That's what I meant. Oswald told us he had a man in mind, who would be just right for the part of "John de Coverley". It was someone who specialised in English gents. Who had the right air about him.'

'I see. Well, Feversham told us a different story,' said Payne. 'He said that you and he went back a long way. He had taken part in previous Murder Weekends which you had organised.'

'He said that? Well, that is simply not true,' Mrs Garrison-Gore said vehemently. 'I'd never met Feversham before … But what possible reason could he have had for lying to you? Was it because he didn't want anyone to know that there was a link between him and Oswald Ramskritt?'

'That seems to be the obvious conclusion. And, as it happens, I have an idea as to what that link might be –' Payne broke off. Bending down, he picked up a shining object from under a piece of statuary. 'Hallo. This, I believe, belongs to you?'

'Yes! My silver bullet pen!' Mrs Garrison-Gore gave a delighted cry. Internally she cursed herself for being the blindest of bats. 'I thought I'd lost it! I'd lent it to Feversham, you see, but he *insisted* he'd given it back to me!'

Major Payne stroked his jaw with his forefinger. 'I don't think that without your pen Oswald Ramskritt's murder would have taken place at all … At least not in the way it did … It was Antonia actually who hit on the idea … Does that make any sense?'

'It most certainly does. I also worked it out.' She took a step towards him and brought her face alarmingly close to his. 'I know exactly what happened. *The pen was hurled across the library*. Like a mini missile. That's what you mean, isn't it? Isn't it?'

'Yes. That was the little light Maisie saw. A metal object flashing in the lamplight. Your silver pen. It was used as a missile, as you so aptly put it. Its target was the French window. When the window exploded,' Payne went on, 'everybody blamed the storm. We assumed the window pane had given way under the strong wind, while in actual fact, it was your pen that broke it.'

'How did you work out it was my pen?'

'We deduced it,' said Payne. 'It fitted the bill. We were there when you reminded Feversham that you'd lent him the pen, remember? We heard him say he'd already given it back to you.'

'That was a lie! Another lie! I believe the man is a pathological liar!'

'I believe you are right. I came down in the hope I might be lucky enough to find your pen, which I have now done. I also wanted to make sure the broken glass *was* on the outside – which it is.' Payne weighed the pen in his hand. 'Yes, it's heavy enough to do the job.'

'You remind me of Hal Jackson. That's my detective. You speak like him, at least that's how I hear him in my head, that's exactly as I imagine him to be.' Mrs Garrison-Gore made a self-deprecating grimace. 'Feversham smashed the window to distract us, to divert our attention, so that he could drop the cyanide into Oswald Ramskritt's glass of champagne unobserved. Simple, yet clever, in its own way.'

Payne nodded. 'It did the trick all right … Everybody was compelled to fix their eyes on the window – we leapt back in shock and terror – staggered away from the mighty wind. Nobody was looking at Ramskritt's glass. That was when the poisoning took place.'

'And did he kill Doctor Klein as well?'

'He did, yes. I found a fibre sticking to Doctor Klein's teeth. *Green and yellow.*' Payne made a significant pause.

'The tartan gloves!' Mrs Garrison-Gore gasped. 'He pushed the cyanide into Doctor Klein's mouth – he was wearing the gloves!'

'Yes.'

'But why – *why* did he do it? I can't imagine Feversham in the grip of a single strong emotion. He is so sham and so shallow. Murder, the unique crime, should *always* arise from strong emotions!'

'I see you know your Orwell.'

She gave a short laugh, which to Payne's ears sounded like the bark of a walrus demanding to be fed. I mustn't be unkind, he thought.

'*Is* that Orwell? I always thought it was one of mine!' She hooted with laughter. 'I am *such* an incorrigible cribber! The thieving magpie, that's me. But what, in heaven's name, does Feversham gain from Ramskritt's death?'

'What did he gain? It's more a question of what he is *about* to gain. The answer is money. A lot of money. Or so Antonia and I believe,' said Payne. 'Feversham is Oswald Ramskritt's half-brother. Or so we believe.'

33

CONFESSIONS OF A JUSTIFIED SINNER

He stood before her as straight as a metal rule, which made him look taller. His chin was shaved to a millimetre of its life. He should grow one of those silver-bristle moustaches on his top lip, Sybil thought. It would be terribly becoming. A moustache would be *thrilling*.

Feversham's neck was throttled by a stiff white collar attached, by a gold stud, to a raspberry-coloured shirt. Above the stud, knotted tightly, was his striped regimental tie. He wore a waisted double-breasted suit in discreet charcoal hues. A yellow silk handkerchief spilled rakishly out of his breast pocket. His stepped-bottom trousers were creased sharper than a knife's edge and his elastic-sided boots would have shamed a mirror.

'Why, Fever, you look exceedingly dashing, but then I wouldn't have it any other way,' Sybil said. Her heart was beating fast. 'A proper Beau Brummel.'

'I was wondering if I might have a word?'

'Of course. Won't you sit down?'

'No, thank you. I prefer to stand.'

'I don't suppose you slept well, did you? Or is it your back? You poor darling. I expect you were cold?'

'Not really. Only a bit.'

'I meant to give you an electric blanket, but it would have been no use since there is no electricity. You could have had a fire in your room of course, if only I'd thought about it!'

'Look here, Sybil –'

'I promised I would teach you to play "bumble-puppy" chess, didn't I? It's rather fun. Shall we have a game? Or is it too early in the morning for games? You look too solemn for words. Do you intend to propose to me?'

He cleared his throat. 'I would very much like to do that – but I need to talk to you first.'

'How infuriatingly intriguing. I need to have a cigarette, I simply must.' She picked up the silver cigarette case from the desk and took out a cigarette. 'De Retzke. They still make them, you know. A small shop in Bond Street. All right, Fever. Out with it.' She flicked a lighter. 'What's all this about?'

'I'll come straight to the point. I am Oswald Ramskritt's half-brother. Or rather was.'

'Go on. Don't stop! Why did you stop?'

'It was Oswald who phoned me. He asked me to come over to Sphinx Island and take the part of your brother. He explained about the Murder Game you were putting on. Neither of us was to divulge that we were related. I was to say that it was Mrs Garrison-Gore who employed my services, that I'd done acting jobs for her in the past.'

'Why didn't Oswald want people to know you were his half-brother?'

Feversham inclined his head. 'He wanted me to spy on Ella.'

'Spy on Ella? Are you serious? Why in heaven's name did he want you to do that?'

'Oswald was an extremely controlling man. He had a very strange relationship with poor Ella, as you may have gathered. She had been his mistress. He no longer loved her, but he enjoyed maintaining a hold over her. Ella's friendship with

Doctor Klein bothered him. It annoyed him that they should have become so close. He talked to me about it. He said it disturbed him. I believe he was also jealous, in an odd kind of way. I don't think he was entirely normal. He seemed to suspect Ella and Doctor Klein were having an affair.'

'Did he really? Of all the grotesque ideas! Do be an angel and pass me that ashtray, would you?'

'He believed they were conspiring against him. Oswald gave every impression of being as arrogant as hell, but I think that deep down he felt terribly insecure. He was keen to know what Ella and Klein did when they were alone together. What they talked about. What she said to Klein and what Klein said to her. He wanted me to eavesdrop on them. To watch them. He thought they would be less suspicious of me if they didn't know I was his half-brother.'

'What exactly *is* a "half-brother"?' Sybil held the cigarette away from her eyes.'

'We had the same mother – but different fathers. My mother is completely ga–ga these days, but she was married to a Ramskritt, then to a Bonwell. Clement Bonwell is my father. He is also still alive.'

'Is your name really Bonwell?'

'Yes. Do you like it?'

'It's a charming name, though I must admit I prefer "Feversham". Do go on, don't stop, don't stop. The whole thing is so utterly, so deliciously bizarre. I don't suppose you enjoyed being Oswald's spy and spying on poor Ella?'

'I didn't spy on Ella. I said I would do it, but I hated the idea, you see, so I only *pretended* to be spying on Ella.'

'I suppose he paid you?'

'He paid me yes. He paid me extremely well.'

'You are one of the most decent fellows I have ever met, Fever … Was that why I kept seeing you walk up and down the stairs and lurking in corridors? You invariably had an insouciant air about you. Hands in pockets, whistling *Ain't Misbehavin'*.'

'That was part of my spying act, yes. I did it *only* when Oswald was about. I didn't really eavesdrop on Ella and Klein. When I reported back to Oswald, I said that their conversations were completely innocent and not of the slightest importance. They were most certainly *not* having an affair. Oswald seemed disappointed. I must admit I didn't care for Oswald, but I wanted him to think I was doing exactly what he'd asked me to do … As I said, I needed the money.'

'My poor darling. Are you poor?'

'Poor as a rat. Completely broke.'

'It would be splendid being married to a man with no money since you tend to appreciate little treats so much. I read that somewhere. I must say I prefer poor people to rich people. In that respect I take after mama. She was a Socialist, you know. The Duke of Westminster should be made to pay more tax; I do feel strongly about it. Rich people incline towards callous egotism and careless extravagance.'

'As a matter of fact, Syb, I am no longer poor. I am getting most of Oswald's fortune.'

'Are you really? This is terribly exciting. Actually, I don't mind you being rich at all. That means you can buy the island off me now – no, sorry. I keep forgetting you abhor the sea. You get *mal-de-mer*. We are so alike! But wait a minute. How *can* you be sure you are getting most of Oswald's fortune?'

'He sent me a copy of the will. He wanted me to know I was his main legatee.'

'That may have been an elaborate practical joke. Oswald was the kind of fellow papa would have dismissed as "second-rate". He wore a toupee.'

'He was unpredictable all right, but I do believe he was serious about the will,' said Feversham. 'He hardly knew me, but he found me amusing. Besides, he was fond of mother – before she lost her mind, that is. He said he couldn't cope with irrational behaviour as it unsettled his equilibrium, though of course he paid all the fees for her upkeep. Mother is in a home in Windsor.'

'Ah the shared mother. Norah, yes? She must have breast-fed the two of you. That's the sort of thing that makes a big difference. Did Oswald leave Ella anything at all in his will, do you know?'

'Not a penny.'

'What a bounder. But he must have left her *something*. They'd lived together for ages. She did so much for him. Running errands and cooking and making phone calls and changing her dresses each time he told her to. No? What a bounder.'

'He was not a good man. Something very wrong with him, actually. He left nothing to Maisie either.'

'Maybe he was waiting to see which way things would go with Maisie?' Sybil mused. 'She did blot her copy-book, poor child, didn't she, when she turned down his advances. These American girls are a mystery to me. An English girl would have taken a thing like that in her stride. She would have lain back and thought of England.'

'I will be a very rich man, Sybil.'

'Why the long face then? You aren't worried someone will say you killed him, are you?'

'Major Payne seems to have tumbled onto my secret,' said Feversham. 'Payne is awfully good at making connections between things. Oswald was very silly, you see. He talked to me about my father. He thought he was being funny. It happened when the Paynes first arrived, remember?'

'You mean the silly talk?'

'Yes. Oswald and I managed to exchange family information under the guise of silly talk. We thought we were being clever, but Major Payne's proved to be cleverer. Major Payne is the kind of fellow who would be terribly good at teasing anagrams from recalcitrant master phrases, wouldn't you say?'

'Oh he is a major pain.' She waved an impatient hand. 'Who does he think he is? An exemplar of a superior purpose? God Himself? You know the kind of thing. *Everything is uncovered and laid bare before the eyes of Him to whom we must give account.* Don't tell me he suspects you of killing Oswald. The idea is preposterous.'

'Not that preposterous. Once my true identity is revealed,' Feversham said, 'I will be suspect number one. The police will take a special interest in me, of that I have no doubt. I am sure I'll make a bad impression. When I am nervous, I find myself reduced to blubbering incoherence.'

'I find that hard to believe.'

'I tend to say all the wrong things. Even if in the end they decide it's Doctor Klein who did it, suspicion will linger. There's bound to be talk …'

'Most people are fools. Never submit to hypocritical hysteria, that's my motto,' Sybil said firmly. 'I never imagined you cared what self-appointed arbiters of moral orthodoxies might be saying.'

Feversham's hand went up to his tie. 'You don't really think I killed Oswald, do you?'

'Of course not … If you killed Oswald, that would mean you killed Doctor Klein as well … Not that it would make a scrap of difference to the way I feel about you, if you did kill them, you know. Souls come in pairs, but when we are born they are split in two and we spend all our lives trying to find the other half … *Now I have found you and you have found me* … I find this public passion for justice and retribution such a bore anyway … But *did* you kill them?'

34

A QUESTION
OF PROOF

'I realised I had all the necessary information at my disposal,' Payne was saying. 'Ramskritt mentioned the fact he had a half-brother when we first arrived, on our way here. He said his half-brother was an actor – "treading the boards" was how he put it – and that he was still chasing the ladies – despite his back injury. He also said that his brother was more English than the English. Well, Feversham's speciality is a certain rarefied kind of an English gent, isn't it?'

'Indeed it is. The kind that never existed.' Mrs Garrison-Gore gave a contemptuous laugh.

'At one point Feversham said he had suffered a back injury … Then there was the reference to Bonwell and Norah … I believe Norah is their mother … Ramskritt apparently had Norah's eyes … Well, suddenly everything clicked into place … I caught Feversham unawares and he admitted his father's name was Bonwell.'

'Most actors are psychotic, though they don't know it, and character actors are the craziest. As for you, Major Payne,' Mrs Garrison-Gore said, 'you are *so* much like Hal Jackson, it's uncanny. That's my detective. That's how I've always pictured Hal, you know – *as someone like you*. Sorry – this sounds like a declaration of love, doesn't it?'

'Are you in love with your detective?'

'Perhaps I am, I don't know. Naval men and military men are a bit alike, aren't they?'

'They most certainly are,' Payne agreed politely. Privately he thought they were nothing of the sort. He found the idea abhorrent.

'Bluff admirals and bluff colonels are practically inter-changeable.' She was rubbing her right hand with her left. Her face twisted. 'I seem to have got a sore patch,' she explained. 'I seem to be – um – allergic to something, don't know what.'

'Hope you haven't been bitten –?'

'Bitten? *Bitten?*' Her face turned the colour of a fire extinguisher. 'Do you mean – *bugs*? You don't think –? Well, it's an old house … I don't believe Sybil has ever had it properly cleaned and fumigated … What's the matter?'

'I've had a brainwave, that's all. I do believe,' Payne said, 'that it is thanks to you that I've got my final proof now.'

'Your *final* proof? Really? You mean – proof of Feversham's guilt? How exciting! What did I say? Was it my reference to Hal Jackson? Or to bugs? Or to bluff admirals? What *is* your proof?'

'If I told you, the story would be over,' he said. 'It isn't time for the denouement yet. You must wait for the right psychological moment.'

'When *is* the right psychological moment? I never seem to know. I tend to write my last chapters several times and I am always left with this deeply dissatisfied feeling –' Mrs Garrison-Gore broke off. 'Oh there's Antonia Darcy! I am sure *she* knows. I am sure she is a much better novelist than I shall ever be! Ahoy there!' She waved her umbrella in the air. 'I must say you look terribly festive. Your husband's been marvellous, truly marvellous. It seems he's managed to solve the mystery! He's beaten us all to it!'

Antonia was wearing a red burgundy dress in fine wool and a short black coat. She was also wearing the new hat. She smiled. 'This morning he was complaining how hard it was to get proof. I advised against despair. I told him that sooner or later he'd get his proof.'

'You are lucky to have a husband who *listens* to you. How I envy you, Antonia Darcy! Oh how I envy you! I haven't had your obvious good fortune.' Mrs Garrison-Gore sighed gustily. 'Your murder mysteries are all set in modern times, aren't they?'

'On the surface they are.'

'Scientific changes have affected all serious writers of mystery novels set in modern times and not necessarily for the better. Don't you find that infuriating? Don't you feel *threatened*? I mean, all that DNA business! I can't help feeling threatened.' Mrs Garrison-Gore rubbed her hand.

'DNA has certainly revolutionised the investigation of murder,' Antonia agreed.

'If you had a corpse with some blood or skin from the killer under their nails, and if you had six suspects, say, well, it wouldn't take the police long at all to solve the mystery, would it? What would you do *then*?' Mrs Garrison-Gore was speaking in her loudest voice. She had a frantic air about her. 'How *do* you produce sixty-five thousand words or thereabouts without losing momentum? How do you manage to maintain that vice-like narrative grip?'

'How indeed … I often find myself struggling.'

'Once the police turn up on the scene, you've simply *got* to introduce DNA as well. If you don't do it, they'll say you are anachronistic and irrelevant. I know what critics are! I'd rather die than write a murder mystery set in modern times!'

'My solution is not to involve the police till the very end of a novel if at all … It seems to me that most modern crime fiction deals in documentary realism rather than creative ingenuity …'

'Jolly well put, Antonia Darcy!' Mrs Garrison-Gore boomed approbation. 'I couldn't agree more!'

'You ladies seem to hold similar views,' said Payne. 'Would I be right in saying that your books are about murder *only* in the sense that *The Importance of Being Ernest* is about child neglect and identity crisis?'

This made Mrs Garrison-Gore choke with laughter.

'The good news is that the network is back and I have managed to make a call.' Antonia held up her mobile phone. 'I have called the police. They are sending a launch.'

'Well done,' Payne said. He glanced at his watch.

'The police are coming? Hoorah! Thank God!' Mrs Garrison-Gore cried. Tears sprung from her eyes. '*Thank God!* At long last! I can't bear to stay on this island a moment longer! How about subplots? Are you keen on subplots?'

Antonia scrunched up her face. 'No, not really. Maybe a hint or two of romance. I try to make everything relate to the main murder ...'

Antonia glanced round. The edge of the cliff was less than ten feet away, bounded by a waist-high crumbling stone wall. A solitary seagull soared above them.

'The sea looks like a mighty mud bath. They say mud baths are extremely good for the nerves,' Mrs Garrison-Gore said with a frown. 'Mud baths were used to be known as a "cure".'

'I have got my final proof now,' Payne told Antonia.

'Really? What is it?'

'Want to see it?'

Antonia blinked. 'Well, yes. Of course I want to see it.'

Mrs Garrison-Gore went on gazing at the sea. For some reason she was remembering what a critic had written about her second novel. *The ending, when it finally stumbles into view, isn't so much contrived as almost meaningless in relation to what had preceded it.*

The next moment she screamed. 'Major Payne! What are you doing?'

Major Payne had got hold of her right hand.

'How dare you? Have you gone mad? Let go of me at once!'

But he didn't.

He pulled off her glove and held her hand up firmly for Antonia to see.

35

OLD LAMPS
FOR THE NEW

It was late afternoon now.

The police had been and gone. Lady Grylls, Sybil de Coverley, Feversham and Ella Gales were sitting in the conservatory listening to Antonia and Hugh Payne's explanation.

'She hit Hugh on the head with her umbrella. Then she ran to the edge of the cliff and jumped into the sea. It was all quite awful,' Antonia said. 'Like something in a dream. Everything happened extremely fast. There she was one moment, the next she was gone.'

Payne rubbed the side of his head. 'Her body hasn't been recovered yet.'

'With great victory, comes great sacrifice,' Feversham said. 'Sorry. Awfully bad form. But the blasted woman did try to frame me, didn't she? She used my gloves to kill Klein and then she replaced them in my room! How did you trap her exactly? By pretending you suspected me, thus lulling her into a false sense of security? You led her on and then you suddenly pounced on her, what?'

'Something like that, yes. Well, she had reached the end of the line. Her nerves were in a dreadful state. She was *not* the cold-blooded killer type.'

'She was a wildly erratic character,' Lady Grylls said.

'She knew it was all over. She could do nothing about it. The proof was there – like the mark of Cain – on her hand. She wore gloves in an attempt to conceal it.'

'A *bite* mark. How extraordinary. How does one get rid of a bite mark? Well, she could have cut her hand off,' Lady Grylls said ruminatively. '*That* would have eliminated the evidence once and for all.'

'The bite mark was flaming red, since it seemed to have got infected. I believe it was *an exact imprint of Doctor Klein's teeth*. Doctor Klein bit her when she tried to push a lump of cyanide into his mouth. He bit her badly, that's how a fibre from the tartan gloves got between his teeth,' Payne explained. 'It was the fibre and his ferocious expression that gave me the idea.'

'Poor plucky Freddie Hansen died fighting,' said Antonia.

'Envisage the scene,' Payne went on. 'Doctor Klein is in his room, lying on the bed, probably dozing. He is not feeling well. Mrs Garrison-Gore sneaks through the balcony door. She'd done it once before, when she ransacked Doctor Klein's chest of drawers. One of the drawers contained a file with pictures tracing Freddie's transformation into Klein. I believe the phial containing the cyanide was also there at the time and Mrs Garrison-Gore helped herself to some of it.'

'Had she already started contemplating killing Oswald?' Lady Grylls asked.

'I believe so, yes … She leans over Klein – he wakes up – a struggled ensues – with her hands in tartan gloves she gets hold of his mouth and prises it open – he bites her – but she manages to push the lump of cyanide into his mouth.'

'How perfectly brutal. There was something of the beast about her, I always thought,' Sybil de Coverley said. She was sitting next to Feversham and they were holding hands.

'So the cyanide belonged to Klein?' Lady Grylls said.

'Yes. Doctor Klein seemed to have wanted to kill Ramskritt but never managed to make up his mind. Remember, he was not a well man. He gave the impression he was suffering from general slowing-down of reactions. He never hinted at what he might do, did he? He never mentioned – revenge?' Payne glanced at Ella Gales.

'No. Never. I think he – she – was fascinated by Oswald – by the discrepancy between the way Oswald saw himself and the way he really was. He was interested in studying him.'

'Explain the mechanics of the murder to me, Hughie, would you?' Lady Grylls urged.

'Mrs Garrison-Gore carried the cyanide in her bag. She was getting quite desperate. The storm gave her the idea, I think. It was she who hurled the silver bullet pen at one of the library's French windows, thus displaying a great power of imaginative improvisation. She wanted to cause a distraction, which she succeeded in doing. In the chaos that followed she dropped the cyanide into Ramskritt's champagne glass. Later on she killed Klein using the remaining cyanide.'

'Why did she kill Doctor Klein?'

'My theory is that she was afraid Klein might have noticed some of his cyanide was missing. She feared he would tell the police about it. She was paranoid. She clearly feared she would have been considered the obvious suspect, you see – since her room was next to Klein's and there was only a low partition separating the two balconies.'

Antonia said, 'She must also have hoped that by killing Doctor Klein, she would bring about a closure to the case. Klein, after all, was the most obvious suspect. He clearly had murder on his mind. Mrs Garrison-Gore wanted to make it look as though Klein killed Ramskritt and then, either tormented by guilt or simply not wanting to go on with his tragic existence, killed himself.'

'Extraordinary. But why *was* the woman so desperate?' Lady Grylls pushed her glasses up her nose. 'It isn't as though Ramskritt had threatened her with exposure, is it?'

'Ramskritt's torture methods were much subtler than any overt threats,' Antonia said. 'Ramskritt specialised in oblique hints and innuendo. He started playing a cat-and-mouse game with her. That was his style. That was the kind of thing Ramskritt enjoyed best. Isn't that so?'

'Yes,' Ella said. 'That's what he liked to do to women. He enjoyed intimidating them. He was a mental sadist.'

'So *la* Garrison-Gore's crime was cribbing ... Passing other people's books off as her own?'

'Oswald Ramskritt cottoned on to the fact that Mrs Garrison-Gore had been plagiarising out-of-print, out-of-copyright whodunnits from the early 1930s, which were in the public domain on the Internet, on Project Gutenberg. Project Gutenberg publishes Shakespeare and Dickens whereas Gutenberg *Lite* specialises in lighter fiction. Completely forgotten authors like Canon Victor L. Whitechurch, Edgar Jepson, Milward Kennedy and so on. When Oswald read bits from the novel she was in the process of writing, he noticed how she was changing names of characters and places.'

'That,' Payne explained, 'was the real meaning of his recurrent teasing – *old lamps for the new.*'

'He congratulated her on being "enterprising". He spoke teasingly, in mocking tones. He made it absolutely clear to her that he was aware of what she was up to. He also suggested he might phone her publisher. He talked about it in front of everybody – he made it sound like a joke but she took it seriously. She felt threatened.'

Payne said, 'Mrs Garrison-Gore had had four flops, but then she published what we could assume was the first of the plagiarised, if modified, whodunnits, to considerable acclaim.

She was worried that, if exposed as a fraud and a cheat, she would face ruin. Incidentally, this is all almost entirely conjectural. Her literary reputation was going to suffer – she might even be taken to court – her publisher would drop her and no other publisher would ever offer her a contract – she would become "untouchable" – beyond the pale!'

'But how *likely* was any of that?' Sybil de Coverley asked.

'Maybe not terribly likely, but that's what she *feared*. We believe she suffered from anxiety and depression and perhaps some sort of paranoid disorder. She was scared Ramskritt would at some point choose to make his discovery public. Well, she couldn't allow that. So she decided to kill him.'

Feversham said, 'She tried to throw suspicion on me – suggested she had lent me the pen and that I'd never returned it to her. I was sure that I had, but she managed to fluster me, blast her.'

Sybil said, 'I can't get the bullet pen out of my head, the way she distracted us by throwing it at the window! Something a stage conjuror might have done.'

'We believe that for a while Mrs Garrison-Gore did work as a conjuror,' said Antonia. 'We didn't know whether to believe it or not, but perhaps that story wasn't as apocryphal as we thought it was. Her sleight of hand was reputed to have become the stuff of legends.'

'How did you know she had a bite mark on her hand, Payne?' Feversham put up his eyeglass.

'I noticed how Mrs Garrison-Gore kept rubbing her right hand. She was in pain. She kept her gloves on. She said she had an allergy but she looked terrified when I suggested she might have been bitten … It was one of my inspired guesses … She gave herself away, but she managed to pull herself together and started talking about the possibility that she might have been bitten by *bugs*.'

'There are no bugs in my house!' Sybil said imperiously.

There was a pause.

'Where *is* Maisie?' Lady Grylls peered round.

'I believe she is upstairs talking to my brother. I have an idea he is proposing marriage to her ... He looked terribly solemn the last time I saw him ... Do get me a light, Fever,' Sybil produced a cigarette. 'Well, John is welcome to the island ... We are going to be very rich anyway, so I couldn't care less what happens to the island. In fact, I don't want to know ... Do get me that ashtray, Fever, there's a good boy.'

'There was one thing Mrs Garrison-Gore got *completely* wrong. She said that naval men and military men were "a bit alike",' Payne said with feeling, '*No* similarity whatever.'

'I believe it was her fear of DNA that killed her,' Antonia said thoughtfully. 'She knew they would have found Doctor Klein's DNA on her ... She said she would rather die than write a murder mystery set in modern times, didn't she? One could quip that Mrs Garrison-Gore chose to die rather than be in a murder mystery set in modern times.'

ABOUT
THE AUTHOR

R.T. Raichev is a writer and researcher who grew up in Bulgaria and wrote his university dissertation on English crime fiction. He has lived in London since 1989, and all seven of his previous Antonia Darcy and Major Payne mysteries have been published by Constable in the UK and Soho Press in the USA. The *Riddle of Sphinx Island* is his first novel with The Mystery Press.

ALSO IN THE ANTONIA DARCY AND MAJOR PAYNE MYSTERY SERIES

PRAISE FOR
R.T. RAICHEV

'Fascinating ... recalls the best from the Golden Age of Detective Fiction.'

Lady Antonia Fraser

'I have read all of Raichev's books. They are very clever. I really am a fan.'

R.L. Stine

'Original and intriguing ... An England of club and country house, with a delicious shot of bitters!'

Emma Tennant

'A most unusual yarn of mystery, imagination, observation and splendidly old-fashioned sleuthery which skilfully probes the surface smoothness of clubland and country house. I couldn't put it down.'

Hugh Massingberd

'The kind of old-school mysteries that fans of Christie and Sayers love … but this will be pleasing to more than traditionalists, because it adds a P.D. Jamesian subtlety to the comfortable formula. Antonia Darcy is a terrific sleuth and Raichev is a very clever writer indeed.'

Booklist

'Deftly mixes dark humour and psychological suspense, its genteel surface masking delicious deviancy.'

Kirkus Reviews (Starred Review)

'Greed, jealousy, rampant emotions and a killer lurk in the wings of this tale that mixes Henry James' psychological insight with Agatha Christie's whodunnit plotting skills … a diabolically clever story line.'

Library Journal (Starred Review)

'An ominous feel, reminiscent of Hitchcock.'

Mystery Morgue

'Recommended for any mystery fan who likes surprises.'

New Mystery Reader Magazine

'Murder is fun again! Each chapter parcels out just a bit more of the story, just enough, drawing open the curtain to reveal the picture behind … A mystery that harkens back to the thirties and forties, but pays respect to modernity … Definitely a keeper.'

Suspense Magazine

'Intricate and inventive … very witty dialogue and a cast of gloriously eccentric characters.'

Francis Wyndham

'Stylish … deft use of literary allusion and well-drawn characterisation.'

Publishers Weekly

'Liberal doses of imagination, experimentation, intelligence and sprinklings of irony, satire and fun … the riveting attention of a game of Cluedo.'

The Hidden Staircase Mystery Books

'A whodunnit with more twists than a snake in a basket!'

Robert Barnard, CWA Diamond Dagger Winner

'Superbly plotted … Raichev delivers this classic with the perfect panache one expects from an author who wrote his doctoral dissertation on English crime fiction … Excellent series!'

Toronto Globe & Mail

Visit our website and discover thousands of other
History Press books.

www.thehistorypress.co.uk